P9-EDH-676

ALIEN
ECHO

A L

I EN

ECHO

MIRA GRANT

[Imprint]
MAKE YOUR MARK

New York

[Imprint]
MAKE YOUR MARK

A part of Macmillan Publishing Group, LLC
175 Fifth Avenue, New York, NY 10010

Library of Congress Cataloging-in-Publication Data is available.

ISBN 978-1-250-30629-6 (hardcover) / ISBN 978-1-250-30630-2 (ebook)

Our books may be purchased in bulk for promotional, educational, or business use.
Please contact your local bookseller or the Macmillan Corporate and
Premium Sales Department at (800) 221-7945 ext. 5442 or by email
at MacmillanSpecialMarkets@macmillan.com.

Book design by Elynn Cohen

Imprint logo designed by Amanda Spielman

First edition, 2019

1   3   5   7   9   10   8   6   4   2

fiercereads.com

People contain many things that can be stolen.
Organs. Blood. Bones.
It's impolite to steal pieces of people.
It's also impolite to steal books.
Don't do the one, and the Bone Gnomes won't do the other.
Sleep tight.

For Jennifer,
and all the horror movie
kids out there.

*"There are wonders in the cosmos beyond
all imagining, creatures we may never
understand and biological processes we may
never unravel. What a miracle, to live in a time
when such things are ready to be discovered."*
–Dr. Katherine Shipp

*"The one constant in the universe is that
life wants to continue living, whatever the
consequence. Whatever the cost. Life endures."*
–Dr. John Shipp

ALIEN
ECHO

1

ZAGREUS

THE SKY IS ORANGE.

That's not the worst part—that's a label I try to reserve for about a hundred things more offensive than an orange sky—but it's the most jarring, even after three months' planetary time spent on this specific chunk of rock and water and stupid colonial politics. If the suns are up at all, the sky is orange. Dark orange at sunrise and sunset, bright, artificial orange during the middle of the day, like someone out there decided the actual, literal *sky* is the best safety alert the universe has ever come up with. "Welcome to Zagreus, hope you enjoy the constant, nagging feeling that something is about to catch fire."

When I complain about it—which, to be fair, is basically every day, since there isn't much else to do around here—Viola starts talking about societal drift and recontextualization of the familiar and how, in a few generations, emergency systems on Zagreus will have to use a different color to catch people's attention, since orange will have become so much background noise. That's going to mess with some standard corporate design schematics. Or maybe it'll just mess with the Zagreans, since I can't really see, say, Weyland-Yutani deciding to change their entire corporate color scheme for the sake of one backwoods colony world.

Too bad the corps don't set the plan for Mom and Dad's research. I might not be looking at a sky like a safety light every time I open the window if they did.

My name is Olivia Shipp, and I am not on this planet of my own free will.

Something rustles deep in the bushes below me. I lean further forward, one foot hooked around the tree branch I'm perched on, for balance, and wait to see what's coming. My dish of bait—some chopped-up local fruits, Mom's special Zagreus "sugar water" recipe that she distills from half a dozen types of flower, and an assortment of native insects with low mobility and high caloric density—sits enticingly below me, ready to lure in at least a dozen types of creature. Maybe more. This is still a new world, as far as humanity is concerned. We're making discoveries every day.

The colony's contract with Mom and Dad covers me as well: when I'm the first one to spot something of interest, the credit goes to the colonists, like *they're* the ones out here risking their necks to document another kind of not-quite-squirrel. I don't mind too much. I get a small payment for every discovery I document, and small payments add up. Viola and I—we're twins—will be eighteen soon, old enough to start making our own decisions about where we go and what we do. I want to take us to Earth. I want to meet distant relatives and let Viola see the best doctors in the known galaxy. That means being prepared to pay whatever it costs.

Besides, it's a beautiful day, orange sky notwithstanding, and Kora isn't coming until this afternoon. The colony schools are closed today for some local holiday. No one's cared enough to explain it to me, a weird outsider girl with the mud under her nails and the pollen on her nose. Vi probably knows. Vi knows everything about a new colony like, five minutes before we land, because she says it makes her feel better about having to pull up roots and move again. I think she just likes to feel like the one who knows things, since she never gets to be the one who goes out and *does* them.

I duck my head, feeling guilty for even thinking that. It's not Vi's fault that she can't go outside as much as we'd both like her to. She has some weird, previously undocumented autoimmune disease. She's seen doctors all over the galaxy, and none of them have been able to help her. Both our parents take extra work, every chance they get, to make sure she has the best care possible. I love my sister. Even when she annoys the pants off of me, I love my sister. I shouldn't be mad at her for things she can't help.

There's another rustle in the bushes. My attention snaps toward the sound, concern for my sister forgotten as I hold my breath and wait to see what emerges.

Slowly, nose pressed to the ground and twitching about a mile a minute, a long, low-slung herbivore comes slithering into the open. I call them "snuffle-squirrels," and my mother calls them something long, scientific, and dull. Either way, it's nothing new, and my shoulders slump in disappointment.

Most of the smaller life-forms on Zagreus skipped evolving proper limbs in favor of fleshy little stumps, like the legs on a caterpillar, or long, fringy things, like cilia. The snuffle-squirrel splits the difference, with four caterpillar legs in front, four more in back, and cilia along the length of its body. They wave as it walks, giving it a full sense of the space around it.

Mom says the cilia serve the same purpose as a cat's whiskers, and that if a snuffle-squirrel or other member of this planet's evolutionary equivalent to rodents loses too many of them, they'll die, because they won't be able to hunt, climb, or forage. She's a xenobiologist and I'm just a student, so I believe her. Doesn't change the part where it's funny looking as all hell, these weird, super-long squirrel things with waving pom-poms sticking out of their sides.

Waving pom-poms, green fur that has a lot in common with cactus thorns, and four eyes, arrayed sort of like the eyes on a spider. Xenobiology is *weird*.

The snuffle-squirrel makes its cautious way over to the plate of fruit, sniffing repeatedly before deciding the risk is worth the prize. It shoves its whole head into a chunk of bright blue pseudo-melon, and begins to eat noisily. Because it doesn't have paws like an Earth mammal, it has to do its caching internally, storing fat in its tail for the lean seasons. This is a juvenile, tail still thin and fur still evenly spiky.

We've seen snuffle-squirrels in every part of the local biosphere— forest and meadow and arid, scrubby foothills. Zagreus is what people call an "Earth-like planet," meaning it mostly has systems that are at least somewhat cognate to the ones humanity is most familiar with. It's a nice change. Our last colony world, I couldn't go out without massive protective gear, and I'm pretty sure Vi never went out at all, not even during the transfer from ship to living quarters. Air I can breathe without a filter and sunlight on my face is a nice change. I'm not going to object, even if I hate the color of the sky.

Familiar or not, the snuffle-squirrel is a cute little thing. I sketch a quick series of studies, pencil on paper, like the pre-space naturalists. I'll re-create it all on my computer later, but getting a sense of motion with my own hand makes it easier for me to translate it into virtual space. I'm pretty good. I'm getting better. Give me a few more years and I'll be able to get work doing all sorts of graphic design, including the kind that people like my parents need, the kind that charts new worlds for humanity to claim.

Whatever kind of design I wind up doing, it won't be the kind that requires me to travel for years at a time. Once I get my butt Earth-side, it's staying there for at least a little while. I want to know what it's like to have a home, not just a residence.

The snuffle-squirrel is still eating, gulping down melon as fast as it can. It's so focused on what it's doing that it doesn't notice when the ground next to it trembles. I sit up straighter. This, too, is something familiar, but sometimes familiar can be wicked cool.

One moment the ground next to the snuffle-squirrel is smooth and unmoving; the next, it explodes into clumps of dirt and shredded roots as the lion-worm—a sightless, ground-dwelling predator that's sort of like a mole, if moles were made of knives and hatred and cilia—lunges forth and clamps its terrible maw over the snuffle-squirrel's upper body. The poor little herbivore doesn't even have time to squeak.

Exhausted by its lunge, the lion-worm allows the portion of its body protruding from the hole to slump into the dish of tasty treats. The cilia along its sides are bright gold, garishly bright against the muted browns and yellows and blues of the forest; they wave constantly, sampling the air, advising the lion-worm of potential danger. I hold very, very still. Lion-worms have been known to attack humans when they feel like they can take us, and they don't have a sense of fear: they *always* think they can take us.

An adult lion-worm is about the size of an Earth pig, which is more than enough to give me nightmares about the things burrowing up through the floor of our residence. This is a baby, about the size of a cat and ten times as vicious. It could still take my foot off if it decided to attack the tree. Better not to risk it.

The lion-worm eventually recovers its strength and sucks the remainder of the snuffle-squirrel into its maw before retreating underground. It's young and weak enough—comparatively, anyway—that it's probably still hiding its kills rather than taking them back to the colony. The bigger lion-worms could get excited and shred it.

It's tough to be a predator sometimes.

With snuffle-squirrel blood all over my fruit and a big hole next to the platter, I should probably pack it in and head for home. Nothing else is likely to come sniffing around. Still, I hold my position and count slowly backward from twenty. Experience has taught me that patience is a virtue, and animals . . . they understand their own ecosystem. The creatures on Zagreus still don't know exactly what to make of humans. Sometimes they run from us, sometimes they attack us, but mostly, they avoid us. It's safer and easier for all concerned.

So I hold still, and I count, and as I hit three, I'm rewarded with a rustling sound from the bushes. I stop breathing and watch as a creature that looks sort of like a deer, and sort of like a Sirius XI glass beast, and sort of like a pile of rotting meat steps out of the brush. It doesn't have any sort of visible skin. How can something be walking around when it doesn't have *skin*?

It approaches the platter of treats, lowers its head, and begins delicately licking up the snuffle-squirrel blood with a long, forked tongue. I pull out my recorder and snap several quick pictures before starting the video.

This pretty little monstrosity is getting me and Vi one step closer to Earth.

It takes a long time, but eventually the meat-deer finishes lapping up the blood and trots off for richer, bloodier pastures. I slide down from the tree and retrieve the rest of my gear from the bush where I concealed it. I always pack more than I need. Tip one for wilderness survival: know exactly how much you can carry, and don't take a scrap more, but don't feel like you have to carry everything the whole time. Caching isn't just for snuffle-squirrels.

I'm feeling pretty good about today. The morning has been beautiful, despite the orange sky—that's never going to feel normal to me—and Kora isn't going to be here for hours. I have plenty of time to get ready. I grin to myself as I trot along the familiar path from the woods to the field behind our residence. Kora's never actually come to *visit* me before. Maybe this is the start of something . . . well, something beautiful.

Or maybe she's just one of those colony kids who likes to get a few kicks in with a transient girl, knowing she won't have to live with the consequences of breaking my heart. I've heard stories about a few girls like that, enough of them to leave me a little anxious and leave Vi fiercely, furiously defensive against anyone who thinks they're good enough for *her* twin but hasn't done anything to prove it.

The thought is enough to knock the smile off my face. It's not that I don't love my sister. I do. I love her more than every sun we've ever lived under, and since every sun is technically a star—as she is grindingly, pedantically fond of reminding me—that means I love her more than all the stars in the sky. She's my mirror, my echo, the other half of my heart. It's just that she's also . . .

She's also *Viola*. Stubborn and sullen and way too willing to prioritize facts she's read on a screen somewhere over things she's experienced for herself. Things like "ninety-five percent of all teenage relationships end in heartbreak, you know," and "colonists don't form permanent bonds with the children of transient scientists," and my personal favorite, "I may not have met her yet, but even I can tell that she is *way* out of your league."

Sometimes my sister can be a massive brat is what I'm saying here.

The wide stretch of flat, empty plain between the edge of the forest and our residence—which we constructed well outside the bounds of the official colony settlement, according to their by-laws, which are weird and restrictive and verge on what Vi primly refers to as a "cult mentality"—is covered in an array of brightly colored grasses. Each color stops growing at a different height, and while they look like they should belong to half a dozen different species, they're all part of the same vast, conjoined vegetable colony.

The green ones are sharp. As in flesh-ripping, blood-drawing sharp. Which makes sense, since they're short enough to be hidden by the purple ones, which are super-absorbent and capable of sucking up any liquid they come into contact with. Mom says the grasses aren't technically carnivorous, just very, very opportunistic, but if you ask me, any plant that wants to drink my blood is *plenty* carnivorous.

I step around the danger spots, keeping an eye on the ground as I head for the residence. Lion-worms like to hunt in the grass, letting the grass's natural dangers herd smaller creatures into supposedly safe areas and then striking from below. I can see the furrows where they've attacked before. I'm big enough, and they're confused enough by bipedal locomotion, that I should be safe . . . for now. Dad says they're learning, and what they're learning is that humans can be delicious. The colonists may find themselves with an extermination assignment on their hands sooner than they expect.

He should know. My father is Dr. John Shipp, the second-best behavioral xenobiologist in the known universe. If he can't predict what an alien life-form is going to do, he turns to the best behavioral xenobiologist in the business . . . who just happens to be my mother, Dr. Katherine Shipp. Between the two of them, they have more degrees in more fields of horrifying alien biology than I would ever have believed possible.

Fat lot of good it does Viola and me. Our parents are independent contractors, meaning they went through all courses necessary to land themselves steady, good-paying jobs with one of the megacorps—Mom even did a tour with the colonial marines, since they have access to restricted worlds with horrifying wildlife she wanted to poke; she's a terrifyingly good shot, which isn't helping our dating prospects—and then after all that, they decided choosing their own jobs was more important than, you know, *stability*.

You'd think people who had two kids the first time they tried would be more interested in going where the money is, but not our parents. They want to go where the *science* is, and where the *science* is, well. Apparently, that's middle-of-nowhere colony worlds, ones where the local wildlife has yet to be cataloged, analyzed, and neatly filed away. We've lived on fifteen different colony worlds since Viola and I were born, and sometimes I feel like our parents would be happier with twice that number. They want to see the cosmos, and we don't get much choice about whether or not we come along.

I step out of the grass and into the perimeter of our residence. The colony we're currently working for is all about reuse and recycling and "minimizing humanity's impact on the galaxy." Pretty words. Not so pretty when the lion-worms are erupting out of the ground and dragging the family cat off to their nest. Our parents burned everything within ten yards of our residence the day we unpacked it, following the burn with the application of quick-setting plast-steel. The stuff hardens in the presence of oxygen, becoming strong enough to be used for repairs that need to hold up to open vacuum, and it dissolves when exposed to certain biodegradable compounds. When we leave, the planet will recover, and by the end of the first growing season, there won't be any sign that we were ever here.

Sometimes it gets to me, living the way we do, skipping across the galaxy, never leaving anything behind. Not even footprints. We're like ghosts, haunting every world we come across.

No one's going to mourn us when we're gone.

2

VIOLA

FIVE FEET PAST THE PERIMETER, OUR
electric fence hums and crackles to itself, prepared to keep anything that wants to cause us trouble at a safe distance. I raise my
wrist, letting its sensors pick up the signal from my ID bracelet. There's a click. The fence deactivates, and two of the panels
swing inward, letting me through.

Visitors have to come through the gate, and have to enter an
actual, manual access code, which Dad changes weekly. I've never
been able to understand why he puts so much weight on security,
since it's not like we're a target. We're the biologists. Without
us, the colony is harder to sustain. If we're ever going to be attacked, it's going to happen when we're on our way out the door,
not while we're doing the job we were hired for.

The residence is the standard model, low, squat, and sturdy,
with solar panels on the roof and deceptively large windows that
are almost always sealed, in case the local pollen aggravates Vi's

allergies. Sometimes her body forgets how to breathe. On those nights I feel like I have to breathe for both of us, sucking air in and pushing it out, willing her lungs to remember a time when we did everything together, when there were no differences between us. If I can live, so can she. She just has to remember how.

The rover is gone. Mom and Dad are in the field, or maybe they've gone to the settlement to give another environmental impact report to the planetary governor. Either way, Viola's alone in there, and I have no idea how long she's been that way. I pick up my steps, keying in the lock code almost without breaking stride. The door opens, and I step into the front room, which has been basically the same for as long as I can remember. Couch; coffee table; vidscreen; shelves of interesting biological samples and fossils collected from a dozen colony worlds; family photos on the walls. It even smells the way it always does, a complex mixture of preservatives and Earth spices that I swear Mom mixes in her lab and aerosolizes while we're all sleeping.

When I was little, I thought we carried the front room with us from world to world. Now I realize that our parents reconstruct it each time we land, getting things positioned *just so* before they even bother with our bedrooms. This is where we're a family together, the public space that bonds and binds us. This is home.

Speaking of . . . "Viola! I'm home!"

"Lies! Foul lies and pretense!"

I groan theatrically as I walk toward our shared bedroom. "Are you watching vids for drama or what?"

"Got bored, read some poetry," she calls back. "Shakespeare will never die."

"Witness our names," I agree, and poke my head into her room. "Hi."

"Hi," says my twin, offering me a wan smile. She's curled on her bed with a vidscreen against her knees and a heart monitor hooked around her elbow like a misguided fashion statement. She's beautiful. "See anything interesting today?"

"I dunno. I'm seeing you right now."

She sticks her tongue out at me.

We were born identical. We still look almost exactly alike, even accounting for all the little differences our lives have sculpted into us. We're both pale, like Dad, although Viola's paler: she never goes outside. We have the same white-blonde hair. Mom says we don't appreciate it enough, usually while patting her own messy brown mop and looking sort of inappropriately jealous. I mean, she made us. She should be delighted by her work, not annoyed that we got a better draw on the DNA than she did.

Only Mom has brown hair and brown eyes and Dad has reddish-blond hair and blue eyes, and they should have had comfortably brown-haired children, brown-eyed and healthy. Instead, they got Viola and me. Everything about us is washed-out, from our hair down to our eyes, which look like someone was playing with graphic filters over standard blue and forgot to set us back to full opacity before saving their work. Sometimes I wonder if us being so pale is somehow related to the genetic condition that's been eating Viola alive since we were born. Maybe it's not jealousy that makes Mom say our hair will eventually change colors. Maybe it's regret.

These days, no one mistakes us for one another, not even when we trade clothes and pretend to be interchangeable. Vi is slimmer than me on every axis, a fairy tale girl locked in a tower that moves from colony to colony without ever opening its doors and letting her go. Neither of us tans—I burn fast and bad, enough

13

so that fears of cancer have kept me covered in sunscreen since I was a toddler—but I've still managed to pick up a scattering of freckles across the bridge of my nose. Vi used to count them every day. These days, she pretends they aren't there. They're one more difference between us, one more piece of permanent proof that twinhood isn't forever.

She's going to keep getting sicker and I'm going to keep getting older, until one day I turn around and she's not there anymore. Just a bunch of holos and the vague memory that I was supposed to have a sister.

I walk across the room to her window, which she's propped open to let the morning air in. I prop my elbows on the windowsill, put my chin in my hands, and sigh. Viola doesn't react. Subprime. I sigh again, heavier this time, really putting my back into it. It's surprisingly satisfying, and I inhale, preparing to keep going.

A pillow hits me on the side of the head. I turn. Viola is glaring at me, her lower lip pushed out in the beginning of a pout, another pillow in her hand.

"*Don't* make me throw this," she says. "I'm weak, remember? Mom will be mad."

I laugh. "If you're weak, most people are already dead."

"Maybe they are. Maybe we're the last people alive in the universe, and all these colony worlds have been our parents trying to refine their holotech to make us feel like we're less alone. It would sure explain all the stupid, wouldn't it?"

I wrinkle my nose. "And then some."

Living a transient life, hopping between colonies, is a great way to remember that no matter how much humanity changes and grows, it's always going to be human, and it's always going to be sort of awful. Technically colonies are still subject to Earth laws, but in functionality, they get to make their own choices and do their own thing, and most of the time, what they choose to do is pretty irritating.

One world didn't let kids talk in the presence of their elders. Another world insisted everyone work if they wanted to be allowed to stay within the established safe zone—and that included the elderly, the disabled, and children who should have been considered too young to do anything but go to school and make weird construction paper art. Our parents had been locked into that contract, and Vi and I had spent six months officially working for them, labeling samples and feeding their lab specimens. Not fun.

Viola waves a hand languidly until she pulls me back from my temporary contemplation. "Earth to Olivia, Earth to Olivia, come in, Olivia. Or maybe that should be 'Zagreus to Olivia,' huh?"

"Shut up." I throw the pillow back at her. She laughs.

"Oh, you've got it *bad* for this colony girl," she says. "Does she have any idea how firmly you're already wrapped around her little finger?"

"Shut up."

"She doesn't!" Vi manages to sound delighted and conspiratorial at the same time. It's a nice trick. "How much will you give me if I don't tell her?"

"I won't suffocate you in your sleep, how's that?" I walk over and plop down on the edge of the bed.

Viola snorts. "As if. You'd miss me too much if I were gone."

"Technically true, I guess." I watch as she tucks the pillow behind her back, makes an unhappy noise, and squirms around until she finds a position that doesn't hurt. Her condition means our room is set up to keep her as comfortable as possible, something I think she resents more than I do. Everything about it—the firmness of our mattresses, the material of the pillows, *everything*—reminds her that she's sick, and more, that there's no gene therapy, no real treatment, just trying to stay comfortable.

It sucks. We left the colony before this one because she had an honestly frightening allergic reaction to one of the local plants. Our folks cut their contract half-finished and got us off-world before Viola could stop breathing. Not good.

We both sort of hoped they'd take us back to Earth after that. We have grandparents there that we've never met, cousins who could show us all the sights—the good stuff, not the tourist trash—and doctors who could maybe do more for Vi than these colony quacks. Instead, we're here. Zagreus. The middle of nowhere's middle of nowhere.

Lucky us.

Viola stops squirming, reaches over, and touches my hand. "What are you and Kora going to do?" she asks, pulling me neatly out of my own head. That's the best thing about having a twin. Even when we're fighting—and we fight a *lot*, it's my second-favorite thing to do, after drawing—she always knows when I need her to distract me from myself. I know the same things about her, even if she doesn't need the save as often as I do. We don't have any secrets from each other. Not one.

"Mom said I could check the traps around the main lion-worm nest this afternoon," I say. "I asked Kora if she wanted to come with me. She's probably going to live here for the rest of her life, and she's never seen most of the local flora and fauna. She thinks it'll be really educational."

Viola's expression turns smug and knowing. "Educational, huh? Wow. So that's how you got her to notice that you're alive? By offering her something that can make you dead?"

My ears burn red. I cover them with my hair and glower at my sister, who laughs.

"It's okay! It's okay. It's really cute, actually." She sobers, laughter fading. "I'm glad you found somebody you like enough to go poking horrifying predatory things with, that's all."

"She's nice," I mumble.

"Wow. That's all you can say about her? 'She's nice'? Because you've been talking like she's a brand-new skycruiser with all the bells and whistles and also a built-in carbon-power laser that can cut through diamond."

I elbow her. "Stop."

Vi laughs, starting to say something—and catches herself, looking at me carefully. "You really like this girl, don't you?"

I nod, silent.

"Well, then, I'm excited to meet her. I'm sure she's amazing, if you like her this much." She gives me a sudden, unexpectedly hard shove. "But now you need to go shower and change your clothes. You look like a farmhand. Everyone knows city girls don't go for agricultural workers."

"Brat," I say, and get out of the bed.

"You know it." Viola grins. She's still grinning when I walk out of the room.

I have the best sister in the galaxy. Sorry for all those other sisters out there, but it's just simple science.

3

KORA

EVERY COLONY WORLD I'VE EVER
been on has come with its own resource problems. One world,
they couldn't get any crops to grow, and they were far enough
off the main shipping channels that they only got restocked every
four local months, meaning there was constant food rationing,
and even more constant threat of robbery by the neighbors if
they thought you had a half can more of beans than you were
supposed to. Not fun. Another world, two-thirds of the colonists
were allergic to some local tree—not anaphylaxis-level allergies,
just sneezing and misery—so it was antihistamines on the constantly rationed table.

Zagreus is weird about metal and water. The whole colony is
made from salvaged and recycled goods. Nothing goes to waste,
nothing gets thrown away, and they expand only at the rate that
they can acquire raw materials from off-world. Even using a native stick to prop a window open would be anathema to the lovely

people of Zagreus, who think it's time for humanity to start giving back to the galaxy.

When Dad handed me the colony charter, I was initially afraid—okay, terrified—that the colonists were going to take their "nothing local, no exploitation of the planet" ideals to the worst possible extreme and make us abide by the local rules about water rationing. I've done water rationing. I *hate* water rationing. Humanity has come up with a lot of amazing stuff, but as far as I'm concerned, all of it was in service to the birth of indoor plumbing.

Fortunately, Dad's a solid negotiator, and managed to get us an exemption from the standard colony restrictions. Not that I'd have paid attention to them anyway. There's nothing like a good hot shower. Zagreus has a high water table and we have a medical-grade water filtration system. One of the few true perks of living in a pre-fab residence is the ability to shower for as long as I want to without worrying about either the tanks or the heat running out. I shampoo twice, condition once, scrub, exfoliate, and am starting to consider the virtues of shaving my legs when the residence proximity alert gives one soft, polite chime. Something larger than a snuffle-squirrel is approaching the boundary.

Tapping the key tile on the shower wall brings up a waterproof vidscreen permanently trained on the yard. The residence security system isn't what it could be—what Mom wishes it actually *were*—but Dad upgrades it every chance he gets, and the image of the girl walking toward our front door is painfully crystalline clear.

Kora is taller than I am. Not hard, given my anatomy, but enough that when I talk to her I have to tilt my head back, ever so slightly, and gaze up at her like I'm an astronomer looking at the moon. Her skin is a rich, warm brown, gifted by genetics and enhanced by regular exposure to Zagreus's twin suns, which move through the sky in a delicate ballet that keeps inspiring local theater groups to choreograph long, boring interpretive dances of what they assume the native creation myths would have been, if there had been anyone here to dream them up.

Her hands are long and slim and her face is perfect, big eyes and soft lips and a chin that comes to a delicate point, so she always looks like she's just heard the cleverest joke ever and is willing to repeat it for you, but only if you feel like being a little bit naughty. She's . . . she's *perfect*. All the geneticists in all the world could work for a thousand years and never build anything as effortlessly flawless as Kora Burton, the love of my life.

I don't care what Viola says about the statistics for teenage love affairs. I don't care if she wants to call this "puppy love" and laugh at my fumbling attempts at convincing Kora I would be the best girlfriend in the known universe. Kora is beautiful and smart and better than I deserve and—

And she's about to ring our buzzer and I'm naked in the shower with suds in my hair.

"Crap!" I grab the nozzle, directing it at my head, ignoring the fact that it means blasting myself in the face with water. Whatever it takes to get myself rinsed off as fast as possible. "Crap, crap, *crap!*"

All right. I've already done all the things that *need* to be done. I slap wildly at the wall until I shut off the water and the vidscreen almost at the same time, then tumble out of the shower and onto the bathroom floor with an almighty *crash*, winding up tangled in my discarded clothes, the bathmat, and my towel, all at the same time.

I'm swearing steadily as I bounce back to my feet, grab my

clean clothes from the rack by the sink, and start jerking them on. Putting socks on wet feet is punishment for anything I may have done wrong in the last year.

The residence proximity alert chimes twice. To make sure I don't miss the relevance of that sound, the buzzer rings a split second later, a loud, piercing sound that punctures every inch of the residence. I wince.

"Olivia?" Viola may be sick, but she can yell when she needs to. Yelling is probably her greatest talent. "You want me to get that?"

"I've got it!" Crap. Crap *crap* crap *crap*.

The buzzer doesn't ring again. I pull my shirt on and race, still dripping, hair wet enough that it's plastered to the sides of my head in a solid, sodden sheet, to get to the door before Kora decides I've changed my mind and don't want her here. *Please don't let her leave,* I think frantically. *Please don't let her be mad.*

I wrench the door open, panting, and she's still there. The world is beautiful, the world is perfect, and *she's still there.* On the spot, I decide Zagreus has an orange sky because it matches her curls, which are a thousand shades of brown and a few scattered shades of gold and red. She's like every tiny fragment of an Earth autumn, wrapped in the skin of a single girl and dropped here on this distant colony world so people won't ever forget that we came from someplace beautiful.

She's also smirking at me.

"Your shirt's on backward," she says. "Am I early?"

"What? No. No!" I touch the front of my shirt, which is definitely riding too high. Dammit. So much for being suave. "I was running late. I saw this deer-thing in the woods, and it was cool, and I lost track of time, and anyway, you're here. I'll just . . . go change my shirt . . . and then we can get going. I'm sure you're eager to see everything, and—"

"Actually, I was sort of hoping I could meet this mysterious sister you've talked about." Kora's smile is wide, sincere, and heartbreakingly lovely. How can anyone tell her "no"? Ever? Her life must be one long succession of "yes," and that's fine. That's exactly the way this ought to work.

Then reality crashes down on me, and brings my thoughts to a stuttering halt. "You want to meet Viola? Really?"

"Of course," says Kora. "All the kids at school are curious about her, and about where you live, I mean—wow!" She spreads her arms. "Look at all this *space*!"

It sounds weird when she puts it like that. The colonists on Zagreus have a whole planet at their disposal. Four continents, a bunch of island clusters, some pretty sweet oceans. They could have their choice of climate zones, most of them reasonably Earth-like, even if the ice caps do have a nasty tendency to start raining sulfur. I'm not sure how that happens, and honestly, I don't really want to know. Planetary geography is creepy when you look at it too hard.

All that space, and what do they do? They cram themselves into a single main settlement, whole families sharing residences barely bigger than the room I share with Viola. It's all part of their "salvage and recycle" mentality, like they can only have more space once they've managed to beg, borrow, or steal the raw materials from off-planet. They never run. They never spin in big circles with their arms out, remembering that the whole *point* of colonization is choosing worlds where they'll have the space to do anything they want, not bound by the population constraints on Earth. As far as I know, apart from two small seasteads and one mining operation in the high mountains, the entire human population of Zagreus is in the main colony settlement. One good disaster and they're done.

People who live like we do, surrounded by nature, with room to breathe . . . we must be a novelty.

I don't want to be a novelty. I want to be a girl, showing another girl beautiful things so she'll think of me when she thinks of them. So she'll think of me as something beautiful. And I love my sister, but we have the same face, and right now, I don't want there to be any confusion when Kora thinks of that face. I want to know that she's thinking of me, and only me, and not Viola at all.

"She's, uh, sleeping," I say, and smile, hoping it looks real, and not like me making excuses for my own neurosis. "But my folks said we could have a party the next time they go on a research run, so you'll be able to meet her then."

"A party?" Kora perks right up. "Here?"

"Yes." No. "We can have a great time, and there's so much space, it'll be the best party of the year." I am so dead. I am officially a corpse with delusions of animation. I can't throw a *party*. My parents will never allow it. They'll skin and pin me for even suggesting it. And I can't *not* throw a party, not with Kora looking at me all bright-eyed and excited, like I'm the coolest girl she's ever met.

Maybe I *am* the coolest girl she's ever met. I have the residence with space for a party, right? I try to look cool, and like I'm not secretly dying inside. "You're totally invited, of course."

"Uh, I should hope so. Oh, wow, this is going to be so good! I'll make sure everyone in our class hears."

Subprime. Either she's not as interested in me as I am in her, or there's stuff about colony flirting that I do *not* understand. I keep my smile in place as I say, "Let me grab my shoes and my field kit, and we're good to go."

Kora blinks those big brown eyes, and I want to do whatever she wants me to do. I am putty in her hands. "I don't even get to come inside?"

I want to do whatever she wants me to do *except* let her into the house, where Viola will absolutely want to talk to her, and she will absolutely find out that I'm a liar, and I'll have to try to explain what I can't even fully articulate to myself. "Not when Vi's asleep," I say, with my best regretful look. "Dad's rule. If I break it . . ."

"No party," she concludes, just like I'd hoped she would. Maybe I'm better at this lying thing than I thought I was.

"I'll be right back," I promise, and duck inside, racing for my room. Need a jacket, need shoes, need my field kit, need—

"Aren't you going to invite Kora in?"

Need to smother my sister with a pillow. I freeze in the doorway, giving Viola an apologetic look. "I don't . . . want . . . to?" I try.

Viola rolls her eyes. "She's going to have to meet me eventually. Being ashamed of me won't make me disappear, or make your room available for heavy petting when our parents aren't looking."

I want to be scandalized, but I've already been trying to figure out whether Kora would be cool with living out an old children's song—Olive and Kora, sitting in a tree, K-I-S-S-I-N-G—and so I just roll my eyes and head for my dresser. "I'm not *ashamed* of you. I just want her to get attached to me as the cool, suave Shipp sister before she gets her pick of twins."

"I don't like girls. I'm not going to steal your protogirlfriend."

"That doesn't mean she won't decide she likes you better. Maybe you'd be the mysterious twin that doesn't want her back, and that'll make all the difference." I sit on the edge of my bed to adjust my socks, trying not to grimace at the way they stick to my damp toes. Mom would yell at me for not taking the time to dry off before dressing. Chafing is a danger in the field. Sorry, Mom. Slowing down is a danger in the field of love.

"If she really likes you, she won't even notice me, and if she doesn't really like you, it's better for us to find out now." Viola looks at me anxiously. "I don't want you to get hurt."

I pull on my boots. They seal themselves around my feet, becoming snug and tight enough to keep any of the nastier local insects from working their way inside. They're not true insects, of course, not in the Earth sense, but humans like to put things into terms we can understand. So we call little skittering things "bugs," and we call soft furry things "bunnies," and we work our way across the galaxy in a river of increasing inaccuracy.

Everything we find gets a scientific name, of course, and colonists usually give things "local names," things that everyone who grows up on that specific world will use to describe the creatures they share it with, but for most of the galaxy, it's bugs, all the way. And there are so many bugs. Almost every world that has life has bugs, something chitinous and quick and impossible to eradicate. It's enough to give a squishy mammalian girl a complex.

"I want to get hurt, Vi," I say, trying—and failing—to keep my voice light, carefree. See? I am Olivia Shipp, adventurer, and I am cool with a little pain. "I want to be in love, and the one thing everyone says is that being in love means getting hurt. So let me get hurt, okay? Let me see what it's like to fall and hope that someone's going to be at the bottom to catch me."

She scowls, disapproval obvious. "*Please* be careful."

"Can't be careful when you're falling." I blow her a kiss and

I'm gone, heading back to the front door with long, loping steps, my kit slung over my shoulder and my hair still dripping. My whole scalp itches from the tacky wetness. I don't care, because when I open the door, there's Kora, waiting patiently.

Okay, not patiently. She's tapping her foot, and I'd have to be terminally distracted to miss the irritated glint in her eye as she asks, "No more last-minute errands? You didn't forget your lucky rock?"

"Hey, everybody needs a lucky rock," I object, stepping outside and closing the door behind me. It locks, audibly. Viola will be safe as long as she stays in bed and doesn't try to push herself. "What else am I going to throw if we get attacked out there? My boots? No, thanks."

For the first time, Kora looks unsure of herself. "You don't really think we're going to get attacked, do you?"

If I weren't so infatuated with her, I'd be annoyed. Colony kids come in two flavors: hard as nails and so soft it's almost offensive. Kora is the second sort. All the kids here on Zagreus are the second sort. Some of them play at being tough, but none of them step foot outside the colony walls when they don't have to; they look at the stars and shake their fists and curse the corps, and they act like that makes them tough. I hate that about most of them.

I don't hate it about Kora. She's soft and she's sweet and I can protect her, I can teach her what it's like to have someone who loves you, someone who's willing to fight for you. I can fight for her. I can do such a good job of fighting for her. I can.

"No, we're not going to get attacked," I assure her, easily. This is my place. Not for long, maybe—we could be on our way to a new assignment tomorrow—but for right now, this is *mine*. No one's getting hurt on my watch, especially not this pretty, pretty girl with her soft, soft hair. "I'm taking you to see the sights, not to suffer."

"I'll hold you to that," she says.

"Please do." I start around the residence to the pop-up garage in the rear. It's a luxury to have a private vehicle, especially on a colony world this new: most vehicles get seized by the planetary government as soon as their erstwhile owners touch down, added to the communal fleet that moves people and supplies around the planet. My parents have a clause in their contracts that forbids the seizure of our family's all-terrain vehicle, because we have to live so far outside the main settlement to observe the native animals behaving normally, and we need to be able to get Viola to the hospital at a moment's notice. We can't wait for the loaner fleet to dispatch an available vehicle to our location, not when my sister's life is potentially on the line.

It's funny, though. That's the reason my folks always give for holding on to the ATV, and Vi's medical history supports it, but I can't remember the last time we had to rush her to the hospital. She's not variable, emergency intervention sick. She's just . . . sick. All the time. Sick but stable.

Kora's gasp when I turn on the garage light to reveal the ATV is gratifying. I puff my chest out as I take the keys down from their hook. "I've been driving since I was eleven," I say, supposedly to reassure but really to brag. Who wouldn't, in my position? "I'm pretty good at it. You'll be totally safe with me."

"Wow," she breathes. "This is *cherry*."

It's not, it's really, really not, it's banged and dented and there's a scrape in the paint that Dad has insisted be left through three rehabs as an object lesson in what happens when I take the ATV out without permission. Which I am technically doing right now. Because I am too cool to ask permission, and also because I'm pretty sure my parents would have said no.

"Yeah, she's a beauty," I say, and cringe, because that was *not* cool. Kora's never going to think I'm anything other than sub-prime if I keep breaking out lines like that.

She doesn't seem to have noticed, thankfully. She's running a hand across the fender of our ATV, and I wish she'd caress me like that, that she'd look at me with that much adoration in her eyes. Maybe I didn't need to worry about introducing her to Viola. Maybe it was the ATV I needed to be afraid of all along.

That's stupid. *I'm* stupid. People have been falling in love and figuring out how to deal with it since the dawn of time, or else there wouldn't be people anymore. I can do this. "Come on, get in," I say. "I'm going to show you something gorgeous."

She grins at me, and her teeth are so white against her skin, and there's nothing on this planet as gorgeous as she is.

4

FIELDS
OF FLOWERS

KORA MAY BE THE BEST THING
Zagreus has to offer, but she's not the only natural wonder of the
world. The trail my parents have painstakingly cut through the
woods opens onto a field of impossible flowers, their petals as
long as my hand and colored in a thousand iridescent shades of
rainbow shine. I can't say what color they are, because they're *all*
the colors, blue from one direction, red from another, yellow and
pink and orange and everything. They catch and refract the light,
scattering it like prisms.

The flowers grow on towering stems that stretch taller than
the neighboring trees. The colonists are going to be arguing for
decades about whether these are bushes or trees or individual
flowers. As if the nomenclature matters. They're beautiful. That's
the only thing that's important. They're so, so beautiful. I hear
Kora's small, half-swallowed gasp and know, without question,
that this was the right decision.

"Are these real?" Kora demands. "These can't be real. They just . . . can't."

"They're real," I say. "If you ask my father, he'll say that they're technically not flowers, they're fruiting bodies, and they're closer to being a very large, very complicated fungus than they are to being true vegetable matter. And then he'll tell you a lot of things you don't need to know about the way humans categorize alien biologics, and why we need to rethink the entire taxonomy of life. Better to stick with me, and the easy answers."

"Which are?" Kora sounds amused. That's good. That's better than I was hoping for.

"They're real."

She laughs, and the sound is even more beautiful than the flowers around us, even more beautiful than the rest of her. I think I'd give just about anything to make her laugh like that again.

"Wow, okay." She wipes tears from the corner of one eye. "Okay. What else have you got?"

I grin. I can't help myself. "Hold on."

The giant flowers furl and unfurl as we pass beneath them, sending little puffs of pollen into the air. It's virtually non-allergenic, even for off-world species like humans; more interestingly, it's virtually sterile. It cancels out scents on contact. An Earth dog would get totally lost in this little flower bed, unable to sniff its own trail. We're still trying to figure out what evolutionary advantage comes with being the opposite of perfume. Clearly there has to be *something*, because these not-really-flowers are thriving. We've found them all over the planet, growing in climates from arid, rocky mountainsides to the humid rainforest riverbanks.

They feed the planet's more mobile creatures, which come

to snack on the sweet fruits that form in clusters around the base of the flowers. They provide shelter for small animals, and good hunting grounds for the large ones. Something about these flowers *works*, and once we figure out what it is, the rest of the ecology of Zagreus will snap into focus.

And then, as always, it will be time for us to leave. I steal a glimpse at Kora, who stares, wide-eyed with wonder, at the flowers all around us. It doesn't matter if she breaks my heart. It's not like I'm going to be here long enough for either one of us to learn to live with the consequences.

The stalks grow thicker, their burdens of purplish-red fruit growing heavier and more frequent. The flowers increase in size at the same rate, like they're trying to maintain a steady ratio. The sprays of pollen become more frequent, too, washing over us in a glittering film.

"Wow," breathes Kora. "Mom was talking about a big score this morning at breakfast, but this is so much *better* than any junker she has in orbit."

I don't want to pry. I don't want to bring Kora's mother into this. I want the moment to last forever. "It's harder to get to orbit, that's for sure," I say, as noncommittally as I can.

"Anyway, Michel was wrong. This is amazing." Kora is laughing as she turns to face me, laughing as she breaks my heart. Not completely: I think it can be mended. But enough.

I stop the ATV. The motion is enough to cause the nearby flowers to shower us in pollen, wiping away any traces of scent that a local predator might follow. Kora blinks, slowly realizing that she's said something to upset me.

"Olivia?" she asks. "What's wrong?"

"Michel," I say. "The kid in our science class? The one who

calls me 'freaky girl' and talks about how weird Vi must be if our parents let her stay home when they're willing to let me out of the house? The one who pushed me off the school porch last week?"

Kora's cheeks flush red. She's embarrassed. I'm startled to realize that I'm glad. If she's saying what I think she's saying, she *should* be embarrassed.

"I've known him since we were kids," she says. "Our parents were on the colony design committee together."

And now Kora's father is gone, off to a colony with less repressive rules for resource allocation, and her mother is the closest thing Zagreus has to a planetary governor, leaving her with little time to keep tabs on her only daughter. I've always envied Kora her freedom, the way no one keeps tabs on her inside the colony. Now I'm starting to wonder whether that same freedom turned her cruel.

"He knew you were coming here today." It isn't a question.

Cheeks growing even redder, Kora nods.

"Does he know *why* you were coming here today?"

She doesn't answer.

"I'm perfectly comfortable walking back to the residence. I've done it before." Not usually from this far, but there's a first time for everything. "Do you want to tell me the truth, or do you want to walk?"

"What? No!" For the first time, she looks more alarmed than embarrassed. "We can't walk from—"

I pull the keys out of the ignition, bounce them twice in my hand, and lob them into the fruiting stalks in front of us. They land with a clatter and a jingle, vanishing into underbrush. Kora sucks in her breath, the sound sharp and horrified. She didn't think I'd do it. *I* didn't think I'd do it. I'm going to be on my hands and knees for, like, an hour before we can get out of here.

Good. I mean, not good, but also good, because she shouldn't have done that. She should have come here because she wanted to, not because . . . because . . .

"Was this a dare?" I ask. "A bet? Did he say that you couldn't stand one afternoon with those freaky off-world kids?" Another idea strikes me. My eyes narrow. "Was that why you wanted to see Viola?"

"He said she didn't exist," Kora blurts.

I stare at her, horrified. "What?" I finally manage to whisper.

"He said . . . he saw the manifest for your transport. He says it only listed three people: Katherine Shipp, John Shipp, and Olivia Shipp. No Viola. And he said that since you were, you know." Her blush is so deep it makes her look bruised. "Since you were sort of into me, he said I could probably get you to invite me over. So I could see whether you really had a sister."

"She comms in for class," I say. This isn't happening. This can't be happening. Kora didn't come out here on a bet, she came out here because she *likes* me, and . . .

And . . .

And I'm not that good at lying to myself. I never have been.

Kora shakes her head. "She comms in, but she looks just like you. It could be a trick. I don't know why you'd be pretending to be your own twin sister, but Michel says your family gets an extra water ration. He thought maybe you were defrauding the colony for extra resources."

The day is warm, but I suddenly feel very cold. I lean back until I'm looking at that awful orange sky, and say, "If he had access to our contract, not just our passage manifests, he'd know that we don't *have* a water ration. We have permission to set up outside the colony grid and filter what we need from the local water table. The colonial government doesn't like it, since they have this weird thing about making as little impact on the planet as possible—"

"It's not a *weird thing*, it's *responsible custodianship*, and—"

I ignore her. I'm angry, I'm so angry, and this isn't fair, this isn't how the day was supposed to go. I was supposed to show her beautiful things, and then she was supposed to just fall into my arms like they do in the movies. She was supposed to love me. "—but we're recycling almost as much water as we take out, and since we're here to study the wildlife, we *can't* be on the grid. We're not defrauding anyone for anything. My sister is real, and my family has a job to do, and this is awful."

Viola was afraid Kora would break my heart. I don't think any of us understood how good she'd be at doing it.

Kora's eyes fill with tears. Part of me wants to comfort her. I've been watching her and wishing I could touch her, hold her, let her hold me, a lot longer than I've been angry with her. But most of me is just furious, and maybe kind of sad. This isn't how I wanted my first crush to go.

"I'm sorry, Olivia," she says. "I shouldn't have said 'yes' when he asked if I'd do it, but I was . . . I wanted an excuse to come see you, and . . ."

"Wait." I blink. "You wanted an excuse to come see me?"

She nods, curls bobbing like they're in agreement, like they have a life of their own. I want to touch them so badly. I keep my hands where they are.

"You kept asking, but we're so far outside the boundary, and my mother *hates* it when I ask about going outside the boundary, I didn't—I didn't want to fight with her, you know? I didn't want to make her mad. But then Michel made it sort of a dare, and it was enough to make me go ahead and ask." She sniffles. "I didn't think she'd say yes. And you kept asking, and she'd said yes, and so I went ahead and said okay, and I'm sorry, honestly I am. I didn't mean for things to go this far."

"Sure you didn't." I shouldn't have thrown the keys away. That was stupid. I should have driven away and left her here, let her understand what it feels like to have someone you trust let you down. Maybe she wouldn't be so quick to be a jerk if she understood the consequences.

I could never have done it. I know myself. When you care about someone, you don't leave them behind.

"I *didn't*!" She sounds sincere. But how much of that is real and how much of that is wishful thinking? She looks at me, a single tear escaping and running down the slope of her perfect cheek. "I don't . . . you're smart, and you're pretty, and you know things about other worlds, you're like this perfect idea of what a teenager is supposed to be, and—"

"Wait. You think I'm pretty?"

Kora nods slowly.

I smile. I can't help it. "So you'd have come out here with me even if Michel hadn't dared you to?"

"I was too nervous."

"Are you still nervous?"

She licks her lips. "Yeah. But not about the same things."

She starts to lean toward me, *Kora starts to lean toward me*, and all I can think is how I'm going to be kissed, I'm going to have my first kiss and it's going to be with the most beautiful girl I've ever seen, and I'm leaning toward her, and this is perfect this is perfect this is—

Something bursts from the ground in front of us, sending the

ATV shaking and knocking Kora out of her seat. She falls hard, shouting when she lands. I stand, ready to jump out and help her, and that's when I see it.

The lion-worm—the *adult* lion-worm—that caused the impact is only a foot from her leg, drawing back to strike.

5

PREDATORY INSTINCTS

"KORA," I WHISPER, AS LOUDLY AS I dare. "Stay very, very still. Try not to make any more noise, okay? Try not to *breathe*."

I can't tell whether she's frozen because she's listening to me or because she's terrified, and I guess it doesn't matter, because the end result is the same: she's not moving. She's balanced on her elbows, one leg—the leg the lion-worm is about to clamp down on—sticking straight out in front of her, the other drawn up toward her body. She's in a good position to get back to her feet, if I can buy her the time she needs to do so.

The ATV is intended to take us into unexplored places and get us home alive. We don't have vehicle-mounted lasers or anything ridiculous like that—it would be impractical *and* sort of silly if we did—but we keep the thing equipped for the problems we're most likely to encounter on a world like Zagreus. Carefully, slowly, I reach behind my seat and feel around until I find the handle of my father's machete.

The lion-worm is still rearing, ready to strike but confused by the combination of Kora's motionlessness and the pollen in the air all around us. Lion-worms hunt by two things: vibrations and smell. I have no idea what attracted this one. Maybe it picked up the cooling rumble of the ATV's engine, or maybe it just came to the surface for the hell of it. They're air-breathers, and behemoths like this probably need to take a deep breath every once in a while. I'd be impressed by the size of it, if not for the situation. It's the biggest lion-worm I've ever seen.

Like the smaller lion-worm I saw earlier, this one has no limbs, only golden, fast-moving cilia waving along its sides. It's strangely beautiful, like lacy, dancing fringe. The creature's head is almost entirely taken up by a razor-sharp beak, and it has no eyes. It has multiple ears instead, running along the sides of its body, and a cluster of nostrils right at the center of its skull, allowing it to detect scents from all different directions. Its skin is waxy white, like the flesh of a corpse. I don't even want to look at it.

I have to get it away from Kora. I jump onto the hood of the ATV, machete in my hand, and jump up and down, shouting as loudly as I can.

"Over here, you stupid, overgrown *worm*! Come on! You call that predation? I see bigger predators in my *breakfast cereal*!"

It swivels, following the sound. Its cilia wave. It's beautiful and it's awful and it's the apex predator for this region, and I don't want it to eat Kora. I jump again, my heels leaving dents in the ATV's hood.

"Over here!"

It finishes its turn, the upper portion of its body dropping as it lunges toward me. This is where I find out whether my plan was actually suicidal, or just really, really stupid.

I throw the machete.

Not at the lion-worm, which has skin thick enough that I'd be lucky to so much as scratch it, but at the fruiting stalk directly behind it. I jump at the same time, straight into the massive cloud of pollen unleashed by the blow.

The lion-worm passes me, heading for the ATV. I land next to Kora, grabbing her and rolling into the shelter of the nearest massive cluster of stalks. Pollen cascades down all around us, covering the world in a yellowish film. The lion-worm sneezes, unable to handle the density of the pollen. I press my lips as close to Kora's ear as I possibly can.

She smells so good. Even with the pollen filling the air and the sharp sweat-smell of panic underscoring everything around us, she smells so good, and she's in my arms, and oh, this is bad. I'm in real trouble here. Viola is going to laugh herself sick. Assuming we don't both get eaten by the lion-worm. That could still happen.

"Consumed by giant carnivore" shouldn't feel like a viable way to get out of being laughed at, but here we are, and there it is, bashing its giant head against the side of the ATV like it can somehow make the vehicle edible.

"Don't move," I breathe, voice barely loud enough to count as a whisper.

Kora nods minutely, her hair brushing against my shoulder. I close my eyes. All we can do now is wait. A lion-worm is faster than a running human across short distances, and a short distance is all we'll have if it turns our way.

It doesn't. It bashes its head against the ATV a few more

times, makes a guttural sound of what I can only interpret as frustration, and dives into the ground, burrowing out of sight in a matter of seconds. I relax fractionally. Kora starts to pull away. I tighten my grip and press my lips back to her ear.

"Wait," I breathe. The lion-worm could come back. They understand enough about the pollen to know that the wind carries it away, that sometimes their prey will hide in the brief blind spots it creates.

I'm not really worried about it, though. A lion-worm that big will have long since learned that there's always better hunting away from the pollen fields. It's not going to come back.

I just want the excuse to hold her.

So I do, counting the seconds as the pollen begins to blow away, measuring them in her breath and the way she shivers, fear slowly giving way to relief. Finally, when I can't put it off any longer, I let go and scoot away before pushing myself back to my feet. Dad's machete is embedded in a nearby stalk. It's bleeding thick, purplish sap that coats the blade and is going to take forever to clean up. Oh, well. Better a little cleanup duty than a lot of being dead.

"If it hasn't come back by now, it's not coming back," I say, pressing a foot against the stalk to steady it and grabbing the machete's handle with both hands. "We need to get out of here. Which means—"

"We need to find the keys," concludes Kora. She stands, brushes herself off, and starts to move toward the scrub where I threw the keys. Then she hesitates, eyeing the multi-hued grass with suspicion. "Is it safe?"

I turn and blink at her, still tugging the machete. It's really wedged in there. I guess I have a better throwing arm than I thought. "Don't you know?"

Kora shakes her head, lips growing thin and pinched. "Why would I?"

"Because . . ." Because Viola never goes outside if she can help it, and she can still name all the most common flora, fauna, and fungus from the territory surrounding our residence. Because Kora *lives* here, Kora was *raised* here: this is her planet. Zagreus belongs to her in a way that it's never going to belong to my sister, or to me. She should know everything about it. She should *want* to know everything about it, the same way the first thing I do when we land on a new colony is start asking for maps. This should matter to her.

She's looking at me, lips still thin and eyes still afraid, and I don't know how to deal with this. She's like one of Mom's hothouse flowers, perfect and beautiful and completely unequipped to live outside the lab.

"Here." I let go of the machete, leaving it embedded in the fruiting stalk. "You get my dad's machete loose, and I'll go find the keys. It should only take me a minute." I'm being optimistic. I still want her to think I'm cool. Isn't that the kicker? This whole date—if I can even call it a date—has been subprime, and I still want her to think I'm cool. Hormones are stupid.

Kora doesn't argue, just moves into position, plants her foot against the base of the stalk, grabs the machete, and yanks. It comes loose with a wet sucking sound, sending her staggering a few feet back. She shoots me a smug grin, and doesn't put it down. I guess she feels better for having a weapon, and I can't blame her for that. I wish *I* had a weapon.

"What was that thing?" she asks.

I don't scold her. If she doesn't know how to tell razorweed from greengrass, there's no way she knows what a lion-worm is. I knew the colony kids were sheltered, but this is sort of scary. What are they going to do when they're the adults and this planet is theirs to take care of? It's like they think they're never going to grow up, like they'll never have to make the hard decisions for themselves.

"We call them 'lion-worms,'" I say. "I mean, there's a scientific name for them, because there's always a scientific name for things, but they look like giant worms with beaks and weird metallic manes, so we go with what's easy. They're the apex predator for this continent."

The grass is the usual mix of types, razorweed and greengrass and yellow butterweed. There's a new kind down toward the bottom, the same pale orange as the sky, with tiny insects stuck to it and apparently half-digested. I make a note to tell Dad that we need to come out here and catalog again.

"Why was it here?"

"I don't know. Maybe it felt the vibrations from the ATV and decided to investigate. Or maybe it was bored and wanted to come up to the surface for a while, and got lucky."

"Got *lucky*?" Kora huffs the words, sounding genuinely offended. "It nearly ate me!"

"Which would have been really lucky for an apex predator that size. Hunting takes energy. Eating you would have meant it got a free meal." A glint of light on metal catches my eye. I squint, and there are the keys.

Naturally, they're right in the middle of a patch of that new orange grass. The stuff that apparently dissolves chitin. Who knows what it might do to my poor, innocent flesh? Nothing good, that's for sure. Subprime.

"Is that all I am to you? A free meal for a *monster*?"

"Okay, so first, the lion-worms are from Zagreus, and humans aren't. Which means your own colony says the lion-worm is more important than we are. Our parents would probably have thrown a party if we'd fed the local wildlife by dying out here." That's not true—my parents, at least, would have been *pissed off* if the one daughter they don't usually have to worry about went and died this stupidly—but as I'm about to fish my keys out of grass that wants to eat me, I'm not as worried about accuracy as maybe I should be. Stupid flesh-eating grass.

Kora makes a small, angry sound. I focus on the keys. They're less confusing.

"Secondly, I mean, I did sort of create a diversion and then pull you away and risk myself in the process, which should be the sort of thing that gets me praise and maybe hugs, not yelled at for thinking you should know about the giant predators that share your planet." I pause. "Not that lion-worms are all that giant, as predators go. You should visit Quincy's Paradise sometime. Worst-named colony *ever*. They have these things that are sort of like bears and sort of like really angry boulders, and they can claw through metal, and—"

I'm babbling to distract myself from what I'm about to do. It almost works. My hand is barely shaking when I reach down into the patch of orange grass and snag the keys. A few blades brush against my fingers. The pain is instantaneous. My skin smokes and bubbles, blistering in sharp lines that exactly match the path of the grass.

I yelp but don't drop the keys. If it's the only thing I do perfectly right today, that's still going to be all right. I do *not* want to reach into that stuff a second time.

"Olivia!" Kora forgets how annoyed she is, how afraid she is of the world outside her safely walled colony home. "What happened?"

"Don't touch the orange grass." Predatory vegetation. Always my favorite thing. I straighten up, transferring the keys to my uninjured hand as I hold my wounded hand out for Kora to examine. Her eyes go wide.

"That looks bad," she says.

I grin. It's hard not to. She's beautiful when she's worried about me. "I've had worse."

"Why do people always say that?"

"Say what?"

"That they've had worse. So what? Even if you've had worse before, that doesn't mean it isn't hurting *now*." She scowls. "It's like saying 'oh, I don't need dinner, I had lunch last week, I've had my quota of solid food.'"

"Some long-haul transports, that's sort of how it works." I climb back into the ATV. "Come on. There's a first aid kit at the house, and you can meet Viola. Tell Michel she exists and everything."

Her cheeks flush dull red. "I sort of hoped you'd forget about that." She still climbs into the seat next to me. I guess embarrassment isn't enough to keep her from getting to safe ground. That's good. I'd hate to think that I have such bad taste I'd fall for a girl with no sense of self-preservation.

"I don't think I'm ever going to forget about that." The lion-worm put some new dents in the ATV, but the engine turns over when I insert the key, and it takes more than a little impact damage to take out these tires. I once watched Mom drive across an active pyroclastic flow. The frame took some damage, and she'd have been dead if she hadn't been wearing protective gear, but the tires were fine.

"I wish . . ." Kora takes a deep breath, and for a while, she doesn't say anything.

We're almost clear of the flowering stalks before she speaks again, head tilted back so she's looking at that wide orange sky, and not at me at all. "I wish I'd just said 'yes' when you asked if I'd come and see where you live. I wish I hadn't needed an excuse to be brave. I don't want you to hate me because I let somebody talk me into thinking your sister was a hoax. I don't want . . ."

She stops. So do I, turning off the ATV in the middle of the trail that cuts through the forest. We won't see any lion-worms big enough to threaten us here: they can't work their way through the roots. Only infants and juveniles hunt in the shadow of the weird Zagreus trees.

"What *do* you want?" I ask.

In answer, she leans over, and she kisses me.

I've never been kissed before. I've never *kissed* anyone before. I was always scared I wouldn't know what to do when the time finally came, but it turns out my body knows *exactly* how this is supposed to work, and it's prime, prime, *prime*. Her lips are soft and they taste the way her skin smells, salty and sweet and with just a hint of motor oil, which shouldn't be appealing—should be sort of revolting, honestly—but somehow the fact that it's her, it's Kora, makes it amazing. She's amazing.

Kissing is amazing. I could keep kissing her forever, just me and her and the shadows of the trees around us, the rulers of Zagreus, the only perfect things in a million miles. Forget colony politics and my parents and their stupid jobs; forget Viola coughing in the middle of the night and fading away one tiny piece at a time because modern medicine can't figure out what's broken in her DNA. Kissing takes it all away. Kissing makes the world perfect.

Hesitantly, I slide a hand into Kora's hair, and she doesn't pull away. Her curls are as soft as I always thought they'd be. A soft cloud of pollen is dislodged by the motion, and she wrinkles her nose against mine, and this is so prime, so prime, I can't understand why people don't just spend all their time kissing. Hook up a feeding tube and let us get to business without worrying about the rest of the world.

Kora pulls away first. Her cheeks are flushed again, a different shade of red this time, bright and vibrant and so appealing that I have to fight to pull my hand out of her hair, to not just lean in and start kissing her all over again.

"Is this safe?" she asks.

"Kissing?" I blink a few times, trying to catch up. She's so pretty. Why are we talking? Kissing would be better. "I don't have any—I mean, we have to get full health screens whenever we come to a new colony, so I know I'm not—"

"I'm not either," she hastens to say. "Sick, I mean. All blood panels clean. But is it safe to be outside like this? Is there going to be another of those monsters?"

"Oh. No. The forest predators are smaller, or at least the ones we've found so far are smaller, and it's unlikely anything we haven't already found would be this close to the residence." Regretfully, I finish the process of pulling away and turn the engine back on. No more kisses for me. "We're almost home, anyway. Viola should be awake."

"Oh. Okay." Kora brightens. "It'll be nice to meet her."

"You can tell everyone at school about it."

She frowns, quick and unhappy. "How long are you going to make me pay for that?"

"I don't know. The kissing helped. I think if we do more kissing, I might stop being annoyed about it pretty quickly." The ground is uneven enough that I have to pay attention to the trail ahead of us, wrestling with the ATV's controls to keep us on an even keel. The tree roots grow so quickly, Dad's sure there has to be something gnawing on them, trapping them in a permanent state of biological war.

Not that that's anything special. Most life is at war with everything around it, fighting to carve out space, resources—food, water, places to raise their young—fighting to grow and mature and reproduce. Some people think that "war" is too serious a word to use for that sort of conflict, but I'm a biologist's daughter, and I say they're wrong. Life is war.

Even the sudden uneasy triangle between me, Kora, and Michel is a sort of battlefield. Does he want her for himself? Is that why he's telling lies about my sister and encouraging Kora to doubt her existence—which would make me a liar in Kora's eyes, and hence unworthy of her kisses? Does he just want to defend what he sees as his territory against an off-world interloper? The competition for resources is the basis for most conflict across human history. Not just human history: the history of all existence.

We leave the shelter of the forest for the wide, flat grassland between the trees and the fence. Kora starts to lean out of the ATV and let her hand brush against the grass. I grab her arm and haul her back, maybe not as gently as I should have, because she turns and gives me a sulky, wounded look.

"What did you do that for?" she demands, and I'm doomed, because even when she's pouting at me, I just want to start kissing her again. Subprime.

"It was grass that did this to me, remember?" I hold up my hand. Inflamed rows of angry blisters mark the place where the orange grasses touched me. Mom's going to be thrilled. That's only half-sarcastic—once she's sure I haven't done myself any permanent damage, she'll drain the blisters and analyze whatever oil or toxin is clinging to my skin, using it to learn more about this new Zagreus party trick. She doesn't like it when I get hurt, but that doesn't mean she'll refuse essential data.

"Oh." Kora stops pouting. She looks around instead, drinking in the grasslands with her eyes, and finally says, "I had no idea it was this beautiful out here. I always thought . . ."

"What?"

She takes a deep breath. "Mom was born on a mining world. It was corps, not independent; it didn't even have a name. Just this twenty-digit numerical designation. Mom can rattle it off in her sleep. I tried to memorize it when I was a kid, and then I realized she didn't want me to. She wanted it to be forgotten. That place is not my past, and it's not my future, either."

I don't say anything. Maybe it's adrenaline and maybe it's hormones, but if Kora wants to share something like this with me, I'm going to let her. Anything to bring us closer together, here, under this orange, alien sky.

"When she talks about the world where she grew up, she always says it was gray, and closed-in, and claustrophobic, and I know it would break her heart if I said this in front of her, but I look at the settlement, and I don't see the difference."

I wince, but I don't contradict her, because she's right. The main colonial settlement on Zagreus is a gray, industrial maze of recycled materials and all the parts and pieces the government has been able to scavenge. There are gardens—ninety percent of the colony's food is grown within the city, and they're hoping to push all their food production to on-planet within the next five years—but they're all concealed behind polarized glass that filters the orange light into something the Earth-standard crops can recognize. Their meat is vat-grown, which is standard but not fun to look at. Even the parks are mostly gray, with bright specks of color where some architect or other has done a molded plastic play structure for the littlest kids, the ones who have no idea that skies are supposed to be blue, and wouldn't believe anyone who tried to tell them.

Maybe those kids, the ones who were born on a Zagreus that already has teenagers chafing against the initial colonial restrictions, maybe they'll be the ones who use my parents' research to turn this planet into a real home, and not just a sort of way station between Earth and somewhere else.

Or maybe it'll be Kora. She keeps stealing glimpses of the grasslands around us, and even as she keeps her hands inside the ATV, it's impossible to overlook her delight.

"I still think we should have a party," I blurt.

Kora turns that delighted look on me. "Really?" she asks.

No. "Sure." *This is a terrible idea.* "I mean, everyone can meet Viola, which might make Michel stop, and it's not fair that there's all this beautiful stuff out here that you never get to see. And it's perfectly safe, as long as you stay on the supply trail between the colony gates and the residence." Unlike our rough-carved forest trails, the supply trail is actually scourged into the earth, cut six inches deep to clear out all the roots and surrounded by sonic beacons to keep the wildlife at bay. Environmentally speaking, it's a disaster. Safety-wise, it's almost better than staying indoors.

Dad says that the trail proves the colonial government is made up of shortsighted hypocrites, since they were the ones who insisted on its design. It's an eyesore that will take at least fifteen years of erosion and exposure to go away, while the footprint of our residence will fade in a single season. But we're the ones exploiting planetary resources. Right.

Kora is looking at me like I'm the most incredible creature in the world. I puff out my chest like she's right.

"I can set up snacks, we can go for a walk—a safe one, safer than we did today—and everyone can see how amazing Zagreus really is. How about it?" Honestly, it's a public service, and one we should have been providing all along. Maybe Michel will be less of a jerk once he understands how amazing it is outside the colony walls.

Probably not, though.

"That sounds like such a good idea," says Kora, and leans over to kiss my cheek.

I'm blushing and trying to think of a response when the residence fence comes into view, and in front of it, Mom and Dad, arms folded, clearly waiting for me to come home.

Busted.

These are my parents:

Dr. Katherine Shipp. Xenobiologist, both practical and behavioral; she specializes in "extraterrestrial zoology," meaning she's happiest when she's working with the things we'd call birds or mammals if we found them on Earth. Big predators are her favorite, and she's the reason we've had cats for most of my life. If it weren't for Zagreus's ridiculously restrictive animal import laws, we'd have a cat right now. One more thing to resent this orange-sky hellhole for. A serious fondness for khaki and the kind of military training that leads to perfect posture and being able to bench-press your own body weight. I want to be her when I grow up.

Oh, and super unforgiving. Did I mention that part? Because

I probably should. Mom holds a grudge like it's made of platinum and she's looking to invest. I take after her, in that regard.

Then there's Dad. Dr. John Shipp. Xenobiologist, yes, but also xenobotanist, xenoparasitologist, and xenoentomologist, since while Mom was running around with the colonial marines, he was collecting degrees like there was some sort of prize for the person who spent the most useless hours in school. He has bugs named after him on, like, six planets, and he's always shooting for a seventh. Or an eighth. Or a ninth. He also has a huge collection of weird teas and a tendency to wander out of the house without his glasses, which makes him seem like the sort of absentminded professor figure that you see in all the science-fiction vids.

Only he's not. He's always watching, always paying attention, and if Mom never lets go of a grudge, Dad doesn't let things progress to the point where he needs to hold one. He'd rather just end them while they're small and simple and controllable. He's like a human flyswatter, and if I'm too much like Mom, Viola's too much like Dad.

Finding them both waiting for me at the fence line is . . . not good. Worse is the way Mom smiles when we get closer.

"Miss Burton," she says to Kora, voice as bright as her expression, and equally as false. "I didn't know you were planning to pay us a visit today."

Oh, I am in so much trouble.

"Hello, Dr. Shipp," says Kora, glancing anxiously at me. "Olivia invited me. I hope that's not a problem . . . ?"

"Of course not," says Dad. "You're a citizen of Zagreus. You're welcome to go wherever you like. I just didn't know you were interested in naturalism. Would you like to join us next week for our tour of the wetlands?"

Kora blanches. I'm not sure she knows what a riparian wet-land environment is, really, but the name gives a lot of it away. "Um," she says. "No, thank you." She climbs out of the ATV, cast-ing a last quick smile in my direction. Not as good as a kiss, but I'll take it. "Thanks for showing me around, Olivia, it was really neat. Give Viola my best, okay?"

"Okay," I say, and before I have time for anything else, she's taking off, heading for the supply trail as fast as her legs can carry her. I watch until she's safely past the first sonic beacon before I turn back to my parents.

Neither of them looks happy.

"How did this happen?" asks my father, touching the ATV's dented front fender.

"Lion-worm," I say. "The biggest one I've ever seen."

"And why was it attacking the ATV?"

There is no answer to that question that is both good and true. They're going to find out eventually. If I lie to them, it's just going to be worse for me. So I swallow, hard, and smile as best I can, and say, "Kora fell out in the pollen stands. The lion-worm thought she looked interesting—"

"Meaning it thought the daughter of the *colonial governor* would make a nice meal," says Mom, in a voice like ice.

Oh, this is so bad. "—and I had to distract it," I say. "It hit the ATV a few times. I can fix it. There's no structural damage, I'll just need a hammer and a belt sander and it'll be as good as new."

"My daughter, the mechanic," mutters Dad. "This is your fault, you know." The last bit is directed at Mom, who arches a brow in response.

"My fault? If she were taking up sharpshooting, I'd accept the blame for that, but how is it my fault that she likes hitting things with a hammer?"

Maybe I'm not in trouble after all. Once they start picking at each other, I can usually slink away. I start the ATV, intending to drive it to the garage.

Mom folds her arms. "Where do you think you're going, young lady?"

Or maybe I'm in the kind of trouble I've previously only dreamt of. "To put the ATV in the garage?" I offer meekly.

"I want you in the residence immediately afterward, do you understand me?"

I understand that I'm about to be grounded for the foreseeable future. Subprime. "Yes, ma'am," I say, and turn the controls toward the hatch in the fence that will allow me to march toward my inevitable destruction.

The garage sensors open at my approach. I slide the ATV into its place, hopping out to connect the charging cables to the port in the wall. A mixture of electrical power and internal combustion means that we can go for miles without worrying about finding fuel. Always important when you're on a world that has yet to be fully charted. Internal combustion has been banned on Earth for decades, but out here, efficiency wins out over environmental impact. One more thing for people like Michel to resent my family for.

It only takes a few moments with the cleaning solution and an old rag to clean Dad's machete. Even my parents won't be mad at me for taking the time. Always leave your tools the way you found them, if you can't somehow find a way to leave them better: that's the family motto, or may as well be. Everything can be improved.

Eventually, though, there's nothing left for me to improve, not without breaking out the heavy tools, and if I do that, my parents will know I'm trying to dodge my punishment. Which seems like a logical thing to do, if you're asking me, but that isn't how my parents think. They always want me to show up and acknowledge the consequences of my actions, as if I weren't there when those actions were happening.

What are the consequences of my actions? I saved a pretty girl's life, and she kissed me. I let the ATV be damaged in a minor, largely cosmetic way, and I already said that I could fix it. I'm not so much seeing what I should be punished for here.

Shoulders slumped, I make my way across the yard to the back door of the residence and let myself in. The kitchen is empty. They never yell at us in the kitchen; some weird superstition Dad has about how bringing bad feelings around food will make the food bad for you. It doesn't make any sense, but that's often the way with Earth-born adults. They have all this cultural baggage even they can't explain, like once something crosses the line into "tradition" it no longer needs to be interrogated. Whatever.

Mom and Dad are in the living room, sitting on the couch, waiting for me. Viola is in her chair, an oxygen tank resting beside her, just in case she has one of her attacks before she can get back to the safety of the monitoring equipment in our bedroom. Sub, sub, *sub*prime. I am in so much trouble.

"Sit down," says Mom coolly. She's always the disciplinarian. Dad's usually happy to sit back and let her mete out punishments, like we won't notice that he's always on her side. There's no good parent–bad parent routine here. There's just two exhausted scientists trying to pretend they have the tactical advantage over two bored, increasingly resourceful teenagers. This is a war they were always destined to lose eventually.

Too bad eventually isn't now. I sit.

"I would like you to explain yourself, please." Her voice is calm, level: she might as well be asking an underling to explain their improperly filed paperwork. Viola winces, flashing me a sympathetic look. She's on my side. She's always been on my side.

I don't know what I'd do if I didn't have my sister. "Which part?" I ask, and hate the whine in my voice. It sounds childish. It sounds like someone who deserves to be punished.

"Start with the whole thing, and we'll ask for details if we need them," says Dad.

Oh, this is bad. If he's abandoning the pretense of neutrality, this is *bad*. I consider the truth, and reject it just as quickly. Maybe—*maybe*—if it were just me, Viola, and Mom, I could get away with saying "hormones made me do it." Mom remembers being a teenage girl, and she's said, more than once, that she hopes we can find a way to start dating before we turn around and realize that we're adults, responsible for our own livelihoods and futures.

Dad, on the other hand, wants to pretend we're still eight years old, and that Viola's illness means she's never going to want to date, and that being a good sister means I'll be more interested in taking care of her than in letting some colony kid touch my boobs, either above or below the shirt. Dad's kind of delusional sometimes.

So I take a deep breath, and give the only answer that leaves me with half a chance of getting out of this alive. "Michel from school has been going around telling people Viola doesn't exist."

6

FAMILY MEETING

SILENCE. VIOLA LOOKS CONFUSED.
Mom looks horrified. Dad looks . . .

I don't have a name for the expression on Dad's face. It's almost like he's going to be sick, which doesn't make any sense. I mean, Vi's sick, she's been sick for a long time, and there are jokes we don't make, because sometimes you don't want to invite the universe to provide you with a punch line, but that look, it's like he's been waiting his whole life to hear he only has one daughter, that Viola has been a particularly vivid figment of our collective imaginations for years.

Mom recovers first. "Why would he say that?" she asks, voice tight and clipped and strangely disciplined. She's really upset. She always goes all ex-marine when she's upset.

This is weird. I don't like it, and I don't like that Vi's on the other side of the room, where it would be super obvious if I went and stood next to her. So I stay where I am, I take a breath, and I say, "He thinks we left her off the arrival manifest for our transport so we could defraud the colony resource grids. Get more than our fair share. I mean, it was an error. We weren't trying to *defraud* anyone, for anything."

Mom snorts. "More than our fair share? We refine everything ourselves. We're actually living off the *land*, not pulling in pieces of other worlds that have already been ravaged and sold off to the highest bidder, then pretending that somehow makes us better than anyone else."

"Kate," says Dad chidingly.

"No, don't start," she says. "These people have a moral framework that falls apart if you so much as look at it funny, and they want to use it to justify claiming my daughter—*my daughter*—doesn't exist? That's not only ridiculous, it's *absurd*."

I'm pretty sure those words mean the same thing. I don't say anything. Mom is furious, and I don't know why, but as long as she's not furious at me, I'm going to let her get it out of her system.

"Olivia," says Dad. "I can understand why a boy saying your sister isn't real might make you angry, but how, exactly, does that lead to you taking the daughter of the planetary governor into the wilderness to be eaten by the local predators?"

Uh-oh. Busted. "I—"

"Kora is in our class," interrupts Viola. "I thought if she came out here and saw me, she'd go back to school and tell everyone else I was real, and this would stop. But we couldn't just have her touch the doorframe and leave, so we offered her a trip to see the pretty flowers." She somehow manages to smile and grimace at the same time, like she's commenting on the ridiculousness of it all. "I'm sorry. Olivia's never said that there were lion-worms out there."

Relief washes over me in a hot, syrupy wave. My sister always has my back. That's what it means to be a sister, to have a twin. I never have to face the world by myself. "I've never seen lion-worms out there before, at least not ones this *big*. I would never have taken a civilian there if I'd had any idea. I'm so sorry. I just wanted them to stop saying those things about Vi."

Mom and Dad exchange an unreadable look. Mom is the first to look away.

"Fine," she says. "Olivia, I'm very disappointed in you . . . but I'm proud of you, too. You were trying to take care of your sister. I can't punish you for that."

I blink. "Really?"

"Really." She narrows her eyes. "Don't make me change my mind."

"No, ma'am! Thank you!" I start to turn toward our room.

Mom puts her hand up. "Wait. We're not finished."

"Oh." I should have known this was too good to be true. "What else?"

"You know better than to take colony children past the fences. They don't understand this world. What you did today wasn't safe."

"They live here," says Viola. "Kora's probably going to be planetary governor someday. I can't even leave the residence, and *I* know more about this world than she does. They're doomed if they don't learn how to work with their environment. How is that right?"

"It's not," says Dad. "It's shortsighted and stupid, and it's going to come back to bite them all in the ass one day. It's also not our place to try to change things for them. Their parents made the rules, and they're going to have to make their own decisions about how they want to handle running their own colony."

"Kora did make a decision today," I object. "She decided she wanted to see what Zagreus has to offer."

"She didn't make an *informed* decision," says Dad, voice prim and faintly hectoring, like he's talking to one of his classes. He'll teach a whole slew of local biologists before we leave this planet, telling them what's dangerous and what's not, helping them understand how to stay alive here. Because they can't possibly do their field research for themselves. That would involve too much time *outside*. "Olivia, you know our position here is tenuous. What you did today could have endangered our jobs."

"So we'd go back to Earth," I say. "You keep promising we will. There's better medtech there, we could get Viola new treatments, maybe get her out of bed for more than an hour at a time."

"Thanks," says Viola dryly.

I look at her. "You're perfect exactly the way you are, you know that, but don't you want to go outside? To do all the things we only ever talk about you getting to do? Earth could change everything for us."

"And we've promised to discuss it *as a family*," says Mom firmly. "Later. When this job is finished. It's not finished yet. You need to be careful. You need to remember that we work best when we work together."

There's something in her voice that I don't like. I frown. "This isn't just you being upset because I took Kora for a joyride," I accuse. "What's really going on?"

Dad reaches over and takes Mom's hand, giving it a firm squeeze before he says, "The governor has purchased a retired scientific research vessel," he says. "They're planning to strip it and refine its by-products for a colony expansion. To give you a sense of scale, it's large enough that most of the work will need to happen in orbit."

That's massive. Not out of line with other ships I've seen taken apart, but still. There's always something sad about seeing something that large stripped down for its component parts, even if those parts will have a new life as part of a colony like this one. Better a recycled future than a haunted, derelict past, I guess.

"Kora mentioned something about a 'big score,'" I say, frowning. "What does that have to do with us?"

"The ship was doing some biological research, and since the crew abandoned it for unknown reasons, we can't be sure that it's been properly sterilized," says Dad. "The colonial government has offered me a hefty bonus in exchange for going up with their scout team to verify that the ship is no longer biologically active, and does not pose a threat to the inhabitants of Zagreus."

I blink. Slowly. "You're going into planetary orbit to scout a dead ship?"

"Yes."

"I want to come." I take an involuntary step forward. "I need more time in isolation suits, and there's always a need for more hands on these runs. I can—"

"No." There's no room for argument in his answer. Even if there were, the way he's frowning means it wouldn't be a good idea. "This is a potentially biologically active site. Do you understand what that means? Maybe the scientists didn't leave. Maybe they liquefied. Maybe there's some unidentified pathogen still moving through the ventilation system, waiting for something new to infect. Why in the world would I take my teenage daughter into that sort of potential disaster?"

"You've always said that 'potential biohazard' sounds scary, but that it usually just means some kind of minor alien virus that we need to identify and eliminate," I say doggedly. "Remember? I'm not supposed to think about disasters, or alien monsters with giant teeth, or biobombs. Those aren't real things."

"It's dangerous, and I'm not taking you up there."

"Why would you go in the first place?" I demand. "If it's that dangerous, stay home."

"The bonus is . . ." He glances, oddly, at Viola, before returning his attention to me. "It's substantial. We're going to need to upgrade some of our equipment soon. We've already put it off long enough. This one mission could pay for everything we need."

None of our equipment is that outdated. Even Viola's monitoring systems were upgraded and completely overhauled before we left for Zagreus. I scowl. "You're making excuses."

"And you're seventeen, which means I can make all the excuses I want." Dad stands. "You're not being punished for what you did today, but you can both go to your room until dinner, and think about the reasons we live the way we do. You need to be more careful, Olivia. Viola is counting on you."

There's nothing I can say to change his mind, and usually he's the flexible one. So I don't argue. I turn, and help Viola out of her chair, and together we walk back to our room.

Our parents don't say anything. They just watch us go, until we're safe together, behind a closed door, until the world narrows again to me and Viola, Viola and me, and it's going to be okay.

Viola has always had the better bed. She needs it, with all the weird machines she has to be hooked up to in order to sleep without being afraid she'll stop breathing in the middle of the night. I was jealous when we were younger. Sometimes we'd have to work out of these cramped little pre-fabs half the size of our current residence, and her bed would swallow most of our room, and I'd be sleeping on a sliver of a mattress crammed into whatever corner was left.

I don't mind anymore. We've both gotten better at moving around her machines. It's like she's one of those fairy tale princesses in the storybooks Mom used to read us before bedtime, sleeping in her dome of thorns and brambles. Only her thorns are IVs and sensors, and her brambles are tubes and wires. No one can get to us when we're tucked into the heart of Viola's bed, not even our parents.

Viola climbs in first, stretching out on her back in the dead center of the briar. I follow, curling myself against her side like a comma, our hair falling together and blending until it's impossible for even us to tell where hers stops and mine begins.

This must be what it was like for us in the beginning, when we were two circles of cells growing and dividing in our mother's womb, pulling apart one step at a time, until we figured out how to be separate beings, separate people. But not all the way. Whenever I think about the future, she's there, no matter what I'm doing. Me, and her, and this big bed.

"So how'd it go?" she asks, skimming a hand along the surface of my hair. She smells, like always, of disinfectant and sterile rooms and just a trace of her favorite vanilla lotion.

"Great." I grin. She won't be able to see it, but she'll feel it, given the way my face is pressed against her shoulder. "It was . . . amazing. She's so good, Viola. She's so, so good."

"Uh-huh. Did you tell her you like her?"

"Not in so many words."

"So what made it so great?"

"I fought off a lion-worm that was going to eat her, and she kissed me to say thank you. She kissed me a whole bunch of times." My cheeks burn red, a belated blush reflex. Thinking of Kora makes my skin feel like it's two sizes too small. It hurts, in a good way. A really, really good way. "I think she likes me."

"Wow."

I push myself up onto one elbow. "Why do you sound so surprised?"

Viola turns to look at me. "I'm not. Who wouldn't like you? You're basically amazing. She's a really smart girl if she's already kissing you. I mean, that's what you wanted, isn't it? For her to start kissing you?"

"Yeah. I just . . . you're okay with this?" For the first time, I'm starting to worry about whether Viola and Kora are going to get along. This was all maybe before today. Maybe Kora will like me. Maybe someday Kora will kiss me, or let me kiss her. Maybe I can have a girlfriend.

Is having a girlfriend so important that I'm willing to let it hurt my sister? I don't know. I should know. It shouldn't even be a *question*. It's always been me and Viola, Viola and me, the Shipp sisters against the entire universe. I want to be able to say, without hesitation, that if Viola doesn't like this, I'll stop, I'll stay here with her and I'll stop watching Kora in class, I'll stop thinking about the way her lips felt when she pressed them against mine,

I'll stop wishing I could plunge my hands back into the tangled glory of her hair.

As if to remind me that Kora's hair wasn't the only thing I plunged my hands into today, the line of blisters on the outside of my right palm begins to throb. I wince and wait for Viola to reply.

She smiles, wan and weak, and says, "You're growing up and I'm not, that's all. It feels like you're going someplace I can't follow. I'm scared that you're going to leave me behind."

"That's never, *ever* going to happen." I lean in and kiss her forehead. Her skin is always so dry. No matter how much lotion we buy for her, she's so dry. "You're my sister. You and me, forever."

"And when I get worse?"

The question is so blunt, so blatant, that it steals the breath out of my lungs and leaves me sitting silent, unable to do anything but sit and stare. Finally, desperately, I stammer, "You—you won't. They're going to keep finding new treatments, and one day they'll find a cure, and then—"

"I don't think there's a cure for what's wrong with me." Viola tweaks my hair, twisting it between her fingers, careful not to pull. "You need to get used to the idea that you're going to be the only Shipp sister. You're the one who's going to carry our shared genetics into the future, and I'm the one who's going to take them gracefully into the past."

"Stop it. Don't talk like that."

"Maybe if we talked like this more, Mom and Dad wouldn't keep spending every cent they get on upgrades I don't need and don't want and never asked for." Viola can be fierce when she wants to. She's fierce now. If she had more blood to spare, I know her cheeks would be flushed. If she had more breath in her body, she'd be shouting. She can't do either of those things. All she can do is glower challengingly, like I'm somehow in control. "When it's just you and me, you're going to stop. You're going to save your money and see the universe, and I'm going to wave while I watch you sail away."

"Vi . . ."

Her eyes widen. She reaches over and grabs my hand. "What did you do to yourself? There's only room for one damaged sister in this bed!"

I try to pull away. I can't. She's surprisingly strong, given how sick she is. "I found a new kind of grass. This one's orange, like the sky. I bet it's invisible to the grazers when it grows on its own."

"Caustic protective layer?"

"True carnivore."

Viola finally lets go. "You need to show Mom, and you need to get that cleaned up. I don't want you leaking nasty fluids in my bed when you have a nightmare and climb in with me."

I grin. "Your self-interest is refreshing."

"I am a hothouse flower; I thrive best in a fully sterile environment." Viola gives me a little shove. "Out. Out of my bed. Away with you and your foul leakage."

I laugh as I crawl back out of the bed, feeling better than I have since I pulled up to the fence and saw my parents waiting there. "What do you think of this mission Dad's going on? I wish he'd let me go with him."

"I don't."

There's a grim note in Viola's voice that grabs my attention and jerks it toward her. I turn, blinking. Normally, she likes it when I go out into the field—or up into orbit—with our parents. We set up a closed-circuit camera and it's like she's there with me, the

Shipp sisters conquering the universe one biological mystery at a time. Maybe that's never going to happen for real, but we've been pretending since we were kids, and it's something we both enjoy.

Something's wrong.

"Vi . . ." I hesitate. This feels wrong. Everything about it feels *wrong*. If I ask this question, I can't take it back, and something tells me I'm going to want to.

I have to ask it anyway.

"What do you know?"

Viola shakes her head. "It's not what I *know*, it's what I don't know," she says. "There's holes in the information I've been able to get my hands on. You know my pen pals?"

I snort. The whole family knows about Viola's "pen pals." She started sending messages to anyone foolish enough to have an open relay when she was five, bored and sick and too smart for her own good, trapped at home with a network interface while I was going off to my first year in a real school, leaving her alone for the first time in our lives. Our parents had traded off who went into the field and who stayed home with Viola back then—I mean, I was too young to really pay attention to their arrangements, but there's no way they would have left *me* home alone when we were five, and I was the healthy daughter. I guess neither of them had seen the harm in letting Viola send virtual waves and cheery greetings to scientists, researchers, anyone with a public address.

And I guess they'd been right not to think of it as harmful, since none of Vi's pen pals has ever done anything to hurt her. Quite the opposite. She was a charming child—we both were—with her big blue eyes and her long blonde pigtails and her endless curiosity about the universe she was never going to see on her own. She's still charming, even if she's bigger now, and she's still writing to people all over the universe. Some of them have been answering her questions and feeding her information that they maybe shouldn't be allowing to slip for more than a decade now.

If she ever wanted to go into politics, she would be *terrifying*.

"There have been some weird rumors circulating recently," she says, and her expression is grave, and I start to pay attention to what she's saying, not just the sheer ludicrousness of the situation. "Nothing concrete, I mean, I think there's *something* concrete out there, because there are too many rumors for them all to be about nothing, but if there's something out there, either it's really good at its job, or someone else is working to make sure word doesn't get out."

That's new. I frown. "What do you mean?"

"That's the problem: I don't *know* what I mean." Viola sighs. "Like, this tourist resort on a terraformed moon went dark overnight. They were there, and then they were gone, and now if you try to ping their relays or request booking information, you don't get anything. It's like the whole thing vanished. Like it never existed."

"Resorts go out of business all the time. Remember that theme park we went to when we were, what, nine?" A whole wonderland of children's entertainment and adult thrill rides carved out of the center of an asteroid. Bring the whole family, enjoy the wonders of freefall in a safe, secure, sterile environment. It had been a big hit with the parents of kids like Vi, whose bodies couldn't handle rides in full gravity, whose lungs were too delicate to risk on unsterilized air.

Our weekend there had been one of the best of our lives. Viola and I had ridden a slow-coaster that flipped us upside down as it

sailed leisurely across the whole park, and we'd giggled and giggled and held each other's hands like it was the best thing in the
universe. Mom and Dad still have the pictures in rotation on the
fridge, our nine-year-old selves fading in and replacing the selves
we are now at preset intervals.

The park closed years ago. Someone had been embezzling
money, and even children's wonderlands can't keep the gates open
when they can't keep the lights on. In the end, the rules are the
same for everybody.

"It's still *there*," Viola objects. "If we got Mom and Dad to
fly us by the asteroid, we'd see the entrance, and all the pieces
that haven't been stolen by scavenger colonies like this one. The
resort I'm talking about, no one's been able to get in to confirm
that it still exists."

I blink. "The moon is gone?"

"It's sealed off. Colonial marines and everything. No one
knows what happened, and they're not letting us find out."

"Then it's something we don't need to know about. The colonial marines wouldn't be keeping up a news blackout over
something that was actually *dangerous*. There was probably some
sort of corporate mixer that went wrong, and now whoever owns
the place is trying to get out from under a bunch of fines and
lawsuits."

Viola shakes her head. "It feels like more than that. I don't
have anything more concrete, but there are just . . . there are whispers around the edges of things. People going missing. Questions
not getting answered. I don't like it. I don't want you going into
orbit until we know more."

"Well, you get your wish, since Dad won't take me." I blow

her a kiss. "I'm going to go ask Mom to look at my hand—and I *won't* ask whether I can go up with Dad, I promise. I'm staying right here with you."

"You better," says Viola. She looks less worried, less wan, and so I hold my promise at the front of my mind as I leave the room.

I will not ask to go into orbit, no matter how amazing it would be, no matter how much I want to. I will not ask to go into orbit, no matter how much I hate this subprime orange sky, no matter how much I want to stand under a sheet of unglittering, unmoving stars and remember that we're not going to be stuck here on Zagreus forever.

I feel a pang at the thought of leaving. Kora kissed me. Shouldn't that be enough to make me change my mind, start thinking about applying for colonial citizenship and finding ways to be happy under a sky the color of canned mango? But it's not. Viola needs better medical care than we can find on a scavenger colony, and I need more choices than a single sky. I'm not staying. We were never going to stay.

I will not ask to go into orbit.

I won't.

The sound of my parents' voices drifts out of the kitchen. I angle in that direction, stepping as lightly as I can. It's not that I *want* to eavesdrop, necessarily. It's more that knowing what's coming is always a good thing.

"—you wouldn't go." Mom. She sounds genuinely upset. Maybe there's more to Viola's rumormongering than meets the eye.

"You know I have to." Dad. He sounds more resigned, like he's already done the risk analysis and come up with the only answers available. "We need more processing power. Otherwise we're going to have to do . . . something. I don't know what. Erase older storage, maybe. This model was never meant to run for so long without some sort of system reset."

"I hate it when you get clinical."

"Sometimes it's necessary."

They must be talking about our transport. It's a nasty little ship, ex–cruise liner, designed to shuttle the wealthy between very carefully placed targets. We've rebuilt the whole thing six times since I've been old enough to help, and it's never enough. It's going to shake apart one day. But I love it. It's freedom, it's continuity, it's the way we come to a planet and the way we leave it again. Viola named it when we were eleven—the *While There's Hope*—and if he's going up because we're going to do another ship rebuild, I am way more cool with the idea.

I step into the kitchen doorway, clearing my throat. Both of their heads whip around. Mom is oddly pale, making her look more like me and Viola than she usually does.

"O-Olivia," she says. "How long have you been standing there?"

"Not long." A ship upgrade is big and exciting, like birthdays and holidays and unexpected days off from school all tied in a single beautiful bow. I don't want to spoil it for myself by letting them know that I know. Instead, I hold out my hand, and say, "I found a new kind of grass."

Mom hisses between her teeth in sympathy as she rises. Dad looks impressed. Leave it to my father to think it's totally prime for a plant to try to eat his daughter.

"Where was this?" he asks as Mom gets the sample kit from the counter.

"The pollen grove. It looked like a normal grass patch, but there were these little orange blades at the center, and they were eating bugs."

His impressed expression melts into excitement. "Are you sure it was *eating* them? Actual predation?"

"The grass that drinks blood is predatory," Mom calls.

"We're still not sure of that."

"Actual predation," I say.

Dad leads me to a seat at the kitchen table while Mom moves to take skin samples, drain the blisters, and bandage my hand, and everything is normal again; this is how our family is supposed to work. Everything is going to be fine.

Viola is asleep by the time I make it back to our room. I look at my own cold, narrow bed, and then I crawl in next to her, curling up with my head on her shoulder, letting the sound of the machines beeping and hissing all around us soothe me into sleep.

7

SCHOOL'S OUT

GOING BACK TO SCHOOL AT THE start of the week is . . . educational.

First off, Michel apparently spread his stupid rumor about Vi a lot further than Kora realized, because *everyone* is looking at me when they think I won't notice. Some of them are appraising, some of them are friendlier than they've been in weeks, but all of them want to see how I'm reacting. Kora is higher in the social pecking order than Michel is, so people must be listening when she tells them my sister exists, but it's hard to let go of gossip, especially the kind of gossip that lets you feel better than somebody. They wanted to see me as a cheater, and now they have to see me as me.

Second off, Kora may be happy to tell everyone about Viola— even if she never actually saw her—but she's less happy to tell them all about me. I don't think anyone knows that we kissed. I'm not sure what that means. Was it just adrenaline that made her make the first move? Do I need to produce an apex predator every time

I want her to kiss me? Because I don't think I can do that, even if I wanted to. We don't have that many predators on this planet.

I'm daydreaming about some heretofore undiscovered predator that's big but not *too* big, dangerous but not *too* dangerous, and most importantly, really, really flashy and difficult to overlook, when my tablet beeps. I glance around. Our teacher is on the other side of the room, trying to negotiate a cease-fire between Andrea and her latest boyfriend, who must have stolen her stylus again. No one's paying attention to me.

I tap the icon. Viola's face appears, captioned, "You got a second?"

She's smart enough not to talk to me when I'm in class. Hooray for that, I guess. I type back, "Just a second. What's up?"

"Dad leaves in three days."

I frown. "Thanks for the reminder," I type back. He's going up to check out that salvaged research vessel. I'm not going with him—subprime—and he and Mom have been fighting about it every night, when they think we can't hear. Sometimes I think they forget how small the residence really is.

"Mom's going out to check that new grass you found, see if she can find any more," Viola types. Her image grins, abrupt and impish. "We'll have the house to ourselves all day."

My eyes widen. "You don't mean . . . ?"

"Party."

"No."

"Big party."

"Big no."

"Miss Shipp?" I lift my head, cheeks burning, to find the teacher looking at me with a measuring expression on her face. "Is there something you'd like to share with the rest of the class?"

I swear I've heard that line used in pre-colony holos. As long as there are schools, there are going to be people being jerks to kids for no reason other than that they can. "No, ma'am," I say. "My sister pinged to ask if we were starting our math unit soon." Viola is officially in this class with me, but she doesn't tend to stay logged on during open study, since it's just a distraction compared to being alone in our residence.

The teacher's face softens. I wonder if *she* believed the rumors about Viola being fake. Probably not. She has to grade both of our papers. She knows Vi and I have different strengths and weaknesses, scholastically speaking. That doesn't mean it wouldn't have been hard to hear the other kids gossiping about my sister.

I decide to like this teacher after all.

"Let Viola know that we'll be starting in ten minutes, if you would?" She turns away, satisfied that I'm not breaking any rules, and I turn back to my tablet.

Vi has been typing while I was distracted. "Come on, Olive. It's not fair that you get to meet all these people and I don't get to meet anyone. They think I don't exist! We need to show them how wrong they are. Dad's going to be off-world, Mom's going to be in the field, we're never going to get a better shot. You won't even technically be breaking any rules. If they come straight from the trail to the boundary fence, they won't ever have gone outside without supervision."

She makes a compelling argument. I want to give in, to say that sure, this is a great idea, we should absolutely go along with it. I want to tell her she always has the best ideas—and she does, she has ever since we were kids. She figured out how to talk adults around to her way of thinking while I was still trying to fit my foot in my mouth. She was our advocate for a thousand child-hood favors, and if she thinks this is a good idea, well, she might be wrong, but at least I know for sure that we'd have a good time before the fire and brimstone came raining from the sky.

"Please. Please. Please."

I half scowl at the screen and type, "Are you just going to keep asking until I give in and you get your way?"

Her image grins. "Yup," says the caption. "Come on, Olive. You know you want this as much as I do. More than I do, even, since you're the one with the girlfriend who could come and sit on the couch and hold your hand. So let's do this."

I hesitate before typing, "Okay."

Her grin is brighter than the orange sky outside, and maybe this is a good idea after all.

The rest of our morning classes pass in relative peace, and it's time for the most status-heavy event of my day: lunch. The popular kids get the prime seating spots, natch, and everyone else arrays themselves around them like the rays of a sun, the brightness and brilliance getting more diffuse the further it gets from the center. Out at the edges, we're dull, we're quiet, we're picking at our food and casting envious glances toward the shimmering brilliance of our betters. In the center . . .

In the center, they shine.

I take my customary spot at the edge long enough to gulp my food—some kind of pickle made from a human-edible local fruit and some sliced meat that Mom probably bought six colonies ago. It's not recognizable, and that's intentional. Half the potted meats on the market are actually potted insect matter, ground and dyed and shaped until we can pretend it's something that would have walked on four legs and lived in a barnyard, once upon a time.

No matter how far humans travel from Earth, we're always going to be trying to take it with us, acting like we can reshape the rest of the universe in the image of the home we left behind. You can see it in the potted meats, and in the pickles, and in the way we set up our social structures, still following the biological imperatives of a savannah that's so deep in the past that it probably doesn't even exist anymore.

When I've finished my lunch—and with it, my last excuse for delaying the inevitable—I surreptitiously breathe into my hand to check for traces of pickle, tug my shirt into place, and start the long, nerve-racking walk along the length of the cafeteria, passing tables with higher social status than my own, aiming for that shimmering center. Viola laughed at me when I told her I had a crush on the most popular girl in school, saying I was just like Mom in at least one serious way: I didn't know how to aim low.

Kora is eating some sort of nutrapaste sandwich, laughing at something Michel said, and she's never been more beautiful, and I can't do this. I should never have thought for a second that I *could* do this. How can a girl like me ask a girl like her to go into the middle of nowhere, not once, but twice?

Michel sees me coming. His eyes narrow, and he leans toward Kora, murmuring something in a voice too low for me to hear. Whatever it is, it must not have been very kind. She looks startled, her own eyes going wide, and then she looks around, finally catching sight of me, and she smiles.

That's how. That's how a girl like me can do this. Because she's beautiful, and she's smart, and funny, and kind, and that smile on her face? That smile is for *me*. I would walk a thousand miles to see that smile, and here she is, giving it to me for nothing.

"Kora, hey." I hope I sound cool. I want to sound cool.

I almost certainly do *not* sound cool.

But she's still smiling, and that makes up for basically everything. "Hey, Olivia. You know you can sit with us at lunch if you want to."

"I know." From the way Michel is glaring, her invitation is far from unanimous—and that's why I don't want to. Colony school social status is nothing. Most of the time I try not to let myself get too attached, since I know we're always going to be moving on soon. Puberty sucks. Before I started noticing girls, it was a lot easier to convince myself I didn't care. "Hey, your mom's the one who brokered the deal for that decommissioned research vessel, right? The 'big score' you talked about."

Kora blinks. Whatever she was expecting from me, it wasn't that. "Right."

"Why, scag?" asks Michel, leaning subtly forward, so that his body is between mine and Kora's. "You looking for something new to steal?"

I guess that answers one question: he's a jerk to me because he wants Kora for himself. Ugh. As if she'd ever have such subprime taste in potential partners. Even on Zagreus, her options aren't *that* limited. "No, I'm good," I say, as sweetly as I can muster. "Maybe you should get in line, though. I'm sure you could use some more metal for that rustbucket you keep trying to pretend is a residence."

Michel bares his teeth at me, actually bares his teeth, like this is some sort of messed-up primate dominance challenge. Ugh. Boys. I am *so* glad that's not where my hormones decided my destiny would one day lie.

Sensing blood in the water, Kora intervenes. "Hey, Olive, why do you ask?"

"Well, my dad's going to be on the team that goes up to clear the vessel for salvage—"

Michel scoffs. I do my best to ignore him.

"—and my mom has some fieldwork to do. So Viola and I are going to have the residence all to ourselves all day. I thought maybe we could have some folks over for that party I promised you. She wants to meet her classmates, since she has to relay in, and that's way subprime."

"So's your outdated slang, spacer," says Michel.

Too little, too late: some of the other popular kids are already starting to murmur with excitement and the good kind of wariness, the kind that comes before a really exciting dare. Kora hasn't told them about the lion-worm—I'd be dead by now if she had, since there's no way Michel would have been able to resist telling her mother, like, five seconds later—but she must have told them about the rest of it, the pollen and the flesh-eating grass and the amazing, frightening beauty of their chosen homeworld.

They're so weirdly sheltered, these colony kids. They wouldn't know real danger if it loomed out of the ground and bit their heads off. Coming to visit me and Vi at the residence won't change that, but maybe it'll convince them that someday they can dare to leave the fences their parents drew for them and see the world the way it really is. If I can help, even a little, then I guess I won't feel as bad about being dragged to this middle-of-nowhere planet by my parents.

Kora's smiling at me like I'm the smartest person in the whole universe, and I guess I already don't feel so bad about it.

"We can't fit *everyone* in the residence, and it's not safe to hang around outside," I say, before people can start calling their friends over to join the fun. "Say six? Plus me and Vi? You're invited, Michel."

"Am I?" asks Kora.

My heart seizes before I realize she was teasing. I smile as nonchalantly as I can manage, hoping she didn't catch my brief flicker of terror. "You're the reason I'm having a party," I say.

And she

Leans over

And she

Kisses me.

In front of everyone. In front of all the popular kids, her social equals, the people she's going to be sharing this colony with long after I'm just a funny memory of that blonde girl whose parents were counting the bugs. In front of all the *un*popular kids, who are suddenly looking at me like I'm some sort of conquering hero. It feels like my blood is freezing and on fire at the same time, it feels like I can do anything, *anything*, because Kora is kissing me again, Kora is kissing me where people can see it happen, where she can't pretend it was all in my imagination.

This is the best day of my life. When she pulls away, cheeks red and lips curved upward in a smile, I stay frozen exactly where I am, unable to find the strength to move.

"I'll get you a guest list," says Kora, and just like that, it's her party, not mine, and I honestly don't care. She can bring whoever she wants, as long as she's willing to kiss me again. And again. And again.

The rest of the day passes in a glorious haze of thinking about Kora, about the way her lips move under mine and the way her breath tastes and the way there's always a hint of motor oil in her perfume. I don't know why, and I can't wait to find out. I collect my homework downloads and head for home, striking out into the main colony without looking back.

Most colony worlds suffer from at least a small conflict between planning and production. The colonists spend all their waking hours on the ship thinking about how *their* world is going to be perfect, with none of the problems of the world they're leaving behind, and so every design is at least part reaction to the last one. If one colony crams residents together in towers that minimize environmental impact but also minimize personal space, the next is going to be nothing but personal residences and big yards and privacy, which means the one after *that* is going to be all about the towers, and on, and on, and on, for as long as there are people, for as long as there are planets to be settled.

Corps colonies are more regulated, and make more consistent sense, because it's not the builders making the decisions, it's the people who issue the payments, and they don't care what their new residents want, they care what's going to work for the new planet. I like corps colonies. They make sense.

But the best plan in the world won't change the limitations of a new world, whether they be gravity, atmosphere, or—in the case of Zagreus—the need to find flat, rocky ground to build on without displacing a bunch of large, charismatic wildlife. It's a self-imposed limitation, and one that makes my parents furious, because there's no such thing as "unused land." There's just land that doesn't have occupants that people feel bad for killing. Bugs and lizards and other, weirder life-forms always get the short end of the stick when colonists come around, because people don't think of them as needing to have homes. But they do.

Every inch of land that humans settle on worlds with their

own preexisting biospheres is stolen. It's sometimes hard to forget that, especially when it's been stolen for something as industrial and, well, *ugly* as the Zagreus colony.

Our school is at one edge of the settlement, where students can look out the window at the blowing rainbow of grasses and shiver, feeling better about the choice to lock the gates and keep the big, scary world outside. There's a gym and a "recreation area," but they're fully enclosed; we never go outside, we never even come within a fence-width of that big beautiful uncharted world. None of the other students seem to understand why that's a problem, and trying to explain it to them only ever makes me tired. I've stopped trying.

Outside the school is a maze of narrow, fully enclosed streets and alleyways, all of them lined by shops and vendors and the stairways that lead up to the residence levels, which tower three and four and five stories above the street. People like Kora live in the bigger, more private residences toward the center of the settlement, established by the new colonial government when they touched down. Funny how Michel doesn't seem to have a problem with *that*. Only with the idea that someone like me could come out of nowhere and disrupt the way he believes things are supposed to be. Doesn't matter how egalitarian and equal a colony sets out to make itself, it always comes down to status somehow.

There are individual transports available for use, but they all require committing to in-colony labor hours to rent, and I don't feel like spending any more time in this gray, lifeless place than I absolutely have to. Everything around me is recycled, but not in that loving, thoughtful way that transforms trash into treasure. Instead, it's like . . . it's like laundry done by someone who doesn't understand how to wash clothes. Everything loses its individual qualities and blends together until it's all the same. Everything here is the same. Even the people start to seem the same, because recycled fabric is a fashion statement that says "I conform," and hair dye is a luxury, and so it's just this mass of sameness that makes my teeth itch and my skin feel funny, like I'm being judged all the time, from all sides.

If it weren't for Kora, I'd be climbing the walls of our residence every night, wishing there was something—anything—I could do to get us off this world faster. Even *with* Kora, I don't dream about building a future here. I dream about somehow convincing her the universe is bigger and better than anything on Zagreus, and I could be the one to show it to her. That's the ultimate fantasy: me and Kora, leaving this colony behind. With Viola, of course. Nothing's worth doing if I can't have my sister there, and no one's worth being with if they can't understand that. But Kora would understand. I know she would.

I'm so lost in thoughts of her mouth and her smile and the way the corners of her eyes crinkle when she kisses me that I don't realize I'm being followed until a hand closes on my shoulder and whips me around, slamming my back into the nearest wall and knocking the air out of me. I gasp, trying to breathe, trying to shout, and Michel slaps his hand down over my mouth, silencing me.

"You do not touch her," he says, voice low and tight and remarkably grim. I never realized how *big* he was before. He's at least a foot taller than me, with a flushed, ruddy face and hair the color of dried grass. He looks like he belongs on Zagreus, like he's trying to match the color of the sky. "You do not look at her, you do not talk to her, you do not kiss her. Do you understand? Nod if you understand."

There's only one person he can mean by "her." So I do the only thing I can do, under the circumstances.

I bite him.

Not hard enough to break the skin, but hard enough to hurt like hell. He yelps and jerks his hand away. Midway through the motion, it becomes a fist and starts swinging back toward me, clearly looking to return the favor of pain. I'm not there anymore. I drop away at the last second, and his knuckles slam into the metal full-force, sending the whole wall clanging.

Michel yells and clutches his wounded hand to his chest, while I half scuttle to a safe distance, balancing my weight on the balls of my feet, waiting to see what he's going to do next.

Cry. That's what he's going to do. He's going to cry and hug his hand and look at me with wounded, betrayed eyes, like I'm the one who did something wrong by refusing to play along with his messed-up little attempt at intimidation.

"You're a big guy," I say. "I'm betting, like, half the kids at school are scared of you, and you like it that way. People don't mess with you when they're scared of you."

"You little—"

"Yup," I agree. "I'm little. Me and Viola both. We've always been tiny people. Dad used to joke that he could lose us in a shipping crate and accidentally mail us back to Earth with the rest of the equipment he was putting into storage. How many of those kids are going to be afraid of you when I tell them I beat you in an unfair fight?"

He pauses, but there's fear in his eyes. Real fear. "All of them, because they'll know you're lying."

"Oh, but see, I won't be." I smile. Brightly. "My parents knew I'd be spending a lot of time alone on colony worlds that don't necessarily have the best manners. I've been taking self-defense classes since I was old enough to walk. If you come at me, if I see you coming at me, I will break you. Understand?"

He doesn't look convinced. That's not . . . great. I'm not lying. I really have been taking self-defense classes since I was practically a baby. We get videos, and Mom goes through the moves with me, and she's told me, over and over again, that if I wind up in a situation where a fight is unavoidable, it's my job to put the other person down as hard and as fast as I can, because my responsibility—my only responsibility—is to come home in one piece. We can deal with colonial governments and assault charges, we can handle hospital bills and accusations of unnecessary force, but we can't do anything about me holding back and getting myself killed.

"You like Kora, don't you?" He jumps. Good. I want to hit him where it hurts, but I'd rather do it verbally if I can. "I get it. She's amazing. She's going to wake up one morning and realize the universe is huge and Zagreus is small and then she's going to be gone, because this place? Is never going to be enough for her."

"That's not going to happen," Michel mutters.

I shrug. "Maybe. Maybe not. But if you want to make *sure* it happens, you'll keep harassing me. The way I see it, right now, I'm a harmless fling. She kissed me—and that wasn't the first time, in case you were wondering—and I bet if you asked her, she'd . . . well, hopefully she wouldn't tell you why, because a lady doesn't kiss and tell, but I bet part of the reason is that she knows I'm not staying. I'm safe."

It hurts to say that. Not a lot, but enough. I don't want to be a harmless fling. I don't want to be the colonial equivalent of a summer romance. I want to be the forever girl, the one she dreams about waking up next to for the rest of her life. And that was never going to be me. When my parents finish their catalog, we're gone, off to another colony, another series of surveys, and Kora will stay here. She'll fall in love with someone like Michel—maybe with Michel himself—and settle down in her mother's residence, raise her kids there, teach them to respect the walls. She's never going to fly away with me and Viola, never going to see the universe.

That's okay. No matter how much I like her—and I like her so much it feels like I've swallowed fire, like I'm burning from the inside out—I don't get to decide who she's going to be.

Neither does Michel.

He looks less scared now. "Why should I care if you're a fling, scag? You're spacer trash. She's playing with you."

I force myself to shrug. "So let her play. Am I really worth risking your reputation over? Because I'll put you on the ground if you make me. Please don't make me."

I don't want to explain to colonial security why I hurt one of their precious kids. Not when half of them think of me—and Viola, weirdly enough—as a "disruptive element," not when some of them argued against letting me attend the colonial school because the other students might not know how to deal with a stranger in their midst. I don't want to deal with any of this. I just want to go home, and think about Kora's lips on mine, and pretend, for a little while, that the world doesn't work the way I know it does.

Michel's lip curls. "I could break you," he says. "But you're not worth my time."

He turns and walks away, vanishing into the dull, gray crowd that throngs along the dull, gray street. I realize, belatedly, that not a single one of them intervened when it looked like he was going to hurt me. To them, I'm just an invasive species, one of those necessary evils that needs to be purged from their precious colony before I do irreparable harm. Michel could have broken me, and they would have kept going about their business.

I hate this planet.

I can't go back to happy daydreams, not after Michel. I finish my walk across the colony as fast as I can, ducking down narrow side alleys and taking every shortcut I can think of in order to reach the gate that will let me out and onto the residence supply trail.

The word "gate" always makes me think of something like the fence in front of the residence, transparent and secure but not showy, not intimidating. I can open the gate to the residence with a pulse from my ID bracelet. This gate is nothing like that one. This gate is two big metal doors set into a metal wall almost three meters across, so wide that I could stretch out on top of it with my arms over my head and still not be able to touch both sides at the same time.

Dad says it makes them feel safe. Mom says if they wanted to feel safe, they should have stayed in a nice orbital colony that would never encounter the natural world and stopped pretending to be anything other than cowards. My parents are fun people who definitely don't hold grudges against colonial security choices. Not.

The guards at the gate know me by now; more than most of the adults in the colony, they've even learned to like me, at least a little. Rockwell nods, a faint smile on her face. Johnson, eyes closed, continues leaning against the wall. I indicate him with my thumb.

"They pay you for this?" I ask.

"It's a living," says Rockwell, and laughs. No one on Zagreus gets paid, except for my parents—one more reason for the colonists to hate us. Instead, individuals old enough to contribute to the colony's well-being are expected to volunteer their labor, and are rewarded accordingly. Basics like housing, bland but nourishing food, medical care, and education are provided free of charge. Everything else takes labor hours.

Including accessing library files, which is why I've done not only my fair share of volunteer time but Viola's, since there aren't colony exemptions for health reasons, and while there's work she could do from her bed, all of it requires travel into the colony proper for training, orientation, and approval. It's easier for me to do six hours than it is to risk her health for the sake of her doing three.

Johnson doesn't say anything. I'm pretty sure he's asleep.

I hold out my hand. Rockwell scans my fingerprints, compares them to the set on record, and nods in the affirmative.

"Have a nice walk home," she says. She punches a series of keys on the pad next to the gate, and it creaks upward, creating a hole in the otherwise seamless surface of the wall. I walk through. I hear it slam behind me, but I don't bother looking back. After a whole day in the colony, even the awful orange sky is beautiful. I walk along the supply trail with my head back and my eyes half-closed, feeling the sunlight on my face, pretending that I'm anywhere but here.

Dad's in the living room when I get home, checking and double-checking the equipment he'll be taking on his salvage run. Mom is nowhere to be seen, probably out in the field somewhere, poking something that doesn't want to be poked.

Viola perks up when I step into our room. "Party?" she asks.

"Party," I confirm.

My sister claps her hands and laughs, and maybe this is a good idea after all. What could it hurt?

8

GET THIS PARTY STARTED

KORA KISSES ME TWICE MORE over the course of the week, once in front of our classroom and once in the library, where she comes up behind me while I'm scrolling through a book on Zagreus customs—historians-for-hire can make you seem like you have a rich cultural story five minutes after you've been founded, if you have the cash. Both times, she leaves me breathless, aching, and confused, unable to figure out exactly what we are to each other. Am I allowed to kiss her the way she kisses me? Am I allowed to leave her with a skin that's too tight and a chest that's too small, so she can't get enough air into her lungs?

I don't know the rules and I don't like it. But she gives me a guest list halfway through the week, and I set the residence harvesting units to pull and purify extra water, to process extra insect protein for our use; we'll have plenty of refreshments, as long as no one decides to be a jerk about where they came from.

The morning of the party dawns bright and clear and way too early. The sound of the front door slamming wakes me, reverberating through the residence like the banging of a gong. I shuffle out of bed and into the living room, wiping the sleep out of my eyes.

Dad is there, a funny look on his face as he stares morosely at the door. I must have made a sound, because he turns toward me and manages a wavering half smile that doesn't entirely fit his face.

"Morning, sunshine," he says. "How did you sleep?"

"Not long enough," I grumble. "I'm a teenager. Science says I need at least another five hours."

"Where's your sister?"

"Following the dictates of science." Almost nothing can wake Viola between the hours of midnight and nine. She adjusts to each new planet with terrifying speed, and once she goes to bed, she stays there. "Where's Mom?"

Dad sighs. "She went out." Punctuating his words, Mom's personal transport—a sort of motorcycle with run-flat tires adapted to the terrain of Zagreus—roars to life in the garage. The engine is too loud. Mom's punching it, and she's not even out of the yard yet.

I stare at him, eyes wide. "What happened?"

"We had a little disagreement about my reasons for going up today. That's all." He picks up his pack, swings it over one shoulder, and bends to kiss me on the forehead. His lips are cool. His mustache tickles my skin. I love him. He's my father, and I love him, and I have the sudden, irrational desire to wrap my arms around him and refuse to let him go. We could cancel the party, we could cancel the shuttle upgrade, and he could stay here. He could be safe.

When he pulls back, he smiles wistfully at me. "You're so big now," he says. "You're almost grown up. Soon, we'll have to take the safeties off and see how far you can fly. You know we're proud of you, don't you? You're so much more amazing than we ever thought you'd be."

I frown. "You and Mom are great. Viola and I couldn't have asked for better parents."

The smile in his eyes flickers. "We did our best," he says. "If we got some parts wrong, I just want you to remember that. We did our best."

"Daddy—"

"I have to go now. Have a nice time today, whatever you wind up doing. I'll see you tomorrow, when I get out of decontamination."

Then he's gone, out the front door before I can protest. I chase him as far as the threshold. I stop there, watching as he walks across the yard to the gate, lets himself out, and starts down the supply trail. The urge to call him back is like a stone in my throat. Bit by bit, he fades into the distance, until no matter how hard I squint, I can't see him anymore. His job has stolen him. Somehow, it feels more like *Zagreus* has stolen him, like the planet has swallowed him whole.

I shut the door as I step back into the residence. We have a few hours before anyone's going to show up. The party should be getting under way right around the time that Dad's shuttle docks with the survey ship in orbit above us. If everything goes well, he'll be back planet-side before Kora and I finish saying good night. He'll spend the night in the colony settlement being tested for possible passengers, and when they give him a clean bill of health, he'll be home again this time tomorrow morning. There's nothing to worry about.

So why do I feel so nervous?

Viola is still sleeping when I step back into our room. I consider waking her, and decide it's a better idea for me to shower and get ready while she's still safely in bed. She doesn't always walk well first thing in the morning. The last thing we need is to be tripping over each other.

So I get ready. I shower, and I brush my teeth, and I put on a green-and-silver tunic over a pair of black leggings—all the rage this season on a colony world so far away from here that the name wouldn't mean anything at all to these Zagreus-born teens. I look prime. I look imported and unattainable and strange in the good way, like something you'd see on a screen, but not right in front of you. Kora won't know what hit her.

This time when I return to our room, Viola is awake. She gives my outfit an approving nod. "Good," she says. "I was worried you'd put on that frumpy jumpsuit you wear to school."

"School is for blending in," I say. "Today is for standing out."

Her grin is quick. "You mean today is for impressing Kora."

"Shut up."

"I'm really excited to meet her."

"I will smother you with a pillow."

"I have machines that breathe for me." Viola waves a hand. "I'm going to tell her all about what you were like as a kid."

"I will disconnect your machines and *then* smother you with a pillow."

If there's a better sound in the universe than my sister's laughter, I've never heard it. She grins at me and says, "How about you pull out my silver and blue and we'll call it square?"

In silver and blue, Viola's coloring won't have anything to complement it. She'll match me, but she'll do it in the most faded, washed-out way possible. I blink. "Really? But you'll look . . ."

"Sick. I'll look sick." Viola's grin turns impish. "You know. Like a girl who totally exists but couldn't possibly go all the way into town to attend class. Also, I'll look like a worse version of you. Keeps Kora from figuring out who the prettier twin is."

I blink. Then I smile. "You always know what to say to make me happy."

"Yeah, well, if there were a doctorate degree in Olivia Shipp, I could make a case for having it awarded to me solely on the basis of practical experience. I get you, stupid sister. Now help me out of bed. I need to take a shower."

Vi's thin, but she's heavier than she looks; it takes some work for me to extricate her from the mattress. Then she's off to the bathroom and I'm off to start getting things set up for the party.

The snacks aren't fancy and there aren't any decorations, and six kids really shouldn't be enough to consider a "party," anyway, but it doesn't matter, because we're doing this; we're going to socialize with people our own age, and maybe I can sneak off with Kora for more kissing, and Michel will have to admit that Viola actually exists, she's not just some figment of my imagination. This is going to be the *best* day.

Viola emerges from the bathroom in her blue-and-silver outfit and settles on the beanbag chair near the living room window. She's having a good day; she doesn't even need her oxygen tank. She still *looks* sick—and I hate that she needs to, but she's right, because people judge even when they shouldn't, and her looking sick will help to convince the others that she *is* sick. I hate it. I hate it more than she does. Viola says other people can't change what she is by refusing to listen, but it's not fair. She should be allowed to exist without people judging her for it.

"You should let me braid your hair," she says.

"I like it down."

"Then you should let me curl it," she says. "It's all flat and lifeless."

"It looks exactly like yours."

Viola grins. "Which means I know what I'm talking about."

There's a chime before I can argue further. I pull up the security screen. Kora's at the gate, with Michel, and Lin and Juan from our statistics class, and Alisa and Paul from history. It's hard not to notice that Kora put together an equal mix of boys and girls, like we were some sort of school dance. I take a deep breath.

"They're here," I say.

"Wow," says Viola, looking at the screen. "Do they always travel in a pack like that, or are they all *that* scared of being outside?"

"I think they're that scared," I say, and turn toward the front door, tugging my tunic into place and putting on my best not-scared smile. They're my classmates. They're my peers. I invited them to come. They shouldn't be this frightening.

All six of them are standing clustered by the gate at the edge of the fenced-off yard when I open the residence door. They're trying to seem unobtrusive and unconcerned. They're failing. Kora perks up. The others huddle closer to her, glancing around like they expect the ground to open up and swallow them whole.

"You made it!" I call.

"Let us in, Shipp," snarls Michel.

I pause in the act of reaching for the gate release, giving him a neutral look. It could go either way, that look. It could let him in or it could lock him out, and there's no way of telling which impulse is going to win.

Kora elbows him in the side, hard. Michel scowls. If I've read the social dynamics correctly . . .

"I mean, please let us in," says Michel. "Your residence looks nice. I'd love to see it from the side of the fence where nothing eats us."

Everything is biology, and biology is war. I allow my neutral expression to shift into a smile as I press the gate release. It swings inward, and six nervous, excited, slightly giddy teenagers spill into our yard, which is as close to perfectly safe as any slice of the great outdoors can be here on Zagreus. The grass is all the friendly, non-carnivorous sort, which keeps most of the bugs away; for the ones it doesn't, we have sonic repulsors. I flip the switch to send the "ants" and "spiders" scattering, hoping none of my classmates will notice.

They don't. They're too busy laughing and hugging one another. Alisa and Paul give each other a high five; Juan spins Lin around by her hands. She throws her head back, eyes on the sky, seeming to drink in the sight of it with nothing to get in her way.

Michel starts to reach for Kora, but she sidesteps him and heads for me, planting a kiss like a flag on the country of my mouth before she grins, cheeks red and curls wild around her face, and asks, "Can we come in?"

"Sure," I say, feeling my own cheeks heat up. "Viola's inside with the snacks."

"Snacks?" asks Paul. Everyone laughs, even Michel. That's a good sign. Maybe he didn't come to challenge me for a better position in the social stack—as if beating me would get him anything. I'm Kora's weird little pet, one more slice of the terrifying outside. It's only the fact that she's at the front of the pack that lets her keep me without hurting her own social standing.

Michel slams his shoulder into mine as he moves past me into the residence, hard enough to hurt. I stagger, catching myself on the doorframe.

Alisa, following behind him, gives me a sympathetic look.

"He hated Paul for, like, two years because he thought Paul liked Kora," she says, voice soft. "Try not to take it personally."

"Bruises are always personal," I say.

They're all inside, and so I shut the door and turn to face the consequences of my own actions.

My schoolmates have spread out through the room like they own it. Paul and Juan are investigating the snacks with the single-minded hunger that is universal to teenage boys. Lin has a tumbler of water big enough to constitute half a daily ration under normal circumstances; she's already drinking, great, blissful gulps, her eyes half-closed as she sucks it down. I hate water rationing, and this reminds me of why.

Michel has stopped halfway across the room, staring at Viola. She smiles back at him, smug as a cat that's gotten into the ship's cream.

"You must be Michel," she says. Her voice sounds just like mine, even down to the inflections. We've been told that it's creepy when people aren't used to it. Right now, nothing could make me happier. "Olivia's told me so much about you. Want to poke me so you'll believe I really exist?"

"I . . . that . . . ," stammers Michel.

Kora laughs and punches him in the arm. "She's got you there. Hi, Viola. It's good to see you again." She winks.

I redden. Kora told the others that she'd already met my sister when she was trying to convince them of Viola's reality. If Viola doesn't play along . . .

"I keep telling Olive that I deserve a social life too, but she wants to keep you all to herself, and I guess I can't blame her for that," says Viola. "I mean, you're not my type, but she likes you a lot."

"What do you mean, she's not your type?" demands Michel.

I resist the urge to put my hand over my eyes. If he decides to challenge my sister over Kora's honor—or whatever—this is going to be a really, really short party.

"She'd break me," says Viola bluntly. "I don't know if you noticed, since Olive's vivacious enough to fill up plenty of space on her own, but I'm too sick to come to school. I don't get crushes on real people. Too much risk of making things worse for myself. Visual novels and dating sims are more than enough for me. Kora's all Olive's, and I'm all my own."

Michel bristles at that characterization of Kora, but Kora laughs and steps away, beckoning for me to come over to her.

"Darn straight," she says, and kisses me, earning herself a whoop from Juan, who has put together some sort of crisps-and-meat sandwich using two of the sweet rolls as bread. Boys have the weirdest taste in food, but I don't care, because I'm kissing Kora. Michel's right there, watching me kiss Kora, and that makes it even better somehow, like if anything was going to spoil things between us, it would have been him, and now I know that he can't. Nothing is going to spoil what we're becoming.

"Best party ever," I murmur dazedly when Kora pulls away, and she laughs, and the party is on.

Except for Michel, who winds up sulking in the corner, arms crossed, looking at the rest of us like he dares us to say a word, everyone seems to have a good time. Lin drinks so much water that she has to sit down, a giddy, almost intoxicated expression on her face. Alisa and Paul get into a good-natured argument about whether going into the yard counts as hanging out in the wilderness, while Juan sits down by Viola, who flirts with good-natured non-commitment, happy to be part of an ordinary social group, doing ordinary things, for once in her life.

Kora and I sit on the couch together, snuggled up so I can feel it when she breathes, so her hair tangles into mine, curls wrapping tight around overly straight strands, and I don't think I've ever been this happy, I don't think life has ever been this good. This is what perfection feels like, this is how the world should be every day, forever.

I should have known it couldn't last.

The lights above the residence vidscreen flash red-white-red, bringing conversation to a grinding halt as everyone whips around to stare at them.

"Cover your ears!" shouts Viola. I realize why a bare second before the screeching wail starts pouring from the vidscreen speakers. Vi is almost always in her room, and this is the emergency transmission alert: we need a way to get her to pay attention when she can't see the lights in the living room.

The sound fills the entire residence, shaking the windows. Kora cries out, pained. I want to comfort her, but I can't bring myself to peel my palms away from my ears. I'm shaking, it's so loud. Then, as abruptly as it started, the sound stops, and the connection is made.

My father's face appears on the screen. His helmet is gone; his environmental security suit has been torn, a great gash down one side that exposes red and bloody skin beneath. There's blood on his cheek. He looks like he's been attacked, or like he's barely evaded being attacked, escaping purely by dint of being willing to throw himself into some piece of machinery. His left arm is dangling, useless. The shoulder is dislocated, or the bones are broken, or both. Both seem suddenly, terribly probable.

"Daddy?" I whisper. I'm sitting up, no longer snuggled into Kora, and I don't remember when that happened, I don't remember moving; I'm staring at my father, beaten and bloody on the vidscreen, and I can't breathe, my lungs are too small and I can't *breathe.*

He doesn't seem to hear me, and I realize this isn't an open channel. This is a recorded message, something sent from orbit to ground with all the emergency keys my father could embed in its message flags. Zagreus only has a small satellite array; incoming messages aren't a priority. This could have happened hours ago. Dread gathers in the pit of my stomach, filling and freezing me. My father is hurt, and I don't know when it happened, and I don't know if—

No. I won't think like that. My father is *fine*, he's *fine*, he's calling to let us know that there's been an accident and he didn't want Viola to miss it, that's all. Nothing's really wrong. This was a salvage run. This was only a salvage run. He's *fine.*

"Katherine." His voice is a rasp, like he's been screaming so much that he's stripped all the skin from the back of his throat. "Kate. God, Kate . . . we messed up. Honey, we messed up so bad. We should never have come here. We shouldn't . . ."

He stops, closing his eyes and forcing himself to take a slow, shuddering breath. I've seen that look on his face before. When I fell out of a tree and broke my wrist; when Viola's equipment malfunctioned and she stopped breathing. Whenever one of us was in danger and he couldn't fix it, he made that face, and he's making it now, or he did make it, whenever this was filmed, and he's so far away, and I can't reach him, and I can't help him.

"Daddy . . . ," I whisper.

Viola is staring at the screen, eyes wide and solemn in her bloodless face, and I want to go to her, I want my sister, and I can't move. No matter how hard I try, I can't make my body listen to me.

My father opens his eyes.

"They took the shuttle. The damn fools took the shuttle, even after what we saw that *thing* do to Petrov. She's dead. They're . . . we're all dead, even if some of us don't know it yet."

Michel stiffens. Petrov is his last name; his mother is one of the people who left this morning for the survey ship.

"They're heading back to Zagreus, and these controls—half these systems are fried. Kate, I don't know how long you have before the shuttle lands. You have to get out of there. Grab the girls, grab whatever you can carry, and *run*. Head for the ship. Don't look back. Don't stop to help anyone, *anyone*, do you understand me? They could be—these things, they—no one is safe. It's you and the girls, and baby, I'm sorry, I'm so sorry, I should never have agreed to this, I should have stayed with you, I should . . ."

He stops. For the first time since this transmission started—for the last time in my life—he smiles. It's soft and it's sad and I realize I'm crying, and I can't stop. The tears have a life of their own, and what they want is to do what Daddy told us to do. They want to escape.

"They would have gone up without me. Maybe it's for the best. At least this way, you have some warning of what's to come. I love you, Kate. I love everything about you, and I'm not sorry, do you understand? But it's time. You have to tell Olivia. She deserves to—"

Something slams into him from the side, something too fast for me to see clearly. I have the brief impression of shining black, not scales, but chitin, something hard and sharp and terrible. A splash of blood hits the lens of whatever camera he's been using to record this. He screams. The sound is mercifully brief. That's the only merciful thing about it.

The transmission is replaced by a blast of static. When that fades, the screen shuts off. All of us are silent, staring, unable to fully process what we just saw.

"No."

The voice sounds like mine, but I know I haven't spoken. Slowly, I turn.

Viola is struggling to her feet, moving jerkily, like she can't remember how her body is supposed to work. Bit by bit, she gets herself under control, until she's standing, straight and strong and pale as skimmed milk, eyes still fixed on the darkened screen.

"*No*," she says again, stronger this time. She whips around to face me. "I told you, I *told* you something bad was happening, I *told* you, and now he's—now they're—we have to find Mom."

She spins on her heel and bolts for the door, moving faster than I've ever seen her move, moving faster than I knew she *could* move. She's running, sprinting, and she hits the door without breaking stride, racing into the yard.

"*Viola!*" I run after her, pausing at the threshold to stare. She's already halfway across the yard, the gate standing open, triggered by the signal from her key. The others pile into the doorway behind me, all stunned and staring.

Then a hand grabs my shoulder and whips me around, slamming me into the doorframe. Michel has his other hand drawn back, fist already formed, ready to strike.

"*What did he do?*" he demands. "*What did your worthless fucking father do?!*"

I don't have time for this. I twist away from his hand and grab his wrist at the same time, digging my thumb into the space between the large bones of his arm. He makes a choked sound, swaying. I dig in harder, feeling the muscle part under the pressure.

"Not. Now," I snarl, and let him go, shoving him away from me as I look for Viola.

She's gone. The gate is closed, and she's gone. My father is—no, he's not dead, I won't think that he's dead, but he's hurt and stranded in orbit, and now I've somehow managed to lose my sister, my sick twin sister, who's supposed to be my responsibility. I can't breathe. How did the day go this wrong, this quickly?

A hand touches my shoulder, right where Michel grabbed me. I duck away, spinning at the same time, and find myself looking into Kora's wide, wounded eyes. She looks like she doesn't understand what's happening. I can't blame her for that. I don't understand it either.

"I have to go after her," I say. "Anyone who wants to come with me, fine—only no, not *anyone*. I can only take three people." I have to save a seat in the ATV for Viola. We only have five seat belts.

"I'm coming with you," says Kora.

"Me too," says Michel.

The others exchange glances, clearly uncomfortable. Paul steps forward.

"If there's a problem, if she's overexerted herself, I can help," he says. "I'm going into med training as soon as we graduate. I can already do first aid."

I don't want him touching Viola. Her problems aren't the kind you solve with CPR and a few compression bandages. I don't want any of these people near her. What was I thinking? I didn't need them to believe in her. I needed to stay home with her, and let them be faces on a screen, and keep her safe. I need to keep her safe.

"Fine," I snap, and turn to the others, Juan and Lin and Alisa. "You all, stay here, keep the door closed, and if my father calls again, contact me immediately. We'll be back as soon as we can. There's no way she's gone far."

I run for the garage then, for the ATV, with the others running behind me, Kora closest, Michel and Paul lagging behind. I trust Kora. The others . . . I don't know, and there's no time to worry about that now. I need to find my sister.

That's the primary thought in my mind as I open the garage, grab the keys, and prep the ATV for the trip. It's fully fueled and charged, ready to go for hundreds of miles if necessary. There's no way I'll need to drive even half that far, not when I'm trying to find Viola. She's probably collapsed somewhere just past the forest's edge, exhausted. The thought makes me work faster. There are too many predators out there. I don't want any of them to hurt her. I *can't* let them hurt her.

Paul touches the side of the ATV, still dented from the lion-worm attack, and whistles, long and low. I ignore him. I have bigger things to worry about.

Our only issue comes when Michel tries to climb into the front seat next to me. Kora grabs his arm, stopping him.

"No," she says. "I ride with Olivia. You ride in the back."

He narrows his eyes, but he doesn't argue, taking up a place in the rear bucket seat with Paul. They fasten their belts. I throw us into gear, and we're off, moving down the narrow driveway with bone-jarring speed. The larger gate at the end is already open, responding to the ATV's engine. Good thing. Right now, I would have been perfectly happy to break the gate off of its moorings if it moved too slowly for me.

Paul cheers. Michel is silent. So is Kora, but she puts her hand on my knee, offering what comfort she can, and I don't nudge it off. I'm so scared. Everything is too bright, and that orange sky, I hate that orange—

I slam on the brakes as a plume of fire streaks across that orange sky like a meteor plummeting toward solid land. It's too big to be a meteor, though, and moving too fast, spinning end over end as it makes its terrible descent. I realize what the shape of it is telling me half a breath before it strikes the distant line of the mountains, sending a jet of dust and smoke and flame billowing into the sky.

Michel makes a guttural, pained noise behind me. I don't bother turning. If he wants to jump out and run for the mountains, that's his call. I need to find my sister. I need to—

This time, when the hand closes on my shoulder, I don't mess around with dodging or trying to play nice. Michel got the drop on me once, and I thought I'd made it clear that we weren't doing this anymore. I drive my elbow back as hard as I can, waiting for the satisfying rush of air that follows impact. Kora makes a squeaking sound. I ignore her, whipping around and grabbing Michel's throat with my other hand. My guess about how far forward he'd bend was right; I catch him just under the chin, forcing his head to stay up, forcing him to look at me.

His eyes are watering. Good. He needs to learn that he doesn't put hands on me.

"I'm sorry if your mother was on that shuttle," I say, voice low. We both know she wasn't. My father wouldn't have said she was dead if he hadn't known, for sure, that she was dead. He's always been careful like that.

He's never going to be careful like that again. Michel and I may both be in denial, but neither of us is stupid enough to think our parents are making it back to this planet alive.

"If you want to go looking for her, I won't stop you," I continue. "The mountains are about five miles to the west of us. There's a lot of bad stuff between here and there, predators and plants that might as well be predators and hostile terrain, but hey, it's your mother. If you want to go, go. But this is *my* ATV, and we are finding *my* sister before we do anything else."

"P . . . please . . ." he manages to rasp. He looks somewhere beyond furious, like he wants nothing more than to shove me out of the ATV and drive off without me. I can understand the sentiment. I even sort of share it, in reverse.

"You don't touch me again. You got two. You don't get any more. We're going to find Viola, and we're going to find my mother, and then, if she says it's all right, we can go looking for your mom." Hopefully, Mom won't say it's all right. There's not going to be anything living in those mountains; nothing that anyone sane would want to find.

"Michel, chill," snaps Kora. "This isn't Olivia's fault."

His anger switches targets in an instant. "Her father—"

"Was a hired biologist, not a magician," says Kora. "If there was something dangerous on that ship, he had no way of knowing

104

before he went up there. Stop. Let her drive. We all get what we want faster if you stop."

"I want to be back inside," says Paul nervously. "This is . . . it's really open out here."

Reluctantly, Michel leans back in his seat, still glaring. I don't make an effort to hold on to him. When his throat slips out of my fingers, I let go, and twist back around in my seat, focusing on the controls.

"Hold on," I say, and start us up again, heading for the forest, while the smoke from the fallen shuttle rises into the air, black and terrible and toxic.

9

AMONG
THE TREES

WE'VE BEEN DRIVING FOR WHAT feels like hours, and we haven't seen my sister. That's impossible. She's not fast enough, she's not strong enough, and we're in a *motorized vehicle*: there's no way she could have gotten this far ahead. It's still happening. The smoke from the crashed shuttle has turned white, like all the dangerous chemicals have burnt off completely, and the sky is trending toward a deeper orange, almost bloody around the edges. The suns will start going down soon, first the primary and then the secondary. I don't know what I'll do when that happens.

Kora hasn't said anything since our first pass along the forest trail without any sign of Viola or my mom. Her hands are pressed to the dash, white-knuckled, and her eyes are fixed on the line of the horizon like she can bring them here through sheer force of will. She has to be remembering the lion-worm, the way it would have dragged her underground if I hadn't been there to stop it.

I know I can't stop thinking about it.

Michel and Paul are more talkative, although they're only talking to each other, not to us. I don't like having Michel behind me. I can't unlock my shoulders. My sister is out there somewhere, in danger, maybe collapsed from the strain of running away, and I just had to go and bring an additional complication into the field. *Keep your friends close and your enemies closer* shouldn't apply when you're talking about a five-person ATV.

We're coming around a curve in the trail, heading into the grove of flowering, fruiting stalks, when I see a flash of white-blonde through the vegetation. Viola. I slam my foot down on the accelerator, and we come around the curve faster than ever, so fast that it isn't entirely safe, and there she is, my sister, standing frozen in the middle of the path. She doesn't look hurt. She has mud on her pants and leaves in her hair, but she's standing, she's breathing, she looks fine. A knot I didn't know I was carrying in my stomach unties itself, and I can breathe again.

The reason for her motionless state is obvious. What looks like a full herd of the meat-deer I saw in the forest a few days ago has filled the path, their muzzles to the ground, rooting up mouthfuls of that strange orange grass. Maybe because the grass eats meat, it fills the same nutritional niche in their diets as actual predation. Mom will be fascinated.

Mom will be broken. Dad is dead. Dad is dead, and I'm thinking about funny grass and predator feeding habits, because it's easier than thinking about my father never coming home, or Mom trying to decide what happens to us now. We'll probably go back to Earth. I've wanted that for so long, and it feels like nothing now, it feels like being a child, because this isn't how I wanted it. This isn't how I wanted it at all.

The ATV didn't startle the meat-deer; they're still feeding, heads down, tails twitching. "Viola," I whisper, as loudly as I dare. "Come on. We need to get you back to the house."

"You can't be here," she whispers back, with genuine fear in her voice. "Go home."

"Vi—"

"Go *home*."

Pollen drifts around us, masking our scents. The meat-deer twitch their ears and keep eating. They must not focus on sound as a source of danger. It makes a certain amount of sense. All the largest predators I've seen are subterrestrial, like the lion-worms. Why listen when what really matters is feeling the vibrations beneath you, reading them for signs of danger?

"Not without you," I whisper back, louder. "You need to get in the ATV. You're sick, you can't be out here, you're going to hurt yourself." It's a miracle that she's still on her feet at all. She should have collapsed hours ago, unable to breathe.

Unless there's something about the atmosphere on Zagreus that agrees with her lungs, and we've been protecting her all this time from a world where she could actually thrive. Maybe I'm going to wind up staying here after all. I'd do it, for Viola. Kora and I could be happy, and we'd laugh and say that it's all down to my sister, and it's a stupid daydream, it's a distraction from the things I *should* be worrying about.

Viola finally looks over her shoulder at me. She's as pale as ever. Either she's been standing here long enough for the flush of exertion to fade, or she's not even winded by running this far from the house. It's strange and confusing and I don't know what to make of it.

"Go home," she says again, a little louder, a little more confidently. "I'll find Mom and bring her back, but I can't do that if I don't know that you're safe."

"Viola—" I begin.

I don't finish.

The thing that drops from the fruiting stalks onto the back of one of the meat-deer is black and chitinous and shines in the fading daylight like it's been dipped in oil, like it's been polished to a mirror sheen by some unknown hand. It's long and angular and insectile and mechanical at the same time. My eyes don't want to focus on it. It's *wrong*, it's an offense, it hurts parts of my brain that normally don't have any say on my daily life.

Its head is long and curved, like a seashell, like a blade. It has no visible eyes or ears, and its mouth, at least initially, is buried in the neck of the meat-deer, ripping out vital arteries and letting the animal bleed out into the patchy orange grass beneath it. The rest of the herd panics and thunders away, scattering in all directions. Some of them are screaming, a warning bellow that sounds like an alarm.

Viola doesn't move. The meat-deer rush past her on both sides, the wind from their passage ruffling her hair, and she doesn't move, doesn't flinch, doesn't even seem to breathe. Kora fumbles for my hand. She's whimpering in the back of her throat, high and tight and agonized. Michel is frozen behind me. I can hear him breathing.

Paul bolts.

I don't have any warning that he's going to move, no chance to tell him to stop and stay where he is. I just hear his feet hitting the ground as he leaps out of the ATV, and then he's running, racing into the tall grass as fast as he can. I start to take a breath, to shout for him to come back, and I stop myself. I catch myself before I can make a sound, and I just watch him go.

The creature lifts its head. Its mouth is a terrible cacophony of angles and lines, teeth like razor blades, a jaw that slots together in a way I can't quite comprehend. How can this be real? How can this be a real thing? It's clearly biological, but it's not at the same time, like someone built it rather than allowing it to evolve. I don't want to look at it. I don't want to share a *world* with it. It shouldn't exist.

Paul keeps running. He doesn't seem to realize what kind of danger he's in. The creature makes a low clicking noise, the sound seeming to resonate through that long, curved head. Then it moves.

I've never seen anything move this *fast*. In an instant, I know that I've seen it before, as a blur on the screen before my father died: maybe not this specific creature, but one very much like it. I want to hate it, but I can't find my way past my fear. This thing, it isn't native to Zagreus, it isn't supposed to *be* here. It came from space, it came from orbit, it . . .

It came down on the shuttle. The one that crashed, the one that burned. This thing somehow survived on a biological survey ship that may or may not have been fully pressurized, that almost certainly lacked a dependable internal atmosphere, and it somehow then stayed alive through reentry and a crash that should have killed anything and everything on board. This thing is a nightmare and I'm awake, and I don't want it.

By the time Kora opens her mouth to shout after Paul, it's already too late, or at least that's what I tell myself as I clamp my hand over her mouth and silence her. I don't want that thing to turn its attention on us, not when it's moving that fast, not when it has a tail like a blackened spine curled over its back, razor-sharp and deadly. Everything about the thing is deadly. It's designed to destroy, nothing more or less.

Paul doesn't stand a chance. The creature slams into him, knocking him over. He has time to scream, and then it's over, and there's blood on the grass, blood that the grass drinks greedily down, as it drinks everything else it finds.

I turn back to Viola, ready to grab her and drag her back to the ATV if necessary, and I freeze.

There's another creature.

This one is slightly smaller, holding itself still enough that I have the opportunity to really understand how it's put together. It's not bipedal in the human sense, not with that tail and that long, curved spine, but it looks comfortable as it draws itself up onto its hind legs to study my sister with its eyeless head. How it sees her, I don't know. Vibrations, maybe, or CO_2, or something else too strange and terrible to name.

The black plating on its thin torso and long limbs is definitely insectile. It looks like someone has taken a wasp, ripped away its wings, and transformed it one sliver at a time to form the perfect terrestrial killing machine. It opens its mouth. A second, smaller mouth appears, driven forward on a retractable jaw, dripping drool and ichor as it moves toward my sister's face. She doesn't flinch or look away. She's staring down death, and she doesn't look afraid.

I'm scared enough for both of us. I can't move. I should be trying to attract the creature's attention, to pull it away from Viola somehow, and I can't move, can barely breathe. Any moment now, it's going to bite down on the flesh of her cheek, or rip her throat away, or do something else, something even more terrible, and I can't move. My sister is right there, right in front of me, and I can't save her.

The creature draws back, like it's preparing to strike. I want to close my eyes. I don't. If I can't save Viola, I can at least watch her die.

"Drive," hisses Michel. "Get us out of here."

The creature pauses. It turns its head slowly, like it's following the sound.

A beast the size of an Earth rhino bursts out of the greenery behind it, bellowing a challenge in the instant before it slams into the creature. It has a whole head of spreading horns, and a maw that's more like a beak, unfolding in floral horror when it goes to bite. I've seen this thing before. Mom calls them "Zagreus hippos," a kind of local omnivore that spends most of its time wallowing in shallow wetlands.

There's a scorch mark on one shoulder, like someone shot it with a bolt of electricity. Even the crash couldn't have done that. In an instant, I realize what that means:

My mother is somewhere near here. She sent the hippo to save us.

I lurch out of the ATV, trusting Kora to keep Michel from moving to the driver's seat and racing off without me, and run for Viola, who still hasn't moved. The creature is occupied with the hippo, the two of them rolling over and over again, the hippo bellowing and the creature hissing in terrible fury. It has speed and vicious natural weaponry on its side, while the hippo has a hide designed to protect it from both the lion-worms and the huge reptilian predators that lurk in the wetland mud; the hippo is already losing, although it doesn't know it yet, but digging deep enough into its flesh for the hippo to bleed out is going to take time. Not much time. Enough.

I grab Viola's arm and yank her away from the scene, dragging her back to the ATV and flinging her bodily into the front before climbing in after her. She winds up sandwiched between me and Kora. There's no seat belt for her, but we're packed in so tightly that I don't think it's going to matter.

"Hold on!" I shout, and hit the accelerator, plunging deeper into the grove, away from the two creatures and the dying hippo, away from whatever remains of Paul's body.

"What's wrong with you, you scag?!" demands Michel, trying to lean forward into the front seat. "You're going the wrong way!"

"Sit *down*," snaps Viola. She twists around and shoves him back into his seat, demonstrating a strength I didn't know she had. Adrenaline is amazing.

"Mom's out here!" I don't want to shout. Those creatures . . . I don't know yet how they hunt, whether they follow sound or something else, and I don't know why they didn't attack Viola when she was standing right there, but I don't want to take more chances than I have to. The ATV motor is already making too much noise. "You saw the hippo—she shot it. She flushed it out to save us. We have to find her."

"What *were* those things?" Kora is hugging herself and shaking, and if Viola is stronger than I thought she was going to be, Kora is not. Kora is falling apart. "I've read all the reports your parents sent to my mom, and they never mentioned anything like that. What *were* they?"

"They're not native to Zagreus," I say. "I think . . . I think they came down on the shuttle. I think one of them, up on the survey ship, one of them killed my father."

"There's no way," says Michel. "My mother would never have transported a biohazard to the planet. You're wrong."

"I don't think your mother had a choice." I don't think any of our parents had a choice. Once they set foot on that ship . . .

Everything changed. We're in danger. The whole planet could be in danger, and nobody knows it except for us. I've never seen anything like those things, not on any planet, not in any record. They're terrible and terrifying, and we need someone who understands them. We need a biologist.

We have to find my mother.

The ATV has a range of several hundred miles with a full charge, and it's been sitting in the garage for days, since we haven't had any family-wide outings, not since Dad started focusing on the plan to head up to the salvaged survey ship. He and Mom had been fighting. I guess we know why now. He didn't know what was up there—he would never have gone if he'd known—and neither did she, but they both knew it was a risk, and now it's all being proven. We're so screwed.

At least Mom took one of the private transports, instead of the ATV. I don't like the fact that Alisa, Lin, and Juan are back at the residence without anyone to keep an eye on them. They could be going through anything, touching anything, and I'm not there to stop them.

Worrying about people going through my stuff is so trivial that I start to laugh, still fighting to keep control of the ATV as we steer through the forest. The trail is far behind us, and we're cutting through virgin brush. Mom's going to be so mad. We're not supposed to disturb anything that hasn't already been studied to death. Well, it's death I'm worried about. Fast-moving, chitinous, terrifying death. Sorry, ecosystem of Zagreus, but I'm willing to run over a few snuffle-squirrels and weird bugs if it keeps me, Kora, and Viola breathing for a little longer.

Michel . . . I'm not so worried about Michel.

Kora gives me an odd look, reaching across Viola to squeeze my knee. "You okay?"

The question is ridiculous enough to make me laugh even harder. That's probably a good thing: it keeps me from talking. *That thing unzipped Paul like a jumpsuit,* I want to say, and *There are two of them, two of them survived the descent from vacuum, if they form a breeding pair, we're finished,* I want to say, and *No, no, I am not okay, none of us are ever going to be okay again.*

Is this what a panic attack feels like? I don't like it. I keep my eyes on the terrain in front of us.

"Where are the others?" Viola looks from Kora to me and back again. "I don't mean . . . I don't mean Paul. I know where Paul is."

We all know where Paul is, except for Paul's parents. They think he's safely at a friend's house. Oh, stars, there's going to be some sort of investigation when this is finished. What was he doing at my house, why did I plan a party to coincide with my parents being gone, did I plan this, did I somehow make this happen, did I yearn for the sight of entrails on the grass and—

And—

And he's *dead,* Paul is *dead,* I barely knew him—he was just a face in a few of my classes, but he was nice, and Kora liked him well enough to put him on the guest list, and Alisa maybe loved him, and this isn't fair. This isn't supposed to be happening.

I stop the ATV before I have time to think better of it, lurching out of the vehicle and dropping to my knees on a patch of open ground. Viola moves into place behind the controls as I vomit everything I've eaten today into the grass. I try to throw up as quietly as I can. Not my favorite new game ever.

"I'll drive for a while," says Viola. "Michel, can you check back there for a red box labeled 'emergency'? I think this qualifies. There should be some bottled water inside."

"There's a gun," reports Michel gleefully.

I vomit again. I'm not letting him drive, but the thought of having him behind me with an actual weapon is almost as disturbing as the constantly recurring image of Paul's broken, gutted body.

"I'll take that." Kora's voice is firm. There's a faint grumbling noise, and then the much more welcome sound of a metal gunstock slapping into Kora's palm. "Don't glare at me like that. You failed your marksmanship classes *twice*. We're all safer if I'm the one with the gun."

"I'm not," says Michel.

"Olive?" Viola sounds concerned. "Honey, I have water if you want it, but we can't stay here. We need to find Mom before that thing finds us."

"I'm okay." I'm lying. Viola knows that, but the others don't have to. We can hide it from them. I'm also terrified. My mother is somewhere out there, alone. Not defenseless—she's never defenseless—but alone isn't good, not right now. My sister needs to be at the residence with her life-support systems, not here, in the wilderness, where anything could go wrong.

She looks as good as she ever does, at least. Her cheeks are bloodless and pale, her eyes are shadowed, surrounded by circles of bruised-seeming skin, but she's not wheezing and she's not collapsing and maybe I can stop worrying about her for a while, until it's safe to focus on something beyond keeping the rest of us alive.

"Are you sure you're good to drive?" I ask, moving toward the ATV. Kora scoots over, making room for me, and I circle the vehicle, climbing into the seat she's vacated.

Viola nods. "Dad taught me the same time as he taught you, and I'm fine. I'm better than you are right now."

"Don't get used to it," I say.

Kora keeps the gun in her lap as Viola starts the ATV up again. It seems to comfort her to know that she can shoot anything that attacks us, and I decide not to point out that it's a false comfort: the thing that killed Paul looked like it could spit bullets out without missing a single, horrifying step. That kind of natural armor is usually designed to protect against claws and teeth, and there were joints between the plates, places where a well-aimed shot could potentially do some damage, but on the whole, we're not going to stop those things with guns.

Nukes, maybe. Massive amounts of crushing damage. Or flamethrowers. I would really, really like a flamethrower right about now. That would be *ultra*-prime.

Viola may be a better driver than I am. She steers us easily through the trees, into a grove of feathery grasses that actually recoil from our passage, opening a clear path toward the glistening disk of the nearest lake. The ground changes consistency under our tires, hard-packed dirt giving way to soft mud. We're entering the wetlands.

A Zagreus hippo bellows in the distance, declaring ownership of this territory. Something with four wings and a razor-sharp bill flashes by overhead. Viola stops the ATV, turning off the engine.

"What are you doing?" demands Michel. "We can't just sit here!"

"You can run." Viola sounds almost serene. "It worked for Paul."

Michel makes a snarling noise. "Paul *died*."

"Then maybe you shouldn't run."

The grass in front of us rustles. I tense, reaching behind me for the machete. Kora raises the gun Michel found in the emergency kit, sighting along its barrel, ready to fire. Viola keeps her hands on the wheel. I can't tell what Michel is doing, and I don't really want to know. Part of me wants him to run. At least if he does, he'll distract the creatures from us for slightly longer. It's a cold, cruel thought, but it's mine, and I'm not sorry.

The rustling gets louder. Kora exhales, settling into a firing stance.

My mother steps out of the greenery.

I grab Kora's arm and yank it upward as her finger twitches on the trigger; she fires safely into the sky before she gasps, drops the gun, and buries her face against my shoulder, shaking. Mom doesn't even blink. She walks toward the ATV, tosses her bag into the back next to Michel, and hops in after it, settling herself on the seat.

"Drive," she says.

"Mom—" I begin.

"*Drive*," she repeats, more sharply. "It's not safe out here."

Viola drives.

She hits the accelerator harder than I would have believed possible, sending us rocketing into a wide turn and then back toward the forest, controlling the ATV with a clinical precision that I would envy, if I wasn't so busy being astonished.

"Where did you learn to drive like this?" I demand.

"Again, Daddy taught me the same time he taught you," she replies.

Daddy. My throat seems to shrink, until I can barely breathe. I glance back at Mom, who has claimed the gun Kora dropped and is checking it over for damage. She doesn't know. She's a widow, we're halfway orphans, and she doesn't know. I can tell her here, in the middle of nowhere, while we're fleeing from a monster we've never seen before and don't fully understand—don't understand even a little—or I can wait until we get back to the residence and tell her in front of a bunch of kids she doesn't know. There are no right answers here.

"Oh," I whisper. I twist in my seat, focusing on Mom. "You shot the hippo."

"I needed to stampede the herd," she says, finally satisfied with the gun's condition. She shoves it into her belt and looks at me challengingly. "You saw them, didn't you?"

I nod. "What are they?"

"I don't know." The admission seems to pain her. "I've never seen anything like them before. They came from the direction of the mountains—I think they arrived in the shuttle. The one that crashed."

I nod again, not trusting myself to speak.

She looks at me with grave, weary eyes, and I know she knows. It should be a relief: I won't be the one telling my mother that my father is dead. It feels like something has been stolen from me, like this was one last thing we could have shared as a family, and now we can't. My whole body aches from stress and fear and impending sorrow. It's going to hit me soon, and I'm going to be useless when it does.

"You can't give in," she says quietly. "This day—this isn't a day we ever wanted to face, and you're going to learn a lot of things you don't want to know, and you can't give in. If you do, you're not going to make it. I can't lose you, too. You're all that I have left."

"Viola and I aren't going to leave you," I say. She grimaces, like something about my words is painful to her, and I remember something that didn't have the room to matter until now. "Daddy managed . . . he managed to call us from the survey ship. It was a pre-recorded message. I don't know how long ago he recorded it. He said you had to tell me something. That it was time for me to know. What was he talking about?"

Fear flashes in her eyes. "Wait until we get home," she says, and looks over the side of the ATV. She chuckles, mirthlessly. "Never thought I'd actually have to do this. Not alone. Goddammit, John, what were you *thinking*?"

"Somebody want to tell me what the hell is going on?" Michel demands. "You're supposed to be the colony's pet biologist, and now you want to say you don't know what those things were? They killed Paul. How come they didn't kill you? Or blondie over there?" He gestures toward Viola.

My throat tightens, but I can't deny that it's a good question. She'd been there, she'd been *right there*, and somehow the creature hadn't attacked her. It should have. By any reasonable standard of predation, it should have.

"The pollen," I blurt.

Mom looks back to me, eyebrows raised. "What?"

"It didn't attack Viola because of the pollen, right? We use it to confuse the lion-worms. It's scent-neutral. The creature didn't attack her because there was so much pollen in the air that it couldn't *find* her." I'm starting to get excited. "Vi, turn around.

We can gather a bunch of the fruiting bodies, use them to keep the creature from finding the house. We can—"

"No," says Mom gently. "That's not what happened."

"But it didn't attack her."

"And it did attack your friend, and he was exposed to the pollen as much as she was. I know how much you want to look for an easy answer, but sweetheart, the answer you're going to get isn't the one you want." She looks over the side of the ATV again, out at the tranquil grassland. "We're almost back to the residence. Hold tight, and I'll explain everything once we get there."

"Mom . . ."

"Everything."

I fall quiet. Kora reaches for my hand, sliding her fingers into mine. She doesn't have the gun anymore, and I'm not foolish enough to think my machete is going to be enough to save us if the creatures find us again. Viola is steering as straight a path as she can toward the residence, but I'm scared, and every rustle in the nearby brush sends another jolt of adrenaline racing along my spine.

I don't want to die. I've never really thought about it in connection with myself before. Viola dying, sure; I think about Viola dying all the time, and how I'd be willing to fight Death itself if it meant she got to stay here, with me, forever. She may have accepted her eventual fate, but that doesn't mean I have to, and all the time I've spent thinking of ways to keep her alive has always started from the assumption that I'm perfectly fine, I'm not someone to worry about. Everything is changing so fast. It's disorienting.

If I'm disoriented, Kora looks like she's about to pass out. I squeeze her hand.

"Is there anything I can do?" I ask.

She starts to shake her head, then stops, looks at me sheepishly, and asks, "Can I have the gun back?"

"You know how to use it?" It's a stupid question, and I regret it as soon as it's out of my mouth. Of course she knows how to use it. She as much as said so, when she mentioned her marksmanship classes.

Her face hardens slightly as she nods. "I do."

"Fine." I twist in my seat, pulling my hand out of hers and holding it out toward Mom. "Give me back the gun."

She raises her eyebrows. "Why should I do that?"

"Because you already have whatever you used to shoot the hippo, and Kora's unarmed. Give me back the gun."

She looks unimpressed. She hands me the gun anyway. I give it to Kora, and watch as some of the lines on her forehead disappear, smoothed away by the simple comfort of knowing she has the ability to defend herself if she has to. She flashes me a quick, half-shy smile. I'm forgiven.

That's nice. Something good has to happen today.

Viola drives on, and the grasslands give way to the more familiar terrain around the residence, and then the fence appears, like a promise of home and hope and harbor. I sit up straighter, waiting for the attack I know has to be coming.

Nothing happens. We reach the fence, and the gate opens, and Viola stops the ATV in the middle of the yard. Unspoken is the fact that we may need to run: putting it in the garage would only slow us down. We climb out of the vehicle and move, in a tight group, toward the door.

Inside, Lin, Juan, and Alisa are sitting on the couch, staring at the silent screen, drinks and snacks forgotten in front of them.

They all look stunned, like they've sunk so deeply into shock that they don't know what to do anymore. They turn when the door slams open, and I notice their expressions of relief when they see Mom—a responsible adult, someone who can maybe make all this go away.

Mom doesn't share their relief. Her face falls when she sees that she has three more teenagers to look after, and she moves quickly to check the front door, making sure that it's locked. Once that's done, she turns to us.

"I don't have time to learn your names, so don't ask me to," she says. "My name is Dr. Katherine Shipp, and as of right now, I am your best chance of getting out of here alive. Do you understand me?"

Silence falls.

10

SECRETS

AS I HAD MORE THAN HALF EXPECTED, Michel is the first to speak.

"What the hell were those things?" he demands. He gestures toward the door behind us, where Viola is still checking the locks. "Why did they kill Paul and not touch your damn daughter? How do we know you didn't bring them here? You're a biologist. You get paid more when you find dangerous animals to warn us all about. Is this your fault?"

Alisa pales, clasping her hands over her mouth. My heart sinks. She didn't know. Of course she didn't know—how could she?

This day just keeps getting worse.

"Kid, my husband is dead, and I don't like your tone," says Mom flatly. "I didn't bring those things here. If I had the kind of skill it would take to control creatures like the ones we saw today, I'd be getting paid way too well for this backwater little colony."

"Creatures?" Juan starts to stand. "What are you talking

about? Paul's not dead. He can't be." He laughs, tight and high and anxious. "This is a really lousy joke. You should tell better jokes."

"If you step toward the door, I'll shoot you myself," says Kora. She manages to make the statement sound calm, even reasonable: if he tries to exit the residence, if he risks drawing attention to us, she'll shoot him. No second chances.

Juan freezes, staring at her. It's clear he believes her threat. I amend, slightly, my opinion of the girl I've been crushing on since we landed here. She may be a sheltered colonial girl who doesn't even understand her own planet, but there's a pretty solid chance she's also secretly a badass.

Mom and Michel are still glaring at each other. Michel looks away first, shaking his head.

"Whatever," he says. "You'll pay for this."

"We're already paying for this," says Mom, and her voice is almost gentle, and I know, without needing to ask, how much danger we're in.

"Mom?" My voice comes out high and frightened, the voice of a child looking for reassurance that the monster in the closet isn't real, isn't going to hurt me. I swallow, and sound a little more normal when I ask, "It was the pollen, wasn't it?"

Mom turns to look at me. "What?"

"The creature didn't attack Viola, because she was surrounded by falling pollen. It masks scents, somehow. I didn't see any eyes on that thing, so maybe it couldn't find her if it couldn't smell her. We have pollen samples in the lab, we can—"

"No." Mom rubs her forehead with one hand, looking suddenly, crushingly weary. "It wasn't the pollen. Goddammit, John." It's like she can't say my father's name anymore without swearing at him. "I wasn't supposed to have to do this alone. I wasn't supposed to have to do this at all."

"Mom?"

Viola moves closer to me, so that I'm flanked, her on one side, Kora on the other. She can't take my hand without taking the machete away. She puts her hand on my shoulder instead, holding on to me, like I'm the only thing keeping her from flying off into space and being lost forever.

Mom looks at us and musters a fragile smile. "My girls," she says. "My perfect, perfect girls. Do you understand how much you were wanted? How hard we worked to have you?"

"I don't feel like I should be hearing this," says Lin uncomfortably. Alisa shushes her. The rest of the room is quiet, watching our mother watching us.

Somewhere outside the residence, a pair of creatures I've never seen before are hunting, and I don't know whether they're going to come hunting for *us*. We should be piling into the ATV and fleeing for the colony, we should be finding a way to fortify and secure our position, and we're not doing any of that. We're seven frightened teenagers looking to the only adult in the room for help, and she's not helping. She's just gazing at me and Viola like she's never seen us before, like she's never going to see us again.

It hurts, the way she's looking at us.

It probably hurt Paul when that thing ripped him apart. We need to move.

I don't move.

"When Viola got sick, we were terrified that it was something infectious, that it was going to spread to the rest of the family. She was so scared. We didn't want her to be locked in a quarantine ward, away from us. The only thing that made her feel better, even a little, was sleeping with her sister." Mom smiles. It's directed at me. Only me. "Co-sleeping, the doctors called it. When she had your arms around her, Olivia, she found it easier to breathe, she cried less, she seemed to get stronger. We thought . . . for a while, we thought . . . she was going to make it."

"She made it, Mom," I say. "She's right here."

Viola doesn't say anything.

"You were only three years old. Our sweet girls. And then we came in to check on Viola, and she wasn't moving. Wasn't breathing. You had your arms wrapped around her, so tightly that it took us both to get the two of you apart, and you were screaming, you wouldn't stop *screaming*, and John . . . John . . ."

Mom stops. A single tear runs down her cheek. I want to hug her. I want to hit her. I want to do anything, *anything* to make her stop talking. The creatures out there in the grass, the burning shuttle in the mountains, even the survey ship in orbit above us, none of them feel as dangerous to me in this moment as my mother and her calm, almost resigned recitation of facts that didn't happen, can't have happened, can't be possible. None of this is possible. I refuse.

"John said we had plenty of footage of Viola," she says finally. "We had brain scans the doctors had taken when we were trying to figure out what was wrong with her, we had dream recordings we'd taken of you both, we *knew* her. She was only three. It might have been harder if she'd been older."

"Stop," I whisper.

"It's easy to build an extrapolative model of a toddler. They're complicated—they're human—but they seem simple to an onlooker, and if we were willing to keep buying more processing power, she'd be able to grow and learn and mature just like the real Viola would have done."

"She *is* the real Viola," I whisper. I can't seem to get enough air in my lungs. I want to shout. I want to scream. I'm lucky to be making a sound.

"The creature didn't attack your sister, because your sister isn't biological. She's synthetic. She's an android."

Viola squeezes my shoulder. I look at her, and she's not upset, she's not confused: she looks sad, maybe, and resigned, like she never wanted this to happen. Like she never wanted me to . . .

"You knew?" I ask.

"I knew," she says. "For years. I didn't at first, but there were so many things that didn't add up, and I was supposed to be sick and stay in bed. It left me with . . . well, it left me with a lot of time to think about things. My pen pals. That started out as me trying to get answers about myself without telling anyone why I needed them. I'm sorry, Olive. I wanted to tell you."

"I *knew* it!" Michel shoves himself between me and Kora, jerking her hand out of mine. He stabs a finger at my chest, knocking me backward, into Viola. Automatically, I place my body between her and him. A wave of relief follows the motion. She's still my sister. If what Mom is saying is true—and it can't be true, and it must be true, because why would she lie to me like that? She's never lied to me before—it doesn't matter, not really, because Viola is still my sister. No matter what, she's my sister.

Michel keeps advancing, forcing me back another step as he jabs his finger at me again. "I *knew* you were a liar! An android? As a member of your family? That's sick and delusional and wrong. You shouldn't go around normal people if you're going to pretend things like that are acceptable. You shouldn't—"

I slap his hand away before he can jab me a third time. His

eyes widen. He pulls his fist back like he's going to swing it at me, and I stay where I am, keeping him away from my sister.

"You get one," I say softly.

"Professor Shipp, can't you make him stop?" demands Kora.

"I just met the young man, I doubt I can make him do anything," says Mom. "We need to focus."

"If you wanted focus, you shouldn't have been telling stories about Viola," I snap, keeping my eyes on Michel.

"This was the *only* time to tell you about Viola," says Mom. "Those creatures—they're perfect apex predators. Didn't you see? Everything about them is tailored for the kill. You said you didn't see eyes. What *did* you see?"

I hate quizzes. Keeping my attention as much on Michel as possible, I say, "They move fast. Too fast to be endurance hunters—that sort of metabolism means they have to kill fast, eat fast, and move on to kill again. I don't think they were mammalian, even by the most generous definition."

"I didn't see them eat anything," says Viola.

"Of course they weren't mammals," says Michel, apparently swayed from his belligerence by the chance to seem smarter than someone else. "They weren't *fuzzy*."

"There are mammals with almost no visible hair, especially when you're talking about the near-mammals we find on Earth-like planets," says Mom. "Olivia's right. They moved like insects. Fast, large, incredibly dangerous insects."

"I don't like this," says Lin in a wavering voice. "I don't like *any* of this. You're scaring me. You're an adult. You're not supposed to be scaring me."

Juan moves to comfort her, but the damage is done: the atmosphere in the room, already fragile, has turned against us. This time, Michel actually swings for me. I catch his hand, spinning on my heel to bring his arm up and around behind him, bending it at an angle that I know from experience has got to hurt like hell. He bellows, flailing, and has the sense not to reach for me again—instead, he lunges for Viola, grabbing for her hair.

The sound of Mom's volt gun going off is massive. It's the biggest sound the world has ever known. My hair stands on end, my skin goes tight, and for a moment, everything is white and electric and impossible to see properly. Viola's hand tightens on my shoulder. Alisa cries out, the sound shrill in the crackling air.

Michel freezes. Slowly, I let go of his arm and step away. Mom levels the volt gun on him. There's a click beside me. Kora has done the same. He looks between them, wide-eyed.

"What?" he demands. "Why am I the bad guy here?"

"You tried to punch my daughter," says Mom.

"You tried to grab my sister," I say.

"She's not your sister," he says with a sneer. "She's a damn machine."

Viola doesn't say anything. She turns her face away, looking faintly ashamed, like she doesn't have anything she *could* say.

I shake my head. "No. She's my sister, and we're going to get out of here. We'll all fit on the ATV if we squish in and don't worry about seat belts." I pause, counting again. No, not quite all: we can fit three in front and three behind, and there are eight of us. Both individual transports are missing. Dad took one to the colony with him, and Mom took one out into the field. She didn't have it when she found us in the wetlands. She must have lost it when she was evading the creature near the hippo pod.

I shake my head again, harder this time. "We'll *fit*," I repeat. If I have to figure out how to drag someone behind us, we'll fit.

"Viola, get your oxygen—" I stop, cutting myself off. When I look at Viola, she has a tiny smile on her face.

"I don't need the oxygen tank," she says. "I don't need any of it, as long as I can charge myself back up every twenty-four hours or so. Don't worry about me. Worry about yourself. I already died once, remember? I can't say I recommend it."

"So we leave the robot," says Michel.

"*Michel*," hisses Kora.

"I'm an android, technically," says Viola. "There's a difference. Robots aren't intelligent, for the most part: they're built to serve a specific function, not to be individuals. I'm as unique a person as you are. I'm just not organic."

I wince when she says that. I can't help myself.

"That's *sick*," sneers Michel.

Juan gets off the couch. "So wait, if she's not organic—if it's not organic—it can go for help, right? We can lock the doors, and wait for it to come back with the colony guards."

"No," I say. "Viola is *not* walking to the colony alone. Put that thought out of your head."

"Why not?" asks Alisa. "We know it can't get hurt."

"Androids can be damaged like anything else," says Viola.

"Stop calling my sister an 'it'!" I shout.

Something hits the roof of the residence. It's a heavy, resonant thump, like something large has landed there. We all freeze, going silent.

"Hold this," whispers Mom, and hands me her volt gun. I take it automatically, passing the machete I've been carrying since we came inside to Viola. She shuffles closer, and I have enough giddy panic to be glad that we—me, Viola, and Kora—have the weapons, while Michel and the others are empty-handed. No one's touching my sister. No one's touching Kora, either. She looks like she's on the verge of a panic attack. I feel a pang of guilt. Someone should be looking out for her. I should be looking out for her.

Some potential girlfriend I am.

We all look up, listening intently as the initial thud is followed by a series of small, percussive tapping sounds, like something is testing the material. I can't help thinking of the claws on the creatures we saw before. They looked like they could tear through virtually anything. The solar panels and insulation of our roof won't be any challenge at all.

"Give me the gun," hisses Michel.

"No," replies Kora, voice low. She steps closer to me. I glance at her, and realize, with a sick, unsurprised horror, that my mother is gone. The place where she should be standing is empty, and we're alone.

Maybe . . . maybe none of this is happening. Maybe it's all some terrible dream, my brain lurching between nightmare scenarios, and any moment now I'm going to wake up and it'll be the morning of the party. Any moment now this is going to go away.

It doesn't go away. There's a horrible scraping sound from above, like the thing on the roof is starting to test how easy it will be to dig its way inside. Kora, Viola, and I huddle together, ready to fight until we lose, which seems inevitable. Alisa, Juan, and Lin are doing the same, still seated on the couch, unarmed, facing their own impending doom with the frozen terror of prey animals facing a predator.

Michel is the wild card. He doesn't have a weapon, but he looks like he wants to fight, and I'm worried that he'll try to disarm us all to prepare himself for a battle he can't win. I don't want to be fighting inside and outside at the same time, and the small, bitter part of me that knows how to hate, that hates every-thing about this day, wishes it had been him, and not Paul, who had decided to break for cover. This would be so much easier if he weren't here.

I want my mother.

As if summoned by the thought, she steps out of the hallway that connects the front room to our bedrooms and the home office she shares—shared—with my father. She has a gray back-pack with the logo of her old marine detachment on the side in her hands. It's seen some things, that bag; there are tears in the canvas and stains on the straps, and it looks like it could take a thousand beatings and still be in better condition than anything I own. She offers it to me.

"I'm so sorry this was how you had to find out," she says. "Your father and I had a plan. We were going to tell you, in pri-vate, on your eighteenth birthday. We were going to give you time to absorb what we were saying. You should have had that. You deserved that. Forgive me?"

There's a strange finality in her words, like she's saying good-bye in the only way she knows how. I take the bag automatically. It's heavy enough to tug at my arm, weighing me down. "I don't understand," I say.

"Take care of your sister. She's always going to do her best to take care of you. You're family, no matter what anyone else says. You're supposed to be together." She turns to Viola, offering her a faint smile. "You weren't supposed to figure it out as early as you did."

"Sorry, Mom," says Viola.

The scraping from above is getting louder. Kora moans and hud-dles against me. Things are happening so fast. Three days ago, Kora pressing herself into me like this was the only thing I could imagine wanting. Right now, I want so much that it could fill the world.

"I love you both," says Mom. Before I can reply, she steps forward, wrapping one arm around my shoulders and one arm around Viola's, and squeezes. Then she lets go, as quickly as she grabbed hold, and walks toward the front door.

On some level, I know what she's about to do. On another, I'm entirely surprised when she shoves the door open and walks into the yard, waving her arms in the air over her head like she's trying to flag down a shuttle.

"Here I am, you biological monstrosity!" she shouts. "Professor Katherine Shipp! Made of meat! Yum, yum, yum! Come and get—"

The creature pounces from above, moving so fast that it becomes a blur of shining black plates and insectile limbs. Mom screams, but not for long. It wraps its arms around her, hissing, and rears back to strike.

Viola grabs my elbow. I turn.

"Run," she whispers.

So we run, all seven of us, me and my sister and Kora and the kids from school, the kids I invited over for a party. We run from the monster that is in the process of murdering my mother, we run from the sound of screams and clicking and unspeakable horror. We run, and we don't look back, no matter how much I want to, because the future is in front of us, and there's nothing for us back there. Nothing but the past, which is dying even as I flee.

Oh, Mom.

I never could have saved you.

I only hope you've saved us all.

11

SWING FOR
THE FENCES

LEAVING THE ATV IN THE YARD WAS
the smartest thing any of us has done all day. I fling the volt gun
and the bag Mom gave me into the footwell and wedge myself
behind the controls, starting the engine without waiting for anyone else to get on. I don't pull away—I'm not a murderer—but I
leave it to Kora and Viola to load the others into their seats.

There are too many of us. Even without Mom, there are too
many of us, and Lin, as the smallest, winds up crouched between
the front and back seats, holding on to Juan's knees to keep herself from falling over.

Kora waits for her to be braced. Then she turns to me, and in
a voice that's barely more than a breath, that's almost swallowed
by the sound of the engine, she whispers, *"Drive."*

So I drive. I slam my foot down and I drag the controls back
and I bid a fond farewell to every lesson I've ever learned about

safe driving. Safe driving is for people whose mothers didn't just get shredded by a giant predatory space bug.

The gate is too close to the front of the house; we'll attract attention if we go there, assuming we haven't attracted attention already. "Everybody *down!*" I snap, and drive straight for the fence.

Part of me is cheering. This feels like the sequence in an action vid where the hero steps up and breaks out of their comfort zone, where the tide of battle turns and suddenly the good guys can't possibly help but win. I know that part of me is delusional, but I let it keep shouting as the front of the ATV slams into the electrified mesh of the fence, tearing it away from its foundations. I'd rather be deluded enough to think I can survive this than sit frozen until the thing that took my mother comes for me.

Kora is pressed against my side, with Viola on her other side, both of them gripping the roll bars with their free hands in an effort to stay as stable as possible. Viola still has the machete I handed her, and when she sees me glancing in her direction, she musters a wan smile. She looks so real. She looks . . .

Of course she looks real. She *is* real. Even if she's not biological, she's my sister. The flesh-and-blood Viola died when we were so young that I honestly can't remember ever having known her. I must have some memories, buried deep under fourteen years of skipping from planet to planet, chasing biological oddities, chasing the payday that would settle us safely back on Earth, of a sister I didn't realize doesn't exist anymore. But they don't *matter.* What matters is the girl I grew up with, the girl I took care of, the girl who took care of me.

What matters is that I love Viola. She's my sister, and she's worth a hundred humans who aren't, and I know she'll do everything she possibly can to keep Kora safe, because she knows that Kora is important to me. Not in the same way, but still, important.

"Shipp sisters forever," I say, and keep driving, shedding broken bits of fence in all directions as we go bumping and rolling away from the residence. I still don't look back. I still don't dare. If I see that thing gaining on us, I'll probably roll the ATV, and I'm not sure how many people took the time to deal with their seat belts, given everything else that's going on. Lin, at the very least, would be thrown free, and she'd be lucky to survive the impact with the ground, traveling at our current speed.

"Where are we going?" demands Kora. She has the gun in her hands, ready to shoot if she has to, ready to defend us. A warm wave of affection washes over me, not enough to cut through the panic, but enough to leaven it. I feel better knowing that she's right here.

Of course, I feel worse knowing that Michel is behind me. "We're going too slow!" he shouts, making no effort at all to keep his voice down. Apparently, the thought that the things might hunt by sound has yet to occur to him.

Although, if they hunt by sound, why aren't they converging on the ATV? Is it just that they don't like the sounds machines make—that they'd prefer to go after prey they know they can rip apart and devour? There's so much we don't know, so much we might never know. The creatures killed our two biologists—it's somehow easier to think of my parents that way, like they were roles, and not real people who loved me, who I loved, who I'm going to grieve for the rest of my life—and now we have no way of learning anything about them. How they work, where they come from, that's all above my paygrade. And maybe that's okay.

The only thing that matters today, the only thing I actually *need* to learn, is how to stay alive.

"It's not safe to go any faster," I hiss back, trying to keep my eyes on the terrain in front of us. If we can make it to the supply trail, with its smooth, level ground and its electric beacons repelling most Zagreus wildlife, we'll have a shot at making it all the way to the colony.

I've always hated the Zagreus colony, with its high walls and its thick metal and its sterile construction. Right now, it's the most beautiful thing I can imagine. We'll be safe there. These creatures may have claws strong enough to rip through the metal roof of a residence, they may be able to leap higher than biology ought to allow and strike faster than anything mammalian could dream of managing, but there's no way they can burrow through the fences. There's no way they can get *inside*.

Even if they somehow did, they'd find dozens of trained guards with weapons waiting to beat them back. I don't know how good the Zagreus security forces are. They've never had any real cause to test their skills.

They may get to test them today.

"Like hell it's not," snarls Michel, and surges forward, trying to wrest the controls out of my hands.

There's no hitting him back this time, no dodging or grabbing his hands to keep him from putting them on me. There's only struggling to keep hold of the controls that let me tell the ATV where to go, keeping him from tipping us over.

"Get the hell *off* me!"

"Michel!" Kora twists in her seat, aiming the gun in her hands at his head. "Let go of her, or I swear—"

"What? You'll shoot? So shoot me already!" Michel grabs a handful of my hair, yanking backward. It hurts so bad that I take one hand off the controls to claw at his fingers, trying to break his grip. I don't succeed. We swerve wildly, and I hear Juan and Lin cry out from the back, distressed.

I'm distressed too, but I'm not wasting time yelling. There isn't time to waste. I do my best to keep my eyes on what's in front of me. We're almost to the supply trail. Once I hit it, it'll be easier to keep the ATV under control, and I'll be able to fight Michel off.

He knows it, too. This isn't just an attempt to take the ATV away from me: it's a mutiny. We've become a crew, whether we want to be or not, and we've thwarted him at every possible opportunity. Suddenly, the refusal to give him a weapon, even knowing that he would probably go out of his way to use it against me, seems like an intentional insult; we've been shutting him out whenever we had the chance.

He deserved it. He earned it with his own behavior. And now he's lashing out. Every part of this is his fault. None of them are stopping him from yanking on my hair.

"I mean it, Michel! Let her go!"

If Kora fires her gun this close to my face, I'll be lucky not to lose the eardrum. I open my mouth to object, and my words turn into a short, sharp shriek as the ATV hits a rock and bounces hard to the left, nearly overbalancing. Michel falls back in his seat, his hand still tangled in my hair. The impact jerks me halfway out of my seat.

Kora has a choice: keep aiming her gun at Michel, or get the ATV under control. Blessedly, brilliantly, she goes for the latter, flinging herself into as much of my space as she safely can and seizing the abandoned controls. She's never driven an ATV before, but she knew enough to call the machine cherry, and the systems are simple enough. The thing was designed to operate under the worst possible conditions.

It doesn't get much worse than this.

I kick and twist, clawing at Michel's hand, wishing the volt gun weren't down in the footwell, outside of my reach. Kora is screaming steadily, but we haven't flipped over yet, which I'm willing to take as a good thing.

It's hard to guess exactly what I'm doing, since most of the action is happening behind me. My questing fingers find Michel's face. I claw at it, and he responds by biting me—*biting* me—to make me stop. He doesn't break the skin, but the shock is enough to make me pull my hands briefly away.

The machete flashes down between us without warning. Viola, who's been watching for her opening, has slashed it through my hair, cutting off more than half of it. Michel falls back in his seat, howling. I duck down, grab the volt gun, and twist around to face him.

He's clutching his hand to his chest. There's a long, shallow cut down the palm, where the very tip of Viola's machete caught the skin.

"That *thing* attacked me!" he snarls.

"I defended my sister," says Viola. "Try again and see if I won't do the same thing twice."

The look he gives her is pure venom, hatred of a kind I can barely comprehend. I shake my head.

"You're an ass," I say. I shift my attention briefly to the others. "You want to get home alive? Keep him where he is." I don't wait to see whether they'll listen and restrain him. I just turn again, settling into my seat.

Kora's hands are white-knuckled on the controls. She's terrified, but we're still moving forward, and I can see the beacon of the supply trail just ahead. We've taken a circuitous route, which makes sense; even if it's not the most efficient way to get there, we needed to evade the thing that killed my mother.

The thought doesn't even make my heart beat faster. Maybe I owe Michel an apology. Thanks to him, I have so much adrenaline in my system that my body can't even remember that it's supposed to be forcing me to mourn.

I tuck the volt gun down between my knees, the muzzle pointing to the sky. Not good gun safety, but under the circumstances, I think I can be forgiven. Carefully, I slide my hands over Kora's, until I'm half driving the ATV even with her still technically in control. I shift my feet back onto the pedals.

"It's okay," I whisper. "You can let go."

She flashes me an unreadable look, half loss and half longing, and then she pulls her hands away, ceding control of the ATV back to me. She twists in her seat as she does, aiming her gun at Michel.

"You drive," she says. "I'll make sure he doesn't do anything else stupid."

I smile. I don't want to—my parents just died, I'm an orphan, my sister has been dead for almost my entire life, everything I thought I could depend on is falling down around my ears—but I do it anyway, because she sounds so *determined*. She's choosing me over him. If there was ever a contest, it's over now. She's choosing me. I'm the one she wants.

My smile falters. She may get me for a long, long time. I don't know if Mom and Dad ever made any sort of arrangement for Viola and me; their work is hazardous, but it's not usually *dangerous* by the time they get to a colony world, and we're close enough to adulthood that maybe there's no one out there prepared to take us in. Take me in. Does Viola even get that kind of consideration? She's not a real person. She's property. She was my parents' property as soon as they put their biological daughter in the cremation trough.

Is she *my* property? Do I own my sister in the eyes of the law? The thought is subprime, enough to turn my stomach and make me want to lean out of the ATV and vomit for the second time today. She can't be property. She's *Viola*. She's as real as I am.

The walls of the colony come into view ahead of us. We're already going as fast as we can, but that doesn't stop me from slamming my foot down harder, like that might be enough to pull a tiny bit more speed from the engine.

"Kora, signal them," I say.

She glances at me in surprise. Then she pulls out her comm unit, thumbing the switch on the side, and says, "This is Kora Burton, Zagreus colonist, returning from an approved visit to the outside. I am in the company of four civilians and two approved off-world visitors. Requesting immediate access. Emergency conditions."

I let out a relieved breath. She's still listing Viola as an approved visitor. Maybe my sister and I can decide together what we want to do about her legal status.

Maybe not. "Tell them we've got a damn robot with us!" shouts Michel. "Tell them we're being followed by monsters! *Tell* them!"

The urge to shove him out of the ATV for the creatures to eat has never been stronger.

The comm beeps, and Rockwell's voice asks, "Emergency conditions? What kind of emergency conditions?"

"Unknown predators in pursuit," says Kora. She sounds so calm. She doesn't look calm. Her face is pale and drawn, and the whites of her eyes are showing all the way around her irises. She looks like she's on the verge of falling over. "We have two confirmed casualties. Requesting immediate access."

"Casualties? What are you talking about, casualties?"

Rockwell sounds like she's on the verge of panic. She's probably never dealt with anything like this.

I wish there were time to comfort her, but there's really not. I grab Kora's hand, bringing her comm to my own mouth as I say, brusquely, "Contamination from the biological survey ship in orbit has made it planet-side. My mother, Dr. Katherine Shipp, is dead. Colonist Paul . . ." I trail off. I don't know his last name.

"Gladney," supplies Kora.

"Paul Gladney is dead," I say, into the comm. "We need immediate access. We're coming in on the supply trail, and we can't slow down."

That's only sort of a lie. I could hit the brakes. I don't know that we're being followed. I haven't looked back since this all began. But . . . that thing followed us from the fruiting grove to the residence. It *tracked* us. Even if they're not visible behind us right now, I know they're out there. Waiting. Hunting. We need to get safely inside the walls, and we need to do it now.

There's a long pause on Rockwell's end before she says, voice brusque, "We'll be waiting for you." The connection clicks off. I let go of Kora's hand.

"Think she means it?" I ask.

Kora nods, and says nothing, and I drive on.

Gloriously, when the wall gets close enough that I can see the details of the structure, I see that the door is standing open, waiting for us. Rockwell and Johnson are on the other side, where they always are. The ATV won't fit through, but that doesn't matter. I hit the brakes when we're about four feet away, creating a barrier for anything that might be following us, and grab my volt gun before sliding out of the vehicle and turning to help Kora down.

For a moment—just a moment—it looks like things are going to be okay. Teens boil out of the ATV like fleas jumping off a carcass, running for the open door. Lin is the first one through, then Juan and Alisa, and then Michel.

That's where the trouble starts. Kora runs after him, her hand clasping mine, and he lets us both through. He glowers at me, bitter and angry, but he doesn't try to step in my way. He doesn't try to stop me. Viola is right behind us. He steps in front of her, blocking her path.

"No," he says flatly. "You're not coming in here."

"Michel!" Kora sounds appalled, like she never dreamt he'd do something like this.

"Yes, I am," says Viola, and tries to dodge past him.

He shoves her.

Rockwell makes a sound of protest, but that's all; she doesn't move. Neither of them do as Michel plants both hands, one bleeding, one not, on my sister's shoulders. He shoves her back, away from the wall, with so much force that she stumbles and almost hits the waiting ATV. She lifts her head to stare at him. There's no surprise in her eyes, only resignation.

"Michel!" Kora grabs for his arm with her free hand. He bats her away. That gives me an opening. I can't fire the volt gun here, not without potentially frying the electrical systems that control the gate and leaving us all stranded. But guns aren't the only option. I shove it into Alisa's hands, not waiting to see what she does, and charge at Michel, bellowing.

My shoulder catches him at the center of the chest, and the impact is enough to rock him back several feet, knocking us both past the threshold. Michel's eyes widen as he realizes what that means. He flails, trying to shove me out of the way, to get to safety. One of his hands catches me in the nose, more out of luck than anything else. Blood gushes out, hot and sticky, flowing down my face, filling my mouth. I spit it at him and punch him in the throat, rocking him back again.

"*Olivia!*" The voice is Kora's, but she's still safely on the other side of the wall, and my sister is out here, my sister is in danger. Michel punches me again, in the shoulder this time, spinning me halfway around before I recover and lunge for him. I have to give Viola time to get inside. I have to be her protector, the way I've always been, because she's all I have left; she's the only family still standing. I may not be able to do this, we may both die here, but I have to try, I have to be able to die *knowing* I tried, I have to—

The sound starts above us, a low, growling click that makes the hairs on the back of my neck stand on end and my skin get tight as every primordial instinct I have left screams, screams, screams for me to run, to get to cover, to get *away*.

Michel staggers away, suddenly no longer interested in hitting me. I slowly tilt my head back and look up at the wall.

The creature doesn't move. It doesn't seem to care about how much effort it should take for something of its size to sit on a flat, vertical surface like the wall: it just crouches, perfectly balanced, preparing to strike. This isn't the creature that took Mom. That one was bigger, even in the brief glimpse I had before it carried her away. This is one of the pair that attacked us before we even reached the residence.

Something thuds against the ATV. I know that if I turned around, I'd see the second creature waiting there.

A hand touches my shoulder. I somehow manage not to scream.

"I love you," whispers Viola, and runs her hand across my face. I don't understand what she's doing until I see her wipe the blood she's gathered onto her own face, lending a sudden air of biological reality to the synthetic materials she's made from. She picks up a rock from the ground. She throws it at the creature on the wall.

And then she turns and runs, hands in the air, screaming with all the force she can find. She runs, and the creature . . . it doesn't run after her. "Run" implies that it ever touches the ground. It leaps, a single terrible, graceful moment, and hits her from behind. Then it leaps again, and there isn't even time for her to scream. In an instant, she's gone.

My sister is gone. Viola is gone. My parents are gone and my sister is gone and I'm alone, I'm the last Shipp on Zagreus, the last in this sector of space. It's me and some relatives on Earth who haven't seen me in a decade, and I can't do this. I can't do this. I can't move. I can't shout, or run after the thing that's taken Viola. All I can do is stand here and wait for the second creature to take me, too.

Maybe that's better. We can all be together again, even if we won't know it. Maybe that's the way this is supposed to end, and it was silly of me to think, even for a moment, that I could fight it.

Michel doesn't share my shock. He screams and bolts for the

gate, leaving me behind. I'd hate him for that, but I already hate him for so many other things, and I'm numb, and I want to stay numb, so that it doesn't hurt as much when I get to go back to my family.

I'm sorry, I think, and close my eyes.

Michel screams. A hand grabs my arm, jerking me away. I open my eyes, and see the second creature, Michel in its long, terrible arms, leaping into the grass on the other side of the supply trail fence. That's all there's time to see before Kora jerks me through the open gate, and the gate slams closed, and there's a wall of metal between me and the outside, between me and the creatures, between me and my family.

I begin to howl, pulling away from Kora and beating my fists against the closed gate like I can change the reality of it through sheer force of will, like I can somehow bring her back. The metal is thick enough that no matter how many times I hit it, I don't leave a dent. There isn't even so much as an echo. I drop to my knees and sob. Viola is gone. My whole family is gone.

I'm alone, and I have never felt so very far from home.

12

SOMETHING TO HOLD ON TO

KORA KNEELS BESIDE ME, SLIDING one arm around my shoulders, offering me my mother's volt gun. How did she get that? I gave it to Alisa. It feels like the world is skipping tracks, refusing to move in the calm, linear way I'm used to. Everything is happening so *fast*.

Someone is sobbing. I think it might be Lin. Honestly, though, it might be all of us. If ever a day has been awful enough to justify a public breakdown, it's this one.

"Here," says Kora, pushing the gun into my hands. Her own gun—hers now, even if it came from my family's ATV; I don't want it back—is clipped to her belt. She's not disarming herself to make me feel better, and somehow *that* is the one thing that actually *does* make me feel a little better. Brains are weird.

"Here," she says again, and this time I take the gun from her, wrap my fingers around the long, familiar shape of it, pull it to myself like a teddy bear. A teddy bear . . .

"The bag!" I straighten, turning to stare at her. My nose aches. I must look awful. There's blood all over my face, and my hair has been whacked short by the machete, which isn't famed for making the most even of cuts.

This is a strange time for vanity. Again, brains are weird. They do what they want, and it's up to us to make them follow along.

Kora blinks at me. Then, understanding dawns, and she says, "It's right over there," gesturing toward the control panel where Rockwell and Johnson still stand, frozen in their terror over what just happened. They saw monsters, confirming every nightmare they've ever had about the world outside the safe walls of the colony. They saw two teenagers taken, carried screaming into the wilds.

They are not handling this very well.

Everyone is crying, shaking and screaming as they try to deal with the situation. That says something about their faith in the wall: they believe we're safe here.

Kora isn't crying.

Now that I have my breath back, neither am I.

I clip the volt gun to my belt as I stand and move to retrieve the bag my mother gave me. Maybe it's nothing. Maybe it's a bunch of photo albums and keepsakes from the original Viola, the one who died before she had the chance to develop a fondness for gossip, a habit of leaving the bedroom window open whenever she could get away with it, all the things *my* Viola's programming may have extrapolated from those early brain scans, or may have come up with entirely on her own. I don't know that Viola. I don't want to know that Viola. I want my Viola back.

It doesn't really matter what's in the bag. It's what I have left. Mom wanted me to have it. That's good enough for me, at least for now.

It fits on my shoulders like it was sized for me. Maybe it was. Dad said it was time to tell me the truth: maybe this is part of that truth. I turn to Kora.

"I need to know more about those things that took my sister," I say, voice flat, with no preamble. "I need to know what they are, and where they came from. I need to talk to your mother."

She looks briefly taken aback. "Why do you need to talk to my mom? I mean, of course you can come home with me, of course you can stay as long as you want to, this is all terrible, but I don't understand—"

Kora is smart and tough and beautiful and I have a crush on her so big that sometimes it feels like it could eclipse the suns, and none of that matters right now, because *she* isn't an orphan, *she* didn't watch her entire family die today. She doesn't understand what I'm talking about. She doesn't need to. All of this is still academic, for her. She can let it be. She can focus on survival.

"Your *mother* arranged for the purchase of that survey ship," I say tightly. "If anyone had any idea, at all, what was going to be up there, it was her. I need to talk to your mother."

Rockwell seems to snap out of her fugue. It's like she's suddenly realized she's standing by a little-used gate with a bunch of panicked teens—and more, that two teens were just taken on her watch. She needs to get things under control, and she needs to report the situation to the colonial authorities.

There's something comforting in that thought. The colonial authorities may be cowards who'd rather hide behind a metal barrier than confront the realities of living on their chosen homeworld, but they're also adults with access to way bigger weapons than an emergency kit pistol and a biologist's volt gun. They can defend us. They can keep the colony safe while they figure out how to kill those *things*, and I can get Viola back. This is how we win. By letting the adults take over.

"All of you need to go home right now," snaps Rockwell, voice as crisp and tight as a folded memo. She's in command, she's taking control, and if her hands are still shaking, we're all grateful enough to ignore it, at least for the moment. "No one should be on the streets."

Johnson moves to lock the gate, a process that involves typing a long alphanumeric code into the control pad. He shifts positions when he sees me looking, blocking the keypad from my view. They don't want anyone using this gate.

There are other gates. There are other codes. I am not staying locked in here while my sister is out there, being held captive by monsters. The only thing that's keeping me from charging for the gate right this second is the knowledge that Viola isn't technically alive. That shouldn't be soothing—should still, in fact, be absolutely horrifying—but weirdly, it helps. They can't kill her. She died a long time ago, when I was too young to notice, and nothing they do to her now is going to change our uniquely messed-up family situation.

Lin clings to Juan as they turn to go. I don't call them back. They deserve to go home to their families, to close the doors and lock the windows and feel, for at least a little while, as if they're actually safe.

They're not safe. I know too much about biology to think, even for a second, that they might be. These creatures . . .

There are at least three of them, and they're tough enough to have survived the conditions on the biological survey ship *and* inside a crashing shuttle. They survived impact and the shuttle exploding after it hit the ground, and they were able to track us across miles and miles of Zagreus grassland. They're not finished. They're out there, and they're hunting, and they're going to come back for another round.

Maybe if they're all males, or sexless drones—assuming these are some kind of new pseudo-insect, and not something different, or something worse—there's a chance. They'll eventually die out there, of old age or whatever, the humans can have another go at taking the planet. But that feels like the kind of luck it's not safe to count on.

I'm already mentally ceding Zagreus to the creatures, and there are only three of them. It's the only sensible reaction to the information we have so far. I could be wrong. I would love to be wrong. My parents are the Shipps, the best xenobiologists in the business.

I'm not wrong.

Kora takes a deep, unsteady breath. "I don't know where she is right now. It's the middle of the day."

"Then we go to your residence," I say. "I need to wash the blood off my face."

She hesitates. Then, finally, she nods. It's time for us to move. So we move.

Walking through the streets of Zagreus's capital city with blood on my face and in my hair is a new experience. The invisibility I'm used to experiencing is gone, replaced by horrified stares and quick motions to avoid getting too close to me. No one offers to help; no one even asks if I'm all right. It's funny. For a colony founded on the ideals of recycling and cooperation, people here sure are fast to pull away. It's like they don't understand what their utopia is supposed to look like.

Kora doesn't pull away. She keeps her hand in mine as she tugs me through the streets, skirting around the areas where the population is likely to be densest. She manages to make it feel less like she's ashamed of me and more like she just doesn't want to stop and explain what we're doing.

She doesn't need to bother. No one seems to want to ask. I guess my face tells its own story, and while that story is far from accurate, it's enough for the people who glance at us, see the blood, and look quickly away.

We reach the stairs that will lead us to the residence she shares with her mother and I pause, partially to catch my breath and partially because my traitorous heart is suddenly beating a little faster, a little less evenly.

Adrenaline can cause all sorts of biological responses, I think, and I hate myself for it. My parents are dead, my sister is missing, and I'm getting all excited because I'm about to see my maybe-girlfriend's residence for the first time. Subprime, Olivia. Seriously subprime.

Kora looks at me and smiles. It doesn't touch the horror still hanging in her eyes. She looks like she's facing the possibility of her own death at the top of those stairs, and I want to take it personally, but I can't. If her mother knew . . .

We could both be losing parents today, in different ways.

"My mother is . . . she's my mother," she says, like that means anything. "She didn't do this on purpose. There's no way. You'll see. This is all just . . . it's all a misunderstanding, that's all. She'll be able to clear all this up."

I'm not sure she can clear up the deaths of three people—four, if you count Michel, and more than that, if you count everyone else who went up to check that survey ship for signs of danger. I don't say that out loud. I just nod, and force myself to offer the slightest of smiles in response, and follow her up the stairs.

Halfway up, there's a door. We pass through it, and we're not in the open air of the domed colony anymore: we're inside, another layer of protection between us and the world. It feels stifling, claustrophobic, like something essential has been shut away. The air-conditioning is turned up too high. I shiver, knots of gooseflesh breaking out on my bare arms and the back of my neck. For the first time, I miss my hair. It would have kept me a little more covered, a little warmer.

Kora doesn't seem to notice. She's a hothouse flower, used to a life where hot and cold are choices, not consequences of the climate. She keeps climbing until we reach a door that's been painted the red of half-dried blood. It's enough to turn my stomach, and even she hesitates, seeming to see the door in a new light, before she swipes her wrist across the lock. It beeps twice, undoing itself. The door swings open.

The residence on the other side is half the size of ours, but twice as opulent. The walls are papered in something plush and soft-looking, like the skin of a vat-grown peach. The floor is covered in a thick carpet that will muffle and steal away our steps. The windows are tempered steel as clear as water, covered with a photosensitive film that changes colors according to the light outside. Right now, they're tinted to filter the Zagreus sunlight into a pleasant twilight, while artificial lights make up the difference.

It's a packaged, curated slice of civilization, and it could be on any planet in the galaxy, it could be *anywhere*, and I hate it, because it's possible to look out those windows and pretend that everything is fine, everything is safe and ordinary and there's nothing to be concerned about. This whole space is a lie.

Humans are so good at lying to ourselves. We should have learned to stop before we left Earth behind. We're too well-suited to the world that bore us. The rest of the galaxy doesn't have nearly as much patience with us.

Unlike my residence, where every room is neatly partitioned off from the rooms around it, this space is wide and open, making the most of the limited space. The entryway bleeds into the living room, which bleeds in turn into the dining room. That's where carpet gives way to shining tile, where bookshelves and curio cases surrender to cabinets and appliances. There's a large island in the center of the kitchen area, built in, to create additional counter and workspace. That's where Kora's mother is, a tablet in her hand, frantically scrolling through screens, posture tense and miserable.

Kora's coloring must have come from her father, because her mother looks nothing like her: Delia Burton is as pale as I am, with hair only a few shades darker than the Zagreus sky, pulled tight and high in a sleek chignon. Every inch of her is polished, poised. She's perfect for this room, for this residence, for her position. She's all wrong for Zagreus. She doesn't reflect her world, its wild reaches, its rugged glory. I wonder if she's been outside the colony walls since they were finished. I wonder what she'd think if she went out there.

Kora takes a step forward, confirming my belief that the carpets are thick enough to muffle all sound. She makes a small coughing noise, following it up with a half-whispered plea of, "Mama? Can you look at me, please?"

There's something achingly vulnerable about the way she says "Mama," like it's a secret I'm being allowed to share, whether I've earned it or not. She's too shaken by the day we've had to keep it from me. It's a gift, and I don't want it.

And Delia Burton looks up from her tablet. It falls from her fingers to clatter on the marble top of the island, the sound seeming very loud in the quiet of the residence. The color drains from her cheeks, leaving her looking more like a wax sculpture, or a corpse, than a living woman.

The thought of death is enough to make me shiver and touch the butt of the volt gun at my belt, reassuring myself that it's still there: I'm not suddenly, impossibly defenseless. Those windows are making me more nervous than I would have believed possible. Anything could smash its way in, and the things we saw outside the wall . . . they wouldn't even see the glass as a challenge. The way it's tinted isn't going to do anything to protect us. It's just going to make it impossible for us to see the danger coming.

"Kora!" Delia stands gracelessly, gripping the island to steady herself. She doesn't even seem to have noticed me yet. A neat trick, considering how much of my own blood I'm wearing.

Then again . . . I glance at Kora, and for the first time I realize how much of my blood *she's* wearing. It's on her hands and in her hair. There's a dainty, almost delicate smear down one cheek, shockingly dark against the creamy brown of her skin. She's not hurt, but she looks prettily damaged, like something out of a horror vid. No wonder Delia's upset.

"I'm all right, Mama," says Kora. She reaches back to grasp my wrist and pull me forward. "Olivia needs our help."

Delia recoils—actually recoils—when she sees the state of me. I try to smile, to be polite, but I can feel the expression coming out twisted and weird, not the sort of thing I should be sharing with my maybe-girlfriend's mother.

"Miss Shipp!" says Delia, voice just a little shrill. "What happened to you?"

"Michel punched her," says Kora quickly, like she's trying to keep me from being the one to answer. I shoot a look in her direction. She's focused on her mother, eyes wide, face innocent. No monsters here, no sir. No impossible problems. Just a boy behaving badly, just a girl with a bloody, maybe broken nose, everything's normal, everything's the way it's meant to be.

I pull my wrist out of her hand. She shoots me a hurt look. I do my best to ignore it.

"He punched me because I was trying to keep him from shutting my sister out of the colony," I say.

Delia frowns. "Viola? What was she doing coming to the—is she unwell?" She takes a step back, apparently willing to abandon her daughter to avoid catching my sister's imaginary illness.

That doesn't make sense. Michel saw our arrival manifest; he's the one who told Kora there were only three people listed. Three living humans, one android. Androids can't get sick. Which is ironic, given how much of our lives Viola has supposedly spent incapacitated by her illness, but—

"You think *I'm* the android," I blurt.

The look Delia gives me is equal parts horror and respect. "You're not?" she asks.

So many things start to make sense. The adults of Zagreus have always been hands-off, viewing independence and self-sufficiency as essential parts of the colonist experience, but most of the kids I go to school with have been treated like they still have things to learn. My teachers, though, they never gave me that treatment. They always left me to my own devices, and their sympathy, when it was extended at all, was given entirely to Viola. Poor, sick, isolated Viola, whose parents loved her enough to keep her enrolled in a school she could never attend in person.

Poor, sweet, doomed Viola, whose parents loved her enough to build her a companion. The adults of Zagreus haven't been shunning me because they thought I was dirty, or an outsider.

They've been doing it because they thought I was an android.

I want to laugh and pull my machete-shortened hair at the same time. I don't know whether my parents did this on purpose or not. It would make sense if they did. Distract, deflect, let me think people were treating me weirdly rather than start to get suspicious. Right now, though, this is not helping the situation.

"I'm not," I say. I touch my nose, and wince from even that slight contact. "Androids don't bleed, remember? Michel hit me hard enough that I think he may have broken something. He found out about Viola. He didn't want to let her in."

"That doesn't make sense," says Delia, with a small frown. "We don't allow android ownership here on Zagreus, but—"

"Why not?" I blurt. Michel must have gotten the idea that androids were somehow wrong from somewhere. If it's going to be just me and Viola from now on—and it's *going* to be just me and Viola, because I'm *going* to get her back—I need to know these things.

"They . . ." She looks uncomfortable. "Ordinary citizens don't have the necessary technology to build or maintain any decent android model, and there's always the risk they've been loaded with spyware that even they may not be aware of. We're trying to be independent out here. Not beholden to the corps. Keeping them from getting a handhold in our operations is essential to that."

"If you're so worried about spyware, why let us come here in the first place?"

"Your parents are the best in the business," says Delia. "Their prices are reasonable, their references are impeccable—honestly, the only question we had was why they'd be willing to take a posting this remote, and the fact that only one of their daughters is technically alive answered it quite nicely. There are worlds where, biological mysteries notwithstanding, you—I'm sorry, I mean, your sister would never have been allowed to be turned on. They showed me and my advisors comprehensive brain maps of their android, and proof that their software build is entirely unique. It may be a corps chassis, but the program running it, the part of it that is, ah, 'Viola,' was designed under such close watch that the usual concerns don't apply. It's much more expensive to do things this way. I suppose that's what makes it so rare."

The expense explains a lot about why we're always running so close to the wire, why things get "upgraded" without any sign of actually improving. Uneasily, I wonder what's going to happen the next time I have a growth spurt. Will I have the funds to get her the new body she's going to need? Or am I going to grow up while she doesn't get to?

I'm still thinking of her like she's out there for me to save. That's good. That means I haven't given up hope. Not yet, anyway.

"Michel found out Viola was an android," I say. My voice is hard. I don't care that much. "He said she didn't get to come into the colony. He pushed her. So I stopped him, and he punched me, and he kept punching me until he couldn't anymore."

For the first time since she realized Kora wasn't hurt, there's a flicker of fear in Delia's eyes. "What happened? Why did he find out about Vi—about your sister?"

"Where did you find that survey ship?" I ask.

Kora has a question of her own, and it's somehow more damning than mine, for all that it's more gently asked. "Mama, when did you lose contact with the shuttle?"

Delia actually staggers backward, only half a step, but enough to broadcast her guilt loud and clear through the room. "I don't—you girls are asking about things that don't concern you. Kora, take your friend to clean herself up. She's going to stain that shirt past recovery."

"Did you lose contact with the shuttle before or after it crashed into the mountains?" Kora asks. "I mean, it sort of caught fire, so I guess you must have lost contact after that happened, but before that. Did they manage to signal the planet before they went down?"

Delia's silence is more than answer enough.

"Mama, what did you do?" Kora whispers.

"I didn't do anything wrong," says Delia. "I followed all protocols, I did everything correctly, I didn't—"

"There was something alive on that ship," I say. Delia goes perfectly still, watching me. I look at her, aware that the blood on my face has to be making it difficult to meet my eyes, and not particularly concerned about her comfort. Not after everything she's cost me.

Because see, here's a thing about people in general, and adults in specific: they only say they didn't do anything wrong when they absolutely, positively did. Maybe not by the letter of the law, but by any reasonable, moral standard. The guilt is in every word she says, and every word she doesn't say.

"Something alive, and vicious, and fast, and strong enough to survive in partial vacuum, and smart enough to stow away on the shuttle," I say. I take a step forward, and I don't take my eyes off of Delia. "It killed my father. It killed them all. Did you know?"

"No," she whispers, and I believe her, and it doesn't matter.

"Where did you get the ship? Where did it *come* from?"

She glances away, back toward the island in the kitchen where her work waits for her, offering the sweet embrace of distraction. She must have known when the shuttle lost contact. None of this is a surprise to her. The only question now is whether she knew the survey ship was potentially dangerous.

She's an adult and I'm not. Every colony has its own rules for the interactions between teenagers and adults, but they all agree that the one is more important than the other. Don't argue, don't talk back, don't act like you understand anything about the way life works, because you don't; you're just getting started, and people with more experience than you have it all figured out.

I've known that was bullshit since I was twelve, when one of my teachers tried to convince his class that humanity was alone in the universe because we were inherently biologically superior to everything else evolution had ever managed to produce. I had already seen my parents wrestle with predators large and small, with tiny, insect-like creatures whose stings could burn out the human nervous system in a matter of seconds, with seemingly fragile winged things that could survive under pressures that would smash my human skeleton into dust. Humans may be the only *intelligent* life in the universe, or at least the only intelligent life we've been able to find so far, but biological superiority? That's not something we get to claim.

Still. This is Kora's mother, and she's the planetary governor. Even if I'm willing to risk alienating Kora—which I'm not; I've lost too much today to lose the hope that she'll kiss me again, stroke my hair and tell me it's all going to be all right—I can't risk getting seized and handed off to some strange family as an unaccompanied minor. Not before I get Viola back, and not even then, because Viola isn't a person in the eyes of the law, she's property, and if I get given to strangers, so does she. If I want my sister to have her freedom, I have to hold on to my own.

I take a deep breath. "Governor Burton, please," I say. "*Please.* Those creatures that were on the ship, they're here now. They're on Zagreus. They've killed people here, on the planet. Not in space. Where did they come from?"

"Killed people?" Her gaze suddenly sharpens, like this is something it's easier for her to understand. I don't want to think too hard about that. "Who? Where?"

"Paul Gladney, Michel Petrov, and Katherine Shipp have all died on Zagreus soil," I say. My voice barely even shakes until I get to the last name. Oh, Mom. I don't know what I'm going to do without you. I can't handle this by myself. "Paul and Katherine were killed in the wilds; Michel was taken at the gate."

Delia's eyes widen so far it would be almost comical, if she didn't also look like she was about to vomit down the front of her starched and pressed blouse. "What? Paul? And Michel? But they're just—they're just children."

I notice that she doesn't object to the idea of my mother dying. We don't belong here. We never have and we never will.

"Apex predators don't care about the age of their prey; they just care about whether they can catch it," I say. The blood drying on my neck itches. "The biological survey ship. Where did it come from? What *are* those things?"

"Mama, you have to answer her." Kora steps up beside me, reaching over to take my hand in hers. I hold on like I'm afraid of falling, and maybe in a way, I am. She's the only thing holding me here. "Those things, they're terrifying, and there's at least three of them."

"They can't get through the wall," says Delia.

"That's what I thought, too, until they followed us for miles just to grab Michel and Viola," I say. "If there's a weak spot, they'll find it."

"Are you calling them intelligent?" Delia sounds horrified. It's a pretty horrifying thought . . . except that the alternative is worse. So much worse.

I shake my head. "No. If they were intelligent, they'd leave us alone. They'd hunt the hippos, or the meat-deer, or anything that isn't smart enough to build machines and fight back. There'd be plenty of room on this planet for both our species, if they were intelligent. They're not. They're acting on instinct, and their instincts are telling them to follow the prey they already know. They've identified us as a solid, reliable source of whatever it is they're looking for. And if they were intelligent, they'd know how to give up. I don't think these things understand what giving up *means*. They'll keep coming, and coming, and coming, until they find a way through the wall."

Delia scoffs, actually scoffs, and that's the moment when I begin to hate Kora's mother. "We have weapons. We have walls. We'll be fine."

"Where did you get the ship?"

She looks at me like she's seeing me for the first time. "You know," she says, in a thoughtful voice, "I don't think I have to tell you that. I don't think it's any of your concern."

I draw the volt gun from my belt and have it aimed at her chest before I have time to think about what I'm doing. The safety clicks off with a flick of my thumb, and the barrel hums as it warms up.

"I think it's absolutely my concern," I say. "I think if you don't want to experience what it's like to be struck by lightning, you'll tell me."

Her eyes narrow. "Little girl, you don't know what you're doing. If you want to walk away from this—"

There's a click beside me. Delia's face falls. I don't have to be a genius to know what just happened.

"Kora?" she asks, in a small, wounded voice.

"Tell us where the ship came from, Mama," says Kora. "You have to tell us."

"You are my daughter," she says. "I don't have to tell you anything."

"I'm an orphan because of you," I say. I dial up the strength on the volt gun. It hums in my hand. "Whether it was an accident or whether it was on purpose doesn't really matter much, because I'm an orphan either way. A monster has my sister because of you." *I know my sister isn't real to most of the universe because of you.* "I think you do have to tell me. Both because it's the right thing to do, and because if you don't, I'm going to shoot you."

"You wouldn't d—"

Her last word dies as I fire at the window behind her. The tinted glass is strong enough to stand up to the blast, mostly. When the crackle of electricity fades from the air, there's a starburst scorch in the film, letting the natural light slide through. It's red compared to the light around it, red as blood, staining the floor where it falls.

Delia looks at me, horrified.

"I'd dare a lot more than people think I would," I say. "My parents are dead. My sister is gone. It's your fault, no matter how I look at it. Where did the ship come from?"

Maybe it's the calm repetition of the situation. Maybe it's the hole in her window covering. Either way, Delia swallows, closes her eyes, and says, "The ship was stolen. Smugglers seized it en route to some big company's scrapyard—but here's the thing: it was fully operational when they took it. There were people on board. Scientists. Why would there be people on a ship that was being scrapped? There's a research facility out there, a secret one, one they don't want people to know about. One they're dedicated enough to concealing that they were willing to write off the loss of the entire ship in order to keep it from being found."

"What happened to the scientists?" Maybe they'll know what those creatures are. If the smugglers still have them, if I can get a message through—

Delia opens her eyes. The look she gives me is pure pity, like she can't believe I've managed to get this far while remaining so ignorant.

"The scientists? They met with unfortunate accidents once the people who'd seized their ship realized that they had no further value. If something could be easily stripped and sold, it was. I had no part in that, you understand—Zagreus is not a haven for thieves. But we keep our eyes and ears open, and when we hear of a potential prize, we don't let little things like where it came from get in our way. That vessel is *massive*. It contains raw materials sufficient to expand this colony tenfold. We could have extended the borders of this settlement, fortified the seasteads, even established a second settlement on the other side of the forest your parents have been charting for us."

"You could have brought the corporations down on our heads," says Kora, sounding softly horrified. "We're *nothing* compared to them. They could wipe us away and not even notice. They'd seize everything we have to compensate themselves for a theft they would barely even notice."

"Ah, but see, that's what we were gambling on. That the theft would barely even be noticed. It's a big universe out there, Kora.

Things go missing all the time. Things disappear without a trace, and no matter how much the corps might like to be able to blame people for every little thing that goes wrong, there simply isn't time to go chasing after every misplaced trinket. The people I bought the ship from know their jobs. They wanted it gone, I wanted raw materials at a below-market price, and we were able to come to an arrangement that benefited everyone."

"Tell that to my father," I say. Delia glances at me, expression as much guilt as loathing. "Tell that to Michel's mother, or to Michel. I didn't like him very much. That doesn't mean he deserved to die. You knew there was something wrong with that ship. The smugglers sold it for such a low price that you were suspicious, weren't you? That's why you sent a team up to look at it before you started sending your own people to dismantle it. That's why, even though you say you care more about this colony than anything else, you didn't go up yourself. You knew there was a chance they wouldn't come back."

She doesn't say anything. She doesn't need to. Her guilt is written across her face, plain for the world to see.

Plain for *Kora* to see. She looks briefly shocked and saddened. Then she adjusts her grip on her gun, keeping it aimed firmly at her mother, and says, "The washroom is to the left of the kitchen, Olivia. Why don't you go scrub the blood off your face, and we'll figure out what we're going to do next? I'll watch her."

It's not fair to ask Kora to keep her own mother under armed guard. Nothing that's happened today has been fair. I nod, and kiss her cheek, and say, "I'll be right back."

Then I walk away. There's nothing else for me to do.

13

BLOOD AND WATER

KORA'S WASHROOM IS SMALLER than the one in our residence, but that's the only place where it falls short. There's a shower *and* a collapsible bath, a sink with two basins, even a ceiling-high mirror that reflects me back at myself before I can realize that I might want to look away. I stand for a few precious seconds, simply staring.

Who is that girl in the mirror, the girl with the chopped-off hair and the blood all over her face, the girl with the blackened eye and the busted nose and the bruise blooming like a flower on one cheekbone? She looks tough, that girl. She looks beaten without looking broken.

She looks like she could take me in a fight.

I grab a washcloth from the stack between the basins and turn the water on, beginning to scrub the mostly dried blood from my face and neck. It hurts to touch my nose. It hurts even more to touch my cheek, which is almost funny; I hadn't even realized I was hurt until it started throbbing.

There's a lot I haven't realized until now. Like Viola. I'd always assumed I would have warning before I lost her, that I'd have time to prepare. And then my mother—our mother—told me I'd already lost her, lost her so long ago and far away that the memory is completely gone. Trauma can cause people to stop forming memories correctly, letting events slide harmlessly into the abyss.

I sort of wish I could decide to let that happen to everything I've seen today. Let me wake up tomorrow in my own bed, with no idea that anything is wrong. Let me flirt with Kora and fight with Michel and love my family and never have to see one of those things again.

The water sliding off my face runs red down the drain. I raise my head and look at myself again. The bruises are still there. Some of the blood is still there, staining my hair almost the color of the Zagreus sky. I look like I've been through hell. I *have* been through hell, and no amount of wishing it weren't like this is going to change the situation I'm in.

If I want Viola back, I'm going to have to fight for her.

I turn off the water and shrug out of the bag Mom gave me, kneeling on the washroom floor as I unbuckle the flaps. It feels weird and almost shameful to be going through her things here, behind a closed door in someone else's residence; it feels like I'm trying to hide the last of her away. And maybe I am. Maybe I want just one minute where my mother is mine and mine alone, and not the legacy she's leaving to xenobiology, and not the screaming, bloodied figure I see every time I close my eyes. Maybe this . . .

Maybe this is how I mourn. I keep that in mind as I dig into the bag, pulling its contents slowly, carefully out into the light.

I run my fingers along the seams of the flap, and pause when they catch on a name embroidered, green on gray, into the fabric. "K. Shipp."

Seeing her name helps a little, weirdly enough. My mother survived when she was in the field wearing this bag, and she died after she gave it to me. Maybe this is a good-luck charm, of sorts. I'm not superstitious, not really, but right now I could use all the luck that I can get.

There's a gun in the bag. A serious gun, a hunter's gun, with a barrel wide enough to be intimidating and a grip sized for hands only a little bigger than mine. I recognize it from trips to the range with Mom. The recoil won't be nearly as bad as it should be for something this size, thanks to some cunning engineering and momentum-dampening tricks. I don't fully understand them. I don't need to. As long as I can clean and load my own weapons, there's no reason for me to be able to reengineer them on the fly.

There's a folder filled with actual paper and plastic flimsies. It seems anachronistic and out of place until I flip through it and realize that the papers, the flimsies . . . they're the user's manual for Viola, including the estimated specs and costs for her next upgrade. This is a roadmap to my sister's existence, a way for her to keep growing up alongside me, at least until we can figure out what she wants to do. Several data chips have been secured to the inside flap, held down with mag-blocking tape that will keep them from being damaged by things like the volt gun. I'd bet anything that they contain the same information as the paper printout, only in a more machine-readable format.

Tears prickle at my eyelids as I stare at the diagrams, making it difficult to see what's right in front of me. My parents have been planning for something like today for I can't even guess how long, preparing themselves for the day when they'd have to let us go out into the universe on our own. I hope they didn't expect to be eaten by unrecognizable creatures from a stolen corporate survey ship. That would be too much of a coincidence for me to handle.

At the bottom of the bag, I find a pile of data cards. Each of them responds to my thumbprint, flashing its contents at me. I have the financial access authority necessary to get to all the money Mom and Dad have saved up over the last seventeen years. I have the routing numbers to move it from bank to bank, according to my needs. I have the medical files for myself, and for Viola, including the full DNA workup they did to try and find the root of the genetic condition that had weakened and eventually killed her.

Best and most importantly of all, I have the access codes and launch keys for our family shuttle. I stare at the card in my hand, reeling from the realization that we can get away from here. *We can leave*. All I have to do is find Viola and get her safely back to the launch port inside the main colony dome, and we can get off this planet and never look back.

I wonder if Kora will come with us.

The thought is sobering. Of course she won't come with us. No matter how angry she might be at her mother right now—and she's *very* angry, anyone who understands humans can see that; she's angry enough that if I don't hurry up and get out there, someone's going to wind up getting shot—she's not going to leave her behind. That's her family. Not everyone cares about family, but Kora does. If Viola and I flee Zagreus, I'm going to have to say goodbye to Kora, and right now, I'm direly afraid that saying goodbye to someone on this planet is as good as pulling the trigger myself.

This is not a safe place. I don't know why I'm so sure of that, why I'm so convinced that three creatures could possibly be enough to spell the end of an entire colony, but I am. It's something in the way they move, something I recognize, even though it's entirely alien to anything I've experienced before. This world, it's theirs now. We're just waiting for them to finish taking over.

I slide my new treasures back into the bag, except for the gun. It has a holster. I strap it around my waist and secure it there, balancing the comforting weight of the volt gun. Then I shrug the pack back over my shoulders, give my damp, blood-streaked reflection one last glance, and start for the door.

It's time to get moving.

Delia is seated at the island in the kitchen when I emerge from the washroom, her hands resting on the marble where Kora can see them. Kora is still holding her borrowed gun on her mother, although her hands are shaking, and there are tears running down her cheeks. She looks like she's on the verge of breaking down. Delia, on the other hand, is perfectly calm, almost serene. She looks like a woman who has faced the worst, and found her peace with it.

"Hello, Shipp girl," she says when I move back into view. "I don't actually care which one you are, the living or the dead: we're all the dead now. You may just have beaten us there."

"I told you, I'm not an android," I say. I step up next to Kora and stop. "I'm as human as you are."

"I don't know about that," says Delia. "Right now, I might count myself as a little less human. I did this, after all."

"Tell her, Mama," says Kora. She sniffles, but the gun doesn't waver. "Tell her about the call."

"I just received communication from one of the seasteads," says Delia. She looks at the tablet in front of her, eyes unfocused. She doesn't seem to see her screen. "They've been overrun by strange creatures. 'They're like knives,' that's what Julian said, before the transmission stopped. 'They're like knives that hunt.' I say 'overrun,' but based on his report, it only took four of the things to kill them all. Twenty people lost. Do you think they were the same creatures that you saw?"

The nearest seastead is almost a hundred miles away. That's a fair amount of distance for anything to cover on foot, no matter how tireless. But we know at least one shuttle made it away from the survey ship, and there may have been more than one in the initial expedition; there may have been escape pods still available for use. It's not hard to imagine someone tricking one of those things into an escape pod, or being pursued when they tried to flee, and launching the whole thing into space.

Sometimes getting away only matters for a few seconds before it turns into a whole new kind of being trapped.

"I think it was the same species, yes," I say carefully. That description, like knives that hunt . . . I can't imagine anything else on Zagreus fitting that description. The wildlife here is strange and diverse and dangerous, but it's not that. It's not impossible.

"But not the same individuals."

I shake my head. Delia sighs heavily.

"All I wanted to do was help my colony," she says. "All I wanted to do was make a life for us here, away from the corporations, away from the greed, away from the human tendency to pick the corpse of every world we claim until it's nothing but bones and ashes. Was that so wrong of me?"

I stare at her. "I don't know," I say finally. "But you messed up. And now the rest of us have got to pay. I'm going to go now. I need to find my sister."

I turn my back on both of them. I know that if I don't go now, I won't go at all, and so I walk without hesitation to the door, and I let myself out, back onto the stairs, heading for the second door.

I'm almost there when I hear a slam behind me.

"Olivia!"

Barely daring to hope, I look back. There's Kora, her hair a tangled corona around her head, the gun still in her hand, my blood still on her cheek. She's never been more beautiful.

"I have to go," I say.

"I know," she says. And then, most miraculously of all: "I'm coming with you."

I should argue with her, tell her why this is a terrible idea, why she needs to stay here with her mother. I don't want to see her die. I don't want to take her outside the walls to where the monsters are and see her die. But even more than that, I don't want her to die here, where I can't see, where I can't ever know for sure.

If she's not going to stay alive, I want her to die knowing that I did everything possible to save her, and that she has never, even for a moment, been alone.

"It's dangerous out there," I say. "Are you sure?"

Kora nods. "My mother . . . she knew she was risking everything, and she did this anyway. My family hurt yours. I owe it to you to try and fix whatever I can."

I don't want her to come with me because she owes me. I want her to come with me because she wants to, because she cares about me the way I care about her and she's afraid of what might happen if I step outside the wall by myself. I look at her face, her wide, earnest eyes, and I know that I'm asking too much; I should be content with what I have, which is honestly more than I deserve. So I offer her the faintest sliver of a smile, and I nod, and I say, "All right. Let's go."

Fewer people stare as we make our way through the streets this time. There's still blood in our hair and on our clothes—on my clothes, especially—but I'm pale enough that washing it off my skin has made a huge difference. We no longer look like a horror story gone for a stroll.

There are fewer people in general. There's no sign of a panic. Nothing has been knocked over or abandoned. But the normal array of pedestrians and workers has just . . . dissipated, vanishing into businesses and residences without comment. As we walk, I see several people's wrist communicators light up. They raise their arms to check the screens, read the messages displayed there, and suddenly find it in themselves to walk faster, exchanging silent, concerned looks. I glance at Kora.

"It's the emergency transmission system," she says, and grimaces. "Which I guess you were never keyed to, since it's locked to colonist IDs."

"What does it . . . ?"

"A lot of our early colonists were former miners, former shipping techs, people from backgrounds that didn't leave them comfortable with open spaces, but did leave them a little twitchy about things possibly going wrong." Kora's eyes track another pedestrian as his communicator alerts and he starts walking, quickly, toward the nearest tunnel opening. "No one wants to start a panic. The alerts go out, and people take themselves to secure locations in a quick, organized fashion."

"No one says anything?" A thought occurs to me. A bad thought. "Who decides which people get notified first?"

"The system is randomized." At my dubious look, she holds up her wrist and shows me her still-silent communicator. "I'm the governor's daughter. If there were some sort of unfair prioritization of so-called 'important people,' Mama would have made sure I got flagged before anyone else."

"I guess." I keep walking, heading for the gate where we came in. I'm not comfortable being here, surrounded by tall buildings and narrow walkways. There are too many places for a predator to hide.

It's funny, but I'll feel better—safer—once we're outside, in the open. The things that killed my parents and took Viola are fast, but all the speed in the world won't keep them from being seen in the middle of a prairie. We'll have a better chance when we can see them coming. And we're armed now, at least enough to make me feel like we could slow them down. Their exoskeletons may provide them with a certain amount of armor, but they have weaknesses. They *must* have weaknesses. All we need to do is find them.

Kora stays close by my side as we walk, although she doesn't reach for my hand this time, and I can't bring myself to reach for her. She must hate me now, after everything that's happened. She's only here because she feels obligated, and obligation isn't the same thing as affection. She'll regret this soon enough, and when she does, she'll be gone.

We come around the final curve, and there's the gate, unguarded, waiting for us. Johnson and Rockwell probably went for cover with the others, assuming no one would be able to get out without them to unlock the mechanisms keeping the gate sealed. I stare at it, dismayed. They weren't wrong.

"I have no idea how to open that," I say. My voice sounds dead to my own ears. This is ridiculous. This can't be what stops me.

But maybe it's going to be. The wall itself is easily fifteen feet high, and where it ends, the polished dome begins, made of clear plastic that's caused a shameful number of fatalities among the flying wildlife of Zagreus. I spent our first week on this planet circling the colony city with my dad, scooping dead and injured flyers off the ground and taking them away to catalog. He'd started providing suggestions for how to reduce the number of impacts almost immediately, and started being ignored just as quickly. The dome is self-cleaning, self-repairing; it absorbs any damage done by the native animals without requiring human intervention. Why would the colonists want to mess with what is probably both their biggest investment and their biggest success?

I can't climb the dome: it's too high and too slippery, made of material that's designed to be as close to non-stick as possible. I can't shoot the dome. If I had a big enough laser, I could probably cut through the dome, but if there's anything that's going to summon the missing security teams back to their posts, it would be an assault on their primary means of protection.

It isn't sealed at the top. The colonists had to leave an opening for the ships to enter and exit through, and to allow the native biosphere to reach the colonists. It's slow acclimatization. They breathe the pollen, they breathe the spores, and bit by bit, their bodies forget they've ever lived anywhere else. They become a part of this world.

For a brief, dizzying moment, I consider the virtues of stealing a shuttle—not my family's transport, which is too big and too precious for something like this—and flying it straight out that opening. I abandon the idea almost as quickly as it came. Even if I could get to the shuttles, even if I could steal one, they all have lockdown overrides that can be activated from the launch port. I'd never make it as far as the residence, much less to the hills.

"Olivia."

I turn to Kora, opening my mouth to ask her what she wants. That's as far as I get before she's grabbing my shoulders, pushing me against the nearest wall, and kissing me.

She's kissed me before. She's been the one to initiate almost all our kisses. Either she's a lot braver than I am, or she's a lot less afraid of rejection. But this kiss . . . this isn't like the others. It's fiercer, harder, like she's afraid that it's the last one we're ever going to have. She lets go of my shoulders, hands dropping to my waist and then sliding up again, until her thumbs graze the sides of my breasts and my knees go weak, threatening to dump me on my butt right here. She stops there, thankfully, or I don't know if I could stand it.

Part of me wants to push her away, to say that this isn't the time and isn't the place and even if it were either of those things, Viola's in danger and I need to stop messing around. The rest of me, the portion that's descended from a million generations of mammals who managed to survive the threats around them, reproducing and improving and fighting and winning until they culminated in me, standing here under an orange, alien sky, that portion says to go for it. This could be my last kiss. I deserve to enjoy it.

When Kora finally pulls away, her cheeks are flushed, making the delicate blood smear I left there stand out even more, and the bridge of my nose is throbbing where Michel punched me. Facial trauma and make-outs are not close personal friends.

"Prime," I whisper.

She smiles, one corner of her mouth quirking up just a little higher than the other, and says, "I swiped Mama's access card while you were in the washroom."

The way she talks about her mother should sound childish—would sound childish, if it were me—but she makes it sound rich and rare and right, like there's no better name in the world for the woman who bore her, raised her, and is now leaving her to her own devices.

I blink. "What?"

"I can open the gate." She dips a hand into her pocket, coming up with a flat, burnished metal keycard. "I can close it again, too. We can get out of here."

This time, I'm the one who kisses her, putting my hands to either side of her face and pulling her close before I can think better about wasting time.

She still tastes salty and sweet at the same time, with that little improbable hint of motor oil. There's a new taste there now, something savory and sharp at the same time, and it's not until I'm pulling away, not until I can see the way she's looking at me, that I realize what it is.

Blood. Everything on this planet is tainted now.

"Come on," I say. "If we hurry, your mother won't have time to send people after us."

Kora nods and holds the card out toward me. I blink. She reddens, and explains, "It's against colony law for me to open the door without an adult present. You have to be eighteen to come and go freely. You aren't bound by colony law. So if you open the door, and I just happen to walk through it . . ."

"You won't have done anything wrong," I conclude. "I mean, apart from stealing your mother's card in the first place."

She nods. "I figure we're already going to be in enough trouble. I don't want to add to it."

The odds are good that either we won't be coming back, or we'll be coming back with a lot more trouble on our tails. It seems cruel to remind her of that, and so I simply smile, and take the card, and say, "You're a miracle. Totally prime."

Kora looks pleased. I turn and press the card to the reader on the gate.

There was a code before. I know there was a code. Apparently, "physical card belonging to the planetary governor" is more important than any silly numerical string, because the gate beeps twice and unseals itself, slowly retracting into the wall and revealing the ATV, still sitting where we left it.

There's a bloody splotch on the ground to one side of the ATV, marking the place where Michel was taken. Several long fronds of the local "grass" are bent double, absorbing it. The blood that had hit the grass is already gone, completely consumed and wiped away. It won't be long before there's nothing left to show what happened here. Zagreus will put itself back together, a perfectly functioning ecosystem that wants nothing to do with humanity, and it will endure.

Maybe. For all that the colonists haven't been willing to fully commit to their new home, they've been treating it gently, holding it at arm's length. The creatures that took my sister aren't going to be nearly that kind.

I pull the volt gun as I step cautiously through the gate, scanning one way, then the other, and finally turning to look up the wall. Part of me is convinced that this is it: that one of the creatures has been waiting there, ready to drop from above onto the first moving thing it sees.

There's nothing there. I relax, marginally, and head for the ATV, beckoning for Kora to follow. She hesitates, and for one dizzying moment I think she's going to turn around and go back the way we came. That might be a good thing. She'll be safe if she stays inside the wall.

She emerges instead, waving her mother's access card at the scanner on this side of the wall. The gate seals itself behind her. That's it; we're committed now.

The creatures haven't attacked the ATV. It's a small blessing. I'll take it. I climb behind the controls, amazed by how much that small action relaxes me. This is mine. It's familiar and it's comfortable and it's *mine*. The entire world is spread out around me, I can see everything in every direction. I'm as close to safe as I'm ever going to be again.

Kora climbs into the passenger seat. I pass her the volt gun. She blinks at me, clearly bewildered.

"If something moves, shoot it," I say. "This is safer to use while we're driving than a standard projectile weapon. All you need to do is make sure it's aimed away from us, and we won't have to worry about ricochets."

"Got it," she says. "Where are we going first?"

"Back to my residence." I start the engine. The ATV rumbles

to life around us. "There might be some things in my parents' office that I can use."

Even if there aren't, I want to say goodbye. We're about to head off on a fool's errand, one that hopefully ends with us getting my sister back, but could just as easily end with both of us dead. I want to see my home one last time before that happens. I want to remember that we were happy there.

If this is where my childhood ends, I want to be the one who closes the door.

"You know the way," says Kora, and she's right. I do. I turn the ATV around, careful not to hit the beacons that maintain the supply trail, and I drive away from the colony, back into the wilds where I belong.

14

YOU CAN'T GO HOME AGAIN

NOTHING JUMPS OUT OF THE TALL grass to attack us on the drive back to the residence. I see a few snuffle-squirrels vanishing into the undergrowth, and one of the larger flying pseudo-reptiles flashes by overhead, but that's all: nothing larger, no meat-deer or hippos or lion-worms. Zagreus seems to be holding its breath, waiting to see what horrors are going to befall it next.

It seems strange to feel bad for an entire planet, but I do. These things, whatever they are, are only here because the human settlers got greedy and decided to risk planetary biosecurity for the sake of short-term profits. The Zagreus colonists might talk a good game about being conscientious and taking good care of their new home, but in the end, they were just as venial and shortsighted as the rest of our species. They risked everything on one good score, and they lost. We all lost.

Kora keeps her eyes on the scenery around us, volt gun raised and ready to fire. It's comforting, having her there. It lets me focus on everything else, on keeping the ATV moving smoothly, avoiding the holes in the road, and most importantly, on maintaining an even speed. The engine barely hums once it settles into a comfortable groove. As long as I don't accelerate, we might even pass for part of the ordinary background noise of the world.

How intelligent *are* the creatures that have been hunting us? Can they actually recognize the sound of a machine, or have they been following the more unique, louder sounds of mammals fleeing for their lives? I sort of miss having multiple bodies at my back, although I can't even muster enough regret to be sorry that Michel was taken. He shoved Viola. He assaulted me. If it weren't for him, Kora, Viola, and I could all be safely inside the colony right now, preparing to take my family's transport and get the hell off this doomed planet.

The residence is silent when we pull up in front of it. The front door is still open where Mom charged out to distract the creature. There are gouges in the solar panels covering the roof, some of them so deep that it looks like the creature was on the verge of breaking through. My unease about the wall surges back. If those things want to get into the colony, they will.

And that needs to be a problem for later. We have plenty of problems already for right now.

I stop the engine and slide out, gesturing for Kora to follow me. She nods, seeming to understand the need for silence. Shoulder to shoulder, we make our way across the yard to the door. I unholster Mom's gun before I step inside.

The living room is trashed. The couch has been overturned, the shelves have been emptied, and something has been chewing on the rug. I catch motion out of the corner of my eye and whirl, barely stopping myself before I pull the trigger and waste a bullet on the snuffle-squirrel that's sitting on one of the end tables, industriously sucking the last of the snacks into its bulging cheeks.

It stares at me for a moment. Then, with a fluting squeak, it flops to the floor and scuttles out the door, taking its prizes along. I follow it, shutting the door and activating the seals that will cut off all sound escaping to the outside. They're standard issue for xenobiology residences, since we never know when we land on a new planet whether we're going to be dealing with creatures that attack at the faintest hint of an unfamiliar life-form. Sometimes we have to cover all the bases.

"We shouldn't stay here long, but this will buy us a little time," I say. "There's food in the kitchen. Water, too. Grab whatever you want. It's not like we're going to be using it."

Viola ate. Mom and Dad always kept the cupboards stocked for four people, not three, even when money was tight; she was an android and she didn't need to eat, but she ate, because they'd been that committed to the fiction that she was still alive. They'd sacrificed everything to give me the shadow of a normal childhood, and I'd never even noticed.

It hurts to realize that. It helps, too, in a strange way, because all their sacrifices had been intended to *keep* me from noticing that something was wrong, to *keep* me from realizing that my sister wasn't like me, wasn't like anyone else. She was Viola, and that was what mattered. That was what always, always should have mattered. By shaping our environment to lie so that they wouldn't have to, my parents gave me the greatest gift they were in a position to give. They gave me a life I didn't feel like I needed to question.

My chest feels like it's getting heavier and my throat feels like it's getting tighter. My vision blurs, swimming behind a veil of tears. I close my eyes, forcing myself to breathe in and out, slowly, carefully, forcing the impending wall of grief away. It's going to hit me soon enough, and when it does, it's not going to be pretty, or useful, or productive. I'm going to fall apart. I'd rather do it while safely on my family's transport, Viola by my side and—hopefully—Kora strapped into one of the passenger seats, getting the hell away from this doomed world. We can't stay here. If I fall apart now, we're not going to have a choice.

"Olivia?" Kora sounds concerned. That's probably the right reaction. "Are you all right?"

"No." I open my eyes. The tears have receded, at least a little; at least enough that I can see. "You root the kitchen, see what you can find. Take anything, take everything, it doesn't matter anymore. I'm going to check the office."

I spin on my heel and walk quickly away. It's not that I specifically mind Kora seeing me cry. It's that if she says one word—one word—that's meant to comfort me or calm me down, I'm going to lose it, and we're not going to get out of here. We're going to wind up huddled on the couch while I cry, and those creatures will come back, and we'll both die. Even with the door sealed, I have all faith that they'll be able to find us if we're not quick about this. So we have to be quick. I refuse to die out here.

The door to my parents' office is closed. I hesitate outside it, resting my fingertips against the knob. They're dead, they're both dead, I know that, and yet opening this door is what's going to make it real forever, not only in my nightmares. Opening this door when they're not inside is the end.

I open the door.

Their office is the largest single room in the residence, easily twice the size of the room I share with Viola. When we've objected, saying two teenage girls deserve room to keep their things, they've always countered with the fact that they know we pile into Viola's bed at night, sleeping in a tangle of legs and hair and silence. We don't need more room. They do.

The walls are lined with storage units, black and smooth and labeled with tiny white designation codes. Some of the drawers contain biological samples. Others contain paper files, a waste of storage space that both of them will defend as necessary when working on planets that don't always guarantee a global communications network. Old school doesn't need electricity, or wireless signaling, or any of the other luxuries on which the modern world is built.

Somewhere in those files, they have every sketchbook I've ever filled, from my early attempts to accurately draw the jarred samples Mom and Dad brought home to field studies of my own. We all thought I was going to be some great xenobiologist, documenting the natural beauties of a hundred thousand worlds humanity hasn't even discovered yet. I don't want that anymore. I can't just go out into the field with a pencil and a sketchbook and trust that someone else is going to take care of me if I get into trouble.

I have to be able to take care of myself.

Mom's terminal is flashing. I walk over and press my thumb to the print reader on the side of the screen. If whatever message waiting is something that I'm approved to see, it'll unlock, and maybe then I can get into the rest of Mom's files.

I wish Viola were here. She's the one who can make any system do what she needs and wants it to do. She'd be able to crack this whole thing wide open with a reproachful look and a few lines of code, and then we'd be prime.

The terminal beeps, flickering once before it clicks to strident, colorful life, and my mother's face fills the screen. I freeze, thumb still pressed to the print reader, putting my other hand over my mouth and staring at her image.

She's smiling. Not a big, happy smile, but the small, wry smile she's always worn when Viola was sick or I was fussy or Dad left his dirty laundry on the hallway floor. It's a smile that says she understands things have costs, and sometimes she feels the need to pay them, whether they were originally hers or not. It's a smile that isn't giving up, exactly, but is ready to find another way to fight.

"Hello, my girls," she says, and my heart sinks further. "If you're seeing this, something has happened to me, and I was able to transmit the unlock code before it was too late. I am so, so sorry, sweethearts. Please believe me when I say that there's nothing I would like more than to know that this message will never need to play, for either one of you."

"Mom," I moan, and touch the screen with the tips of my fingers. "Mommy."

"Now, there's a good chance that there isn't much time. This message shouldn't play if your father is there, so we have to assume you girls are alone now. Please listen carefully." She leans closer to the camera, smile fading, expression turning grim. "My brother, your Uncle Sebastian, is on Earth. He works for Weyland-Yutani, in their research and development branch, and in the event that something has happened to your father and I, he is now your legal guardian. I know you girls are almost eighteen, I know you probably feel like you don't need a legal guardian anymore, but believe me when I say that family always matters. Family always makes things easier to bear. He'll take care of you. He'll make sure you have a place to sleep, and someone to support you in whatever it is you decide to do with your life. Lives."

She stops, and laughs bitterly. "Olivia, my sweet girl, my first baby, there are things—as I'm recording this, there are things you still don't know, and if no one's told you what they are, I don't want this to be the way you find out. Viola knows. Viola has always known, even if we both pretend that she doesn't. Listen to your sister, honey. She doesn't want to hurt you any more than I do, and if we did this right, she's going to be staying with you for a long, long time. I . . . talk to your sister. Believe her."

My mother takes a deep breath. "Viola, darling, you were my second born, and as soon as I saw you, I knew I was done having children. I had everything. How many people are lucky enough to get everything they want before they even know they want it? You have always been perfect in my eyes. No matter how much things have changed between us, no matter how much you may feel like you're less than you were meant to be, you are perfect. Your sister loves you. Stay with Olivia. Trust and believe and hold on to Olivia. She'll take care of you."

She reaches up and wipes her eyes with the side of one hand. I want to go to her. I want to put my arms around her, hold her, comfort her, tell her that everything is going to be all right. I can't. I don't know when she recorded this, but the world that existed when she did isn't there anymore. Viola and I are alone, orphans, and in the eyes of the law, I'm the last surviving member of our little family. Everything has changed.

I miss my mother.

"All the accounts will have transferred into Olivia's name

upon transmission of this message. The transport is yours. Go to Earth. Go to your uncle. He'll make sure you have the time to make any necessary decisions about where you're going to go next, and what you're going to do once you get there. Stay together. As long as you stay together, I'll be there with you, and as long as I'm with you, I'll know that you're all right." A tear runs down her cheek.

It's impossible not to wonder whether she knew something, or suspected something, about that transport ship. The universe is full of dangerous things, but I can't imagine that she's been recording variations on this same message for years. She had a feeling. She knew something was wrong. And she did what she could to get us ready for the future, where we'd be going on alone, without her.

"I love you, Mom," I say.

"If you're seeing this message, something terrible has happened to both your father and I. It doesn't matter where you are. It doesn't matter how safe you think your current position could potentially be. You're standing in a graveyard. Whether or not the people who claim to be in charge are aware of it, they're already dead. I don't want my little girls to join them. Take our transport and get off the planet as quickly as you can. Run, my darlings. Run, and don't look back. I love you both, more than you will ever know."

The message ends, blinking out to reveal the main screen of her terminal. All her files are available to me. Prime. I sit down, quickly pulling up the geographic surveys of the local mountains.

Xenobiologists study the life indigenous to the worlds humanity chooses to settle on, trying to understand the shape of it before we inevitably change everything through our very presence. Observation changes things. Colonization, messy and exploitative and invasive as it always is, even when it's something as intentionally narrow in focus as the settlements on Zagreus, displaces the wildlife that was there before we came. Humans like "Earth-like" planets, choosing new homes that are already capable of supporting life whenever we possibly can, and way too few people like to think about the fact that a place that *can* support life probably already *does* support life, or that any reasonable ecosystem will have already done its best to fill all available niches.

Before any fieldwork can begin, the planets where my parents work need to be mapped and charted, sometimes down to the millimeter, because any chamber they don't think to peer inside could be the chamber where the next great threat to humanity is lurking. The average colony doesn't contact a xenobiologist until something tries to eat a colonist. In the case of Zagreus, that was a lion-worm, and it succeeded in eating the colonist in question. Subterranean tunnel maps were supplied before we even touched down on the planetary surface.

The maps come up with dizzying speed, showing the network of caves and passageways that riddle the nearby mountains. The original assumption had been that the lion-worms denned there, before my father followed a gravid female back to a hole and realized that they dug themselves vast subterranean nests, choosing to burrow so far below the surface that most conventional eradication methods were just barely shy of useless. Zagreus will always have lion-worms.

Unless these new apex predators decide to devour them all, which seems suddenly very possible. Maybe these were a sort of genetically engineered pest control gone terribly wrong. People sure do love creating life. They forget that life, once created, carries no innate obligation toward whoever made it. Life does what it wants, and screw anyone who gets in its way.

The cave system nearest where we saw the shuttle go down has a large enough opening to allow me and Kora to walk inside without blasting equipment or drills. Once there, we'll have a limited amount of territory we can reasonably cover—but these things are *big*. Even if they like to slither through narrow passageways and hide in crevices, that armor that protects them from things like bullets means that they'll be limited in how much they can manage to compress themselves. The tunnel networks on the map show a distinct lack of deeper chambers. Unless these things burrow, they should still be relatively near the surface.

I run off a flimsy, grabbing it from the printer before I eye Dad's rack of biological samples and snag several jars of the scent-dampening pollen. There's no way of knowing whether these creatures track by scent or through some other, less comprehensible mechanism, but they're not the only dangerous creatures on Zagreus. It would be seriously subprime to have our rescue op shut down when a lion-worm decides to eat my girlfriend. Again.

Kora is waiting in the living room when I emerge. She has one of Dad's field bags slung over her shoulder, pockets bulging with provisions snatched from the kitchen. We have the ATV: she won't have to carry anything for long. I look at her wearily.

"You ready?"

She nods.

I nod back.

This is where we leave the last safe place: this is where we step out into the world, and hope that what we find there is kinder than we expect it to be. I'd linger here forever if I could, trapped in the middle of the crisis, but with four walls around me and a roof over my head and the illusion of safety still pooling in my hands. I can't do that. We both know it's not possible. So I offer Kora my hand, and she takes it, and together we walk away from all the broken things, toward the future; toward the claws that broke them.

We have one shot at doing this. And I'll be damned if we're not going to do this the right way.

15

THE NARROW PLACES

THE ATV'S BATTERIES STILL REGISTER as nearly full. I switch us over to battery power completely, reducing the sound of the engine. We run a little faster when we're burning fuel rather than electricity, and that's another good reason to conserve what we have left until we're heading back to the colony with Viola. If those things come after us, we're going to want to be in a position to make the fastest escape possible.

Kora sits rigidly in the passenger seat, the volt gun in her hands and her eyes scanning the horizon. She looks like she's running out of resources, like she's nearing the point where she snaps and starts shooting at anything that moves. I'm so sorry I dragged her into all this. If I hadn't been so interested in impressing her . . .

"Stop thinking like that," she says abruptly, pitching her voice low, so it won't be heard above the rumble of the engine.

I manage not to swerve off-course, but it's a near thing. "I—what?" I squeak.

She looks briefly, bleakly amused. "I can't read your mind, if that's what you're worried about. But you had that look, the one you get when you think I'm too good for you, or that you're making me do something I don't want to do, or—you really think I'd be here if I didn't want to be? If I didn't *need* to be?"

She shakes her head, the motion and the wind making her curls bounce in all directions. "You know how I knew you were staring at me all the time in class? Because I was staring at you, too. None of this has ever been one-sided. I kissed you *first*. I liked you *first*."

"You only came out to see me because you wanted to know if Viola was real."

"Well, yeah." She looks at me like she thinks I might be a little bit stupid. "If you were lying about whether you had a sister, you were a creep, and I didn't want to date a creep. Michel gave me the excuse to do a field test without actually committing either of us to anything. Maybe we would have realized we didn't get along as well as we thought we did. Or maybe we would have had time. I wanted us to have time."

She looks out at the horizon, at the rapidly approaching line of the mountains.

"I wanted us to have time," she repeats, and I feel the same way, and so I don't say anything at all. I just keep driving.

I know we're going the right way when we pass the carcass of the lion-worm. It's massive, maybe the same massive one that tried to attack Kora on our first date together, and something has ripped it open from just below the jawline all the way to the base of its tail. Organs and viscera spill onto the ground, cooling slowly in the open air. I stop the ATV, studying it.

The lion-worms are the apex predators for this part of the ecosystem. For something to kill one of them at all is a horrifying statement of strength and power. For something to kill one this *large* is . . .

Well, it's terrifying.

"What happened?" whispers Kora.

"Something bigger than it was wanted its territory," I answer. The claw patterns on the lion-worm's hide don't match anything native to this area, but they do match what I saw of the new predators. This is one of their kills. "We're heading the right way."

Kora shudders. "I don't know if I'd go that far."

"We're heading the way we need to go, how's that?"

"I hate that you're right. But you're right. We're going the way we need to go." Kora gives the horizon another anxious glance before she turns to me. "I want to ask you something right now, and I want you to answer."

"All right." I start the ATV again. Something about the lion-worm's carcass makes me uncomfortable. Maybe it's the missing pieces. Maybe it's that not enough pieces are missing. Something about it is just . . . wrong. "What is it?"

She's going to ask me whether I think we're going to make it out of this alive. She's going to ask me whether I plan to stay on Zagreus. She's going to ask me—

"Will you take me with you?"

I barely succeed in keeping myself from slamming on the ATV's brakes. As it stands, I take my eyes off the terrain in front of us, several times, as I turn to gape at her. I have to keep looking back at where we're going, since there's no road or trail out here: a moment's distraction could end in an accident. But she came up with about the most distracting thing she could possibly have asked me.

"*What?*"

"I know you're going to leave once you have Viola back. You have to. Your parents are . . ." She hesitates before practically spitting, "dead, and we don't allow androids here, and I wouldn't stay if I were you. I'm not you, and I don't want to stay. Will you take me with you?"

"What about your mother?"

Kora shakes her head, very slowly. "She loves me. I know she loves me. But she loves the idea of Zagreus more. She loves what she thinks the colony is *going* to be, and she loves the idea of being the person who makes that happen. That's why my father didn't stay here with us. He couldn't stand sitting by and watching her eat herself alive."

And now these creatures from the survey ship are going to eat the planet alive. It would be darkly funny, if we weren't stuck in the middle of it. I worry my lip between my teeth for a moment.

"It's not a luxurious transport," I say finally. "There's plenty of room—it's sized for four—but we won't be comfortable, and we won't be coming back. If you change your mind, you'll have to find someone else to bring you home."

"I know all those things," she says. "I still want to come with you."

She sounds like she genuinely means it: she sounds like her mind's made up. I try, for just a moment, to see things from her perspective. She's pretty and she's popular and she's funny and she's trapped. She's trapped on this backwater colony, where her mother's position means she'll be watched no matter what she does, judged no matter what she does. She'll always be in her mother's shadow, expected to keep her hands clean and her chin high, expected to represent Zagreus in everything she does.

Every time I've kissed her, she's tasted, distantly, like engine oil. She knew enough about field vehicles to call our ATV cherry, and compared to the machines on Zagreus, I guess it is. I fell for her because of the pieces she has to show the public, the pieces of her that fit the role she's been forced to play. I'm still falling, because bit by bit, I'm seeing the Kora under that public design, and she's amazing.

"You have to say goodbye to your mother, because I don't want you to hate me when you realize you've done something you can't take back, and it has to be all right with Viola," I say. "She's my sister. She's an android, and she's been an android since we were too small for me to remember her any other way, and if you're not going to be comfortable with her having a say in all the decisions I make and where we go and—"

"I don't really know her yet," says Kora. "If I push back on anything she says or does or whatever, it's going to be because I don't know her, not because I think she's not a person. Of course she's a person. She's your *sister*. That's what matters. Not all the rest of this 'who's real, who isn't' garbage. If you say she's real, she's real, and of course I'm going to listen to her."

I nod. "Then yeah. You can come."

Kora smiles. She opens her mouth like she's going to say something as we pass the first rank of rocks marking the edge of the mountains. She doesn't speak. She doesn't close her mouth, either. She sits there, slack-jawed, staring at the devastation in front of us.

I stop the ATV and join her in staring.

The shuttle crashed into the ground about ten yards from the entrance to the cave network. If it had hit the actual mountain, it might have exploded; it might have spared us from its deadly cargo. Instead, it looks like it slid across the ground, ripping up rocks and destroying brush, until it came to a stop and burst into flames.

Everything is blackened and charred, creating a perfect environment to camouflage the creatures. There could be a dozen of them, pressed motionless against the mountain, and we wouldn't know until they struck. The grasses have burned away, the larger bushes and trees have been reduced to lumps of charcoal. Nothing lives here. Nothing is ever going to live here again. It's like standing on the surface of a mined-out moon, one that's about to be abandoned by its corporate owners for having nothing left to exploit.

There are a few spots that are less charred than the rest, spots where the ash has been scraped away by the passage of chitinous bodies, or rubbed away by terrible claws. They all point toward the mouth of the largest cave, slowly converging together.

I reach into the bag I scavenged from the office, pulling out two jars of thick, yellowish pollen. "Here," I whisper, passing one to Kora.

She looks at me, eyes wide and cheeks pale. "Why?" she whispers back.

I open my own jar and dust it over myself, covering my clothing, skin, and hair in a dusty film. "We don't know if it works on them, but if it does, it might buy us a few seconds," I say. The lion-worm makes me suspect that it won't do a thing. They can't be hunting subterranean predators *and* hunting by scent. Still, anything to take that look of terror out of Kora's eyes. Anything to make her think we're going to survive this.

This day has been horrible and hectic and life-changing, if not in the good way, and on top of everything else, I'm pretty sure I know whether or not I love Kora now. I do. I love her. I've fallen in love with her. And yeah, that's trauma and adrenaline speaking, and maybe I won't be in love with her tomorrow, or next week, but right now, I love her. I want her to stay with me, now and always, and I'm ashamed of the fact that I love my sister more. If I didn't, I would turn this ATV around and head straight for the launch port. I would get Kora off this doomed world and run for the nearest safe haven.

But I love Kora, and I love Viola, and I'm going to save them both, or die trying. I have to die trying. It's the only thing I have left to offer them.

Kora opens the jar and dusts the pollen all over herself, until she's a ghost sketched in dusty yellow, the volt gun still in her hands. I take the jar gently away and screw the lid back on, before slipping a few more vials into my pockets. I hope I won't need to use them.

Mom's gun is a comforting, deadly weight in my hand. "Ready?" I whisper.

"Yes," says Kora. She's trembling. I don't have time to make sure she means it. We have to go. I slide out of the ATV and start across the blasted ground toward the mouth of the cave. Kora follows, and by the time we reach our destination, we're walking side by side. We stay that way, as Zagreus opens its terrible geological jaws and swallows us both whole.

16

INTO THE BLACK

THE SUNLIGHT ONLY REACHES FOR the first ten feet or so of the cave, which is cold and dark and smells like mold and rot and petrichor. Kora moves closer as the light begins to fade. I can feel her trembling. I pat her shoulder with my free hand, trying to be reassuring, and stay silent. I should have anticipated this. It's too late for me to say anything.

Bioluminescence is a lot more common than most people realize. Even humans are bioluminescent, technically—we glow in the dark. We just do it so faintly that our own eyes can't detect the light, and so we assume that it's not there. During the day, Zagreus is as devoted to camouflage and predictable coloration as any other world. At night, however . . .

Maybe it's because their primary predators don't use sight as a hunting tool, or maybe it's because nature is funky and doesn't like to be told what to do, but Zagreus doesn't believe in rules when it comes to bioluminescence. We pass beyond the reach of the sunlight, and we step around a narrow bend in the tunnel, and suddenly the walls are ablaze all around us. Kora gasps.

Under other circumstances, I would probably be delighted to have surprised her like this. Considering the danger we're in right now, all I do is shoot her a tight, chiding glance. She nods, looking properly chagrined.

It *is* pretty impressive. The walls aren't just glowing, they're glowing in a dozen different shades of green and blue and red and yellow, all of them spiraling and crisscrossing together in carefully segregated bands as the different species of moss war for territory. They mirror the colors of the grasses outside. Dad used to argue that they might *be* the grasses outside, just adapted for a different environment.

The thought causes me to pause and squint at the glittering wall, following the patterns until I find a few small patches of orange. The orange grass is a flesh-eater. Maybe the orange moss is, too. I'm not sure what I'll be able to do with that knowledge, but knowledge is power, and I have so little of that right now that every scrap feels valuable.

Kora stays close by my side, but she looks less frightened now, and more amazed. This is a whole new side of the planet she's lived on for most of her life. It hurts a little, how awed she is. How many more secrets does Zagreus have? How many of them are we never going to have the opportunity to see?

I put my foot down in something wet. I stop, looking at the ground. It's a thick, asymmetrical puddle, barely an inch deep, and I know what it has to be even before I crouch down and touch it with the tips of my fingers, testing it. It's had time to chill, but it's blood. Human blood. Nothing on Zagreus has quite this consistency when it clots. I straighten up, giving Kora a firm nod.

We're going the right way.

That should make me feel better. It doesn't. I feel almost numb, like all of this is happening to someone else, like maybe Kora's mother was right in her assumptions and I'm the android after all. Part of me wants to seize on that idea, to cling to it for all that I'm worth. It would make more sense, wouldn't it, to build an android replacement for a dead daughter and make it as healthy as possible, so that it could go out and see the worlds on the behalf of the daughter you still had left? The one who was damaged by the illness that had carried off her sibling?

Viola's—the original Viola's—genetic condition was all too real. I can say that with confidence. I've seen her medical files. Mom and Dad sat me down with them the year we turned fifteen. It was part of the sex talk. Use protection even if you don't think you can get pregnant, because some diseases don't care about the gender of your partner; don't do anything you don't want to do, no matter how much someone says they love you; your sister has a genetic condition and we still don't know where it came from, so if you *do* decide to have children, you need to be very, very careful about your medical care.

I should have noticed that all those files were from genetic tests performed before we turned three. Hindsight is its own special kind of monster.

I wish I were the android. I wish I could convince myself that I'm unkillable, that no matter what happens here, I'm going to save my sister and get her to the transport and get Kora off this planet and do it all with a smile on my lips, because I can't die. I'm not, though. I'm a flesh-and-blood girl who just stepped in a puddle of blood that may have come from my mother, that may have come from my classmate, and nothing I can try to tell myself is going to make this any better.

Then we come around another curve, and instead of getting better, things get worse.

Michel is hanging from the wall. No, not hanging from the wall: he's *stuck* to the wall, encased in a thick, almost gelatinous-looking substance that manages to be simultaneously viscous and hard. It looks almost like he wandered into a cloud of repair foam, and got himself stuck when it hardened in response to exposure to the air. His head is bowed. His eyes are closed. He isn't moving. I want to tell myself that he's dead, that there's nothing we could possibly do for him, but there's one little problem with that idea:

Corpses don't bleed, and Michel is bleeding. It's a slow, steady trickle from his ear down the side of his neck, dripping from there onto the front of the foamy substance that's keeping him suspended. If it were just gravity pulling blood from a dead body, he would have run out by now. The fact that the blood's still falling means his heart is still beating, still working to do its job.

I glance at Kora. She seems horrified and disgusted, but also . . . sad, like she's silently mourning for someone that she's known almost her entire life. She doesn't understand what the blood means.

I don't want to tell her.

I don't *have* to tell her.

He's hurt. Badly. He's hurt, and he's trapped in some substance I've never seen before and don't want to mess with, because what if touching it is what alerts the creatures that we're here? They have yet to put in an appearance, but that doesn't mean they *won't.* He's not going to make it. If we try to get him off the wall, he's only going to slow us down.

Guilt blooms in my chest like a poisonous flower, choking me. If I don't tell her that he's still alive, I might as well have killed him myself. He's not my friend. I don't owe him anything. But Kora . . .

Loving someone and lying to them are not the same thing. If I start lying to her now, I may as well give up on the idea of loving her. No matter how much danger it puts us in, I have to tell her the truth.

Leaning as close to her as I dare, I press my lips against her ear, and breathe, "He's alive."

Her eyes widen. She gives me a quizzical look. I touch my own neck, then point at him, guiding her attention toward the blood that trickles down his neck.

Slowly, Kora nods, and mouths, "What now?"

It should be flattering, the way she expects me to have all the answers. It's honestly a little scary. I don't have *any* of the answers. I just have a gun, and a missing sister, and a lot of monsters between me and the end of this unwanted adventure.

I can't refuse to act, not with her looking at me like that. So I inch carefully forward, toward Michel. He doesn't react to my approach. He doesn't even seem to know that I'm there. The closer I get, the firmer the stuff holding him to the wall appears. My initial impression seems to be accurate: it looks like a single solid piece, somehow extruded from a biological source. There's a slickness to it that hurts my eyes when I look too closely . . . so I don't look too closely.

I focus on Michel. That trickle of blood is continuing, which means he hasn't died on me, however much I halfway wish he would. Cautiously, I reach up with my free hand and check his pulse. It's surprisingly steady, if a little weaker than it should be. He's holding on.

There's a cut above his left eyebrow, and some split skin around the corners of his mouth and cracking his lips, like his mouth was pried open with a lot of force and held that way for a distressing amount of time. I slap his cheek, very lightly. He doesn't react at all, but the sound echoes down the tunnel. I freeze. Behind me, I glimpse Kora doing the same, both of us waiting to see whether the sound is going to be enough to bring something terrible running.

Nothing comes. Nothing moves. And in the silence, I hear the faintest whisper, closer to a sigh, drift through the motionless air:

"*Run.*"

My skin is suddenly too tight and my pulse is racing and I can't breathe, because I know my sister's voice even better than I know my own: I know the sound of her sighs and the hitches in her breath, and even knowing that those things have always been mechanical doesn't make them any less familiar. Viola is here. Viola is here, in this cave, and more, she's awake. The creatures haven't ripped her apart. She's here, waiting for me, and all I have to do is go and get her.

I start to take a step deeper into the tunnel. Kora catches my arm, stopping me. I'm stronger than she is, but I don't dare fight to break free, not when we don't know where the creatures are. Any sort of a ruckus could bring them running, and then we both die here, and no one comes to save my sister, ever.

That's a chilling thought. She's an android. I don't know how long her power supply can last, but if she's been hurt—damaged is a better word, I guess—she's not going to be moving much, and it could take a long, long time for it to run out. I try to remember the longest time I've seen her unplugged from her supposed "life-support" machines. Hours. Whole days, sometimes. Assuming that the camouflage that allowed her to pass as a sick human included refilling her power reserves so that she'd never run down enough for me to notice her behaving oddly . . .

She could be awake and aware and trapped, alone, in a cavern filled with monsters, for weeks, maybe. Months. Even years. I don't know. I didn't have time to read her specs, and now it's too late. All I *do* know is that I can't leave her here. She's my sister. She's my responsibility.

I try to pull my arm away from Kora. She looks at me, eyes wide, and gives a little shake of her head. I nod, pulling again. She doesn't let go. Instead, she steps closer, until our lips are almost touching, until I can feel the heat coming off of her skin and smell the pollen in her hair. I can't smell anything else. It's doing an excellent job of masking the scent of her. I still don't know whether that will help. I hope so. We need a break.

After the day we've had, I honestly don't expect that we're going to get one.

"Michel needs our help," she whispers.

Michel is beyond our help. He's breathing, but we don't have the tools to get him down from the wall, and even if we did, we don't have any way of fixing whatever damage has been done to him. I feel like a monster for even thinking this, but . . . I'm not sure he can be saved. The kindest thing to do might be to put a bullet in his head on our way out of the caves. Which isn't going to *happen* if we get caught and killed while we're standing right here.

As if thinking about getting caught were enough to make it

happen, I hear something move deeper in the cave. Viola's voice drifts back a split second later, now loud and hectoring.

"Where are you going, you big, ugly bug? You hungry again? Do you even *eat*? Or do you just goop things to the wall so you can save them for later? Hey! I'm talking to you!"

Kora pales. I realize what Viola is trying to do and grab Kora by the arm, dragging her in the only direction I can think of that might stand a chance of saving us: toward Michel. She doesn't fight, not even as I shove her up against the strange shell that binds him to the wall.

The cocoon hangs over the mouth of another, smaller tunnel opening, all but blocking it. There's room, barely, for me to squeeze through; room for me to pull Kora in after me. Once we're both through I slip my hand over her mouth, pulling her tight against my chest. The space is too small and the air is too stale and we're going to die here, I know we are.

"Don't make a sound," I whisper. A thought occurs to me. We don't know how these things hunt. If it's sound, we may still be screwed—it'll hear our heartbeats, although we're close enough to Michel that his may confuse the issue—but there are some predators that follow CO_2 to find their prey. They follow our *breath*. "Don't exhale," I add, and take a great gulp of air, filling my lungs as far as they'll go. Then I push Kora farther behind me, shielding her with my body, and I wait.

"Don't go!" shouts Viola. "I don't want you to go, you ugly, predatory horror show of an evolutionary mistake!"

The sound of motion comes closer. The creatures may be smart enough to set ambushes and follow trails, but they're not intelligent enough to know what she's saying to them. They've decided that she isn't good prey. The noises she makes now don't mean anything.

I don't breathe. I huddle with Kora in the narrow space be-hind the vast, terrible cocoon that surrounds most of Michel, one hand over her mouth and the other resting on the butt of my mother's gun, the one that fires bullets designed to pierce through steel plating. If we're seen, I'll shoot. I'll shoot, and I'll shoot, and my last bullet will be for Kora, because I can't stand the thought of her going into one of these cocoons, saved to be a later meal for a monster.

No one's coming to save us. Not the frightened, untrained colonists, not my parents, not some kind of miracle. The corps don't care about Zagreus. They haven't dispatched a platoon of marines to come and get us out of here. We do this alone, or we don't do this at all.

The creature steps around the corner, barely visible in the narrow slice of open space between us and the main chamber. Kora, frozen against me, doesn't make a sound.

The thing is moving slowly, casually, like it doesn't have a care in the world. Maybe it doesn't. Maybe being a horrifying apex predator from space, on a planet where nothing seems to be in its league, has left it fully relaxed.

It's impossible not to remember what the seastead said about the creatures, that they were made of knives, because it's true. Every line, every angle is perfectly designed for killing, from the sinuous curve of its spine to the bladed shape of its limbs and curling tail. My lungs are starting to ache, but I can't stop myself from admiring the thing, even as it moves closer. It's beautiful. It's perfect and it's terrible and it's going to be the death of so many, and none of that can stop it from being beautiful. I can feel the shape of it in my fingers, where it aches to be drawn, put down on paper and pinned in place, so that I can study it at my leisure.

I wonder if there's a clear image on the recording of my father's death, a single still shot that I could study. I wonder if I'll ever have the chance.

My lungs are starting to burn. Not badly, not yet, but that's coming. People need to breathe. If Kora and I won't do it on purpose, our bodies will eventually overrule us, and we'll breathe anyway.

And then we'll die.

The creature doesn't seem to have noticed us yet. I want to attribute that to the pollen, but somehow, I don't think so. That would be too easy of an answer, and if there's anything today has taught me, it's that the easy answers are rarely the right ones. We're pressed up against Michel's cocoon, we're not moving or breathing, maybe that's enough to keep us—

Michel moans. It's a small sound, barely audible even in the silence, but the change in the creature is instantaneous. It moves so quickly that its outline seems to blur, going from the middle of the cavern to only a few feet away, its long, terrible head trained on Michel's. Not moving takes everything I have in me. I remain perfectly still, my hand locked over Kora's mouth, fighting the animal instinct that orders me to run, run, *run* as fast as I can. Even knowing that it could never be fast enough, it would still be better than standing here, waiting to die.

The creature makes a cooing, clicking sound. It's nothing that could ever have emerged from a mammalian throat. Part of me wonders idly what the structure of its throat and larynx must look like—does it have vocal cords? Is it capable of more complex vocalizations? Does it even need them? The rest of me is frozen in animal terror.

Then the creature opens its mouth.

It seems to keep opening forever, sliding down, down, down, not gaping wide like a normal predator. A second mouth edges forward, tiny and fetal and terrible, dripping with strings of thick mucus. It extends until it almost brushes Michel's cheek, then clicks, the sound soft, delicate, and appalling in a way I don't have words to describe, a way that makes my skin crawl until it feels like it might rip itself clean off my body and slither away into the depths of the cave.

The second mouth opens again. This time, it croons, low and oddly sweet, like it's calling to an infant. Michel moans again. The second mouth closes, and withdraws, vanishing back into the creature's jaws. I can smell it. It smells like hot metal and formic acid, a dark, feral, oddly insectile scent that reminds me of sitting by my father's hip while he performed dissections on wild-caught examples of the native fauna.

My lungs hurt. Badly. I'm going to lose control of conscious breath control if I have to wait much longer, and that means Kora's time must be even shorter: she doesn't have the physical conditioning I do.

Please, I think. *Hold on. Just a little bit longer. I need you to hold on, for Viola. I need you to hold on for me.*

The creature closes its primary mouth and steps backward. It stays there for a moment, perfectly frozen, head slightly cocked, like it's trying to make sense of something complicated. Then it turns and scurries away, moving with more urgency than it was before, heading toward the mouth of the cave.

I wait where I am until the creature is gone. Then I take my hand away from Kora's mouth and slowly exhale, trying to make the sound as silent as possible. It isn't easy. My body fights me, wanting to cough, to gasp, to glut itself on air until there's no more room in my lungs. Kora shakes beside me, her body pressed to mine, and clearly joining in the same rebellion. Our eyes lock. She gives a very small, very tight nod. She's fighting as hard as I am to keep things under control.

Bit by bit, I calm my breath, until I feel like I can safely straighten up and pull away, letting her stand on her own. I don't know if the creature missed us because we were silent, because we didn't move, or because of the pollen . . . but I have a terrible suspicion. I squeeze through the opening, Kora behind me. Once we're in the clear, I reach up and press my fingers to the side of Michel's neck.

His heart is racing even faster than before. Whatever's happening inside that cocoon, it's putting the kind of stress on his system that he may never be able to survive. If the creatures can hear our heartbeats, his may have been enough to mask ours, making them inconsequential. The boy who tried to kill my sister probably just saved my life.

"I forgive you," I breathe, softly, and pull Kora with me as I step away from him, heading deeper into the cave. I don't look back. If Kora does, I don't see it.

It's time to save my sister.

17

BROKEN PIECES
OF ME

THE BIOLUMINESCENCE IS STEADY, and bright enough that we can see the cocoons studding the walls. Michel was the first, but he's far from the last, or the only. Paul is here. Several larger animals are here—a few hippos, a meat-deer, and what looks like an entire family of lion-worms, some of them even larger than the one outside. Their bulk blocks out the glow from the walls in patches, casting those slices of the cave into shadow. I try not to look at them. It's impossible. There are too many, and they're everywhere.

Then we come around another bend in the cave, and I stop, my own heart suddenly beating even harder than Michel's, beating until it feels like it's going to burst inside my chest. I don't think I can survive this. I'm going to drop dead where I stand. Kora will have to leave my body behind, and that's fine, that's absolutely prime, because when she does, she'll be leaving me with my family.

My mother is cocooned on the wall.

Like Michel, her head is exposed, lolling forward, her hair covering half of her face. What I can see of her looks mostly undamaged, and almost peaceful, like she's only sleeping. Please, she's only sleeping. There's a smear of blood on her temple, but she has no visible wounds. Unlike Michel, she isn't bleeding. That could mean she's dead. Maybe she's dead.

She can't be dead. She's my *mother*. My mother isn't allowed to be dead. And on the ground at her feet . . .

Viola raises her head, looking at me with desperate misery in her eyes, and presses a finger to her lips, signaling me to silence. Her left leg is gone, severed cleanly at mid-thigh. I can see wires and metallic cables, exposed to the air for maybe the first time since she left the factory. Ugh. Factory. My sister came from a factory. Any hope I'd had that this was somehow a nightmare, that I might wake up, dies with the sight of those wires. She's an android. A damaged android, and our mother—

I take a step forward. Kora grabs my arm, trying to stop me. I shake her off and keep walking, one unsteady step at a time, until I reach the cocoon, the great dark bulk of the cocoon, until I press my hands against my mother's cheeks and push her head up.

"Mom?" I whisper. My voice seems horrifyingly loud. "Mommy?"

"She can't hear you."

I look down. Viola's eyes meet my own.

"I tried. I yelled and I screamed and I tried to break off pieces of the cocoon. Those *things* just put another layer on. When I kicked them, they kicked back." She grimaces, nose wrinkling. "That's what happened to my leg. They're *sharp*. I don't suggest kicking them."

She's whispering, but not as quietly as I was. I raise my eyebrows. She shakes her head.

"They don't care if I make noise. There's nothing in here for them to hunt, and they don't see me as prey, since I'm not fighting them and they can't . . . kill me."

I don't like that pause. Something in that pause whispers about "killing" not being her only concern, about bodies being used for things other than something to save for later. I look at Mom's face again, studying it, not only for the familiar, but for the *un*familiar, the things that seem even a little out of place.

If, you know, being glued to the wall in a creepy glowing cave wasn't subprime enough.

It only takes a few seconds for me to realize what's wrong. She has the same tears around her mouth as Michel, the same splits in her lip. With him, I'd been able to attribute it to rough handling from his capture and imprisonment. With her . . . it doesn't make sense for that same, very specific pattern of damage to appear on both of them unless it means something.

I leave my thumb resting against the soft, warm slope of my mother's chin as I try to think. I've seen native creatures on a dozen worlds. I've studied them from three dozen more, preparing for the day when I'd be old enough to take a more active role in my parents' work. I've seen injuries like this before. Never on anything the size of a human, and never with this much regularity, but similar enough that a feeling of dread settles in my stomach, growing heavy there, weighing me down. I turn to Viola.

She nods. It's a small gesture. It's enough to tell me that she knows where my thoughts have gone—that she was waiting for me to finish—and worst of all, that I'm right.

"Kora." My voice sounds exactly like Viola's, and the

creatures are used to her. I have to risk speaking a little louder, because I need to be heard. "Come on. We need to get Vi out of here before they come back."

"What? No!" Viola grabs the hem of my tunic, alarm written plainly across her face. "I'll slow you down too much. I'm damaged. You have to leave me here."

"You're not *damaged*." I stare at her, appalled. "You're my sister. Shipp sisters forever, remember? I'm not leaving you behind."

"I'm not your sister," insists Viola. "I'm an android. I'm a *thing*, and your life is more important than anything I am ever going to be. You have to go. I'll stay here."

Viola glances at Mom as she speaks. She'll stay here with our mother, and this cave will be a tomb for the two Shipps who never get to leave Zagreus.

Like hell.

"You were my sister yesterday, you'll be my sister tomorrow, and you're my sister right now," I say. "You don't even have to pretend to be sick anymore. Can you imagine how much trouble we're going to get into? You and me. Forever. That's how it's supposed to be. That's how it's *going* to be. Kora, come on, help me lift Viola up."

I reach for Viola. She bats my hands away before she takes a deep, deep breath and looks at me resolutely. She's always been stubborn, even more stubborn than I am, and every drop of dogged determination she has is shining in her eyes.

"I know you have a knife or a saw or something in that pack," she says. "If you want me to go with you, you need to cut off my head."

I stare at her. Kora stares at her. Viola shakes her head. She won't be able to do that if I *decapitate my own sister*. This is ridiculous. I don't understand why—

"All my essential systems, all my memory and processing power, they're all stored exactly where my brain would be, if I had one," she says. "And without my body, my head only weighs about ten pounds. You can carry ten pounds. You can fit ten pounds in your backpack. You can't fit my whole body in your backpack." She looks at the place where her leg isn't and chuckles, darkly. "Not that I have a whole body. C'mon, Olive. You're already going to have to pay for repairs. Why not get started?"

"I don't want to hurt you," I whisper.

Her expression softens. "You won't. As long as you cut here," she touches the soft center of her throat, below the chin, above the collarbone, "you can't hit any vital systems. I won't feel any pain, and I won't black out. My head has its own power supply, in case of damage to the body. This is the only way we get out of here together."

Slowly, I move toward her, and kneel, slipping out of my backpack. "You promise?"

Our mother's body hangs above me as Viola nods, expression solemn. "I swear."

"Kora, keep watch." I glance over my shoulder to my maybe-girlfriend. She looks back at me, eyes huge and grave. She looks terrified. That's probably a wise decision.

"I don't want to be here," she whispers. "I want to leave."

"That's what we're doing," I say, and unzip the backpack. The sound is horrifyingly loud in the enclosed confines of the cave. It echoes, metallic and unnatural and strange. The sound of claws clicking on stone follows immediately afterward, and the blood drains from my face as I realize, with numb certainty, what that has to mean.

Viola's face goes slack as the same realization hits her. "Run," she says.

"Not without you," I reply, and grab her under the arms, hoisting her as I stand. She's lighter than I remember her being—the missing leg must have contained some pretty substantial hydraulics—and I've been picking her up since we were babies. Me and my sister. As long as I can lift her, she'll be fine.

Viola drums a fist against my back as I stand. "This is *stupid*," she hisses.

"Don't care," I say, and take a step toward Kora, and there it is, the creature made of knives, looming out of the darkness behind her, jaws already open, saliva pooling and dripping from their horrific, chitinous edges. Kora sees the look on my face and starts to turn, but she's going to be too slow, we were always going to be too slow, we're only soft, mammalian flesh, we were never designed to fight this kind of monster, we were never going to win this—

"Throw me," says Viola. "Throw me *now*."

I love my sister.

I listen to my sister.

I've spent my whole life doing what my sister tells me to do, because she's sick, she's delicate, she needs me to stand up for her. She needs me to be the strong one, the decisive one, the one who isn't scared of what happens when her ailing lungs finally stop working. It doesn't matter if so much of that was based on a lie, because habit is stronger than horror, and I love Kora, too, I love her as she is, not in pieces on the floor. The hard part is already finished. I'm already standing, Viola slung over my shoulder like a sack of laundry, and it's surprisingly easy to swing her down, into my arms, and throw her as hard as I can at the creature.

Whatever it was expecting us to do, it wasn't this. Viola strikes it squarely in the narrow, armored center of its thorax. She grabs hold, slicing through the skin of her hands in the process, and there's blood, blood, blood, because she was designed to pass as human; she needed to bleed when someone cut her. There's blood as she begins to punch and kick the creature, which makes a terrible sound, thin and insectile and somehow carrying, like a roar pushed through a different sort of lungs.

Kora grabs for my hand, but I'm fumbling in my pocket, digging down until my fingers find one of the vials I took from my mother's office. I turn away from the terrible creature that's slashing at my sister's body with bladed fingers, pulling the vial out of my pocket and flinging it, as hard as I can, at the cave wall.

It shatters on impact, broken glass and clear fluid going everywhere. I dance back before any of the fluid can hit me, stepping away so my shoulders bump into Kora's chest. She puts her arms around me, and I grasp her wrists, holding on for dear life.

Viola is still hitting the creature, but it's hurting her a lot more than she could possibly hurt it. She's just one unarmed android shaped like a sickly teenage girl, and it's a knife that hunts, a weapon that moves and thinks and kills. This fight was never hers to win.

I don't *need* her to win it. All I need her to do is buy us time. Because the thing is between us and escape, and even terrified as I am, I'm smart enough not to think that running deeper into the cave is the solution to anything but not wanting to be alive any longer. We're at the opening to a hive. A young hive, sure, and one that's still figuring itself out, but I'm the daughter of two xenobiologists, and I know a hive when I see one. If we run deeper, we'll find the rest of the creatures, the rest of the cocoons.

We'll find the terrible thing that tore the mouths of Michel and my mother, the thing that filled their bellies or chests or lungs with something I can't even allow myself to think about yet. Not when I still have to keep running, keep fighting, keep myself *alive*.

That same desire to live is why I'm not shooting, yet. The sound of gunfire would draw the other creatures as fast as anything. Kill all threats to the hive. That's the primary motivation of the eusocial creature. Protect the hive, protect the young. Sacrifice the few in service to the many. That's how ants can overwhelm creatures a hundred times their size. As long as the hive is fed, they don't care about the cost to the individuals who die in the process.

Humanity has always been living on borrowed time, waiting for the moment when we find something that lives in hives, something that cares more about winning than it does about the lives it loses in the process.

Viola isn't bleeding anymore. All her blood has been spilled, and both of her arms have been torn from her body. As I look on in horror, the creature rips out her chest and throws her aside, a broken, motionless husk. There's exposed circuitry where half my mind insists there should be muscle, should be bone, and something thin and oily drips from her wounds. Hydraulic fluid, probably. Cleaning solution. The vital substance of robotics.

The creature turns its long, glistening head toward us, jaws parted, making a strange, menacing clicking sound. It may be summoning other members of the hive. It may be declaring its intent to claim us for itself. I don't know, and it doesn't matter, because if the substance I threw at the wall doesn't do its job soon, we're no longer going to be alive to care what happens next.

Viola lifts her head, as much as her ravaged muscles will allow, and shouts, "Run!"

I don't run. Neither does Kora. There's nowhere for us to run *to*, no possible way for us to evade the disaster that's coming. The creature is adjusting its stance, preparing to strike.

The wall explodes.

Dirt and stone blows outward in all directions, chunks of it striking me. Kora cries out, and Mom's cocoon, detached from its mooring, crashes to the floor, shattering. That seems to enrage the creature, which whips around to face the massive, monstrous lion-worm that has burst through the cave wall. The creature roars. The lion-worm, summoned by the concentrated phero-mones I stole from the lab, roars back.

The sounds couldn't be more different. The creature roars like it's already the ruler of the world, offended by this intrusion into its space, ready to defend, to fight, to kill. There's no warn-ing in the creature's voice. It doesn't sound like it knows what a warning is. The lion-worm's cry is mammalian, hot and furious and willing to be appeased. The lion-worm would be happy—if lion-worms can be happy—to avoid conflict. All the creature has to do is give up this marked territory, retreat, and be spared.

That was never going to happen. The creature lunges for the lion-worm, which it has correctly identified as the greater threat, and Kora and I are, however temporarily, forgotten.

I immediately break into a run, dragging Kora with me to-ward Viola's broken, discarded body. She offers me a wan smile when I drop to my knees beside her.

"Bet now you wish you'd run, huh?" she asks. Her voice sounds normal, which is disturbing in a way I don't have a word for. Her chest has been cracked open. Her lungs—or whatever interior structures serve as her lungs—have been pulverized. I've worried about those lungs for my entire life, worried about the day when they'd acquire an infection or develop a tumor or something and finally cease to work.

I never realized I was worried about all the wrong things.

"Kora, lift her head," I say, and shift like I'm going to reach into my backpack.

It isn't there. It's behind me, near the two fighting behemoths, which are continuing to shriek and scream and roar as they rip at each other. The lion-worm is holding its own, for now, but I know that's not going to last: the knife that hunts is cutting deeper with every blow, and soon, the lion-worm is going to lose. We're running out of time.

That just means we don't have time to waste. I lurch back to my feet and run past them, grabbing my backpack from the shattered shards of Mom's cocoon. She's facedown on the floor, and she's not moving, she's not visibly breathing, and maybe it makes me a terrible daughter, but I hope she's dead. I hope the impact killed her, and that she won't have to live through the process of birthing whatever awful thing has been tucked away inside her.

Most creatures who birth their young through incubation inside another species don't care much about survival of the host. Why should they? Use something else's body as a life-support system for your own young, and then use their corpses as a food source. It's efficient. If the host needs to be fed and cared for, it's inefficient; incubating your own young would work better.

I drop to my knees next to my sister again, and dig the hacksaw out of my backpack. Kora grabs my elbow. I look at her, struggling to contain my growing nausea over what I'm about to do, what I don't have a choice about doing.

"Hurry," she hisses.

I nod, and I bend over my sister's broken body, and I begin to cut.

The false skin covering Viola's frame has been good enough to fool me since infancy, and it's still good enough to fool me now: for the first few cuts, it genuinely feels like I'm slicing into my sister's living body. All the blood has run out of her system, escaping through larger wounds. That doesn't help make this any less disturbing. I cut, and her flesh parts, bloodless but otherwise perfectly realistic. It's like performing an autopsy, right up until I slice through the last layer of dermis and reveal the mechanical structure beneath.

Behind me, the lion-worm howls in what I can only interpret as pain. We never had a lot of time. Now we have even less.

"It's all right," says Viola. She closes her eyes. "I trust you."

I push down harder, slicing into the metal, and continue to cut.

There are moments that, even as they happen, you know will keep happening forever in your nightmares. Moments too terrible to have endured even once, that you're going to have the rare pleasure of enduring over and over and over again, because the human mind isn't good at letting things go.

This is one of those moments. I cut, driving the blade deeper and deeper, until I'm cutting into artificial skin again, and my sister's head comes loose in my hands. Viola manages to smile, despite the helpless horror of her situation.

"I'm all right," she assures me. "Now run."

I stuff the blade back into my bag and sling the strap over my shoulder, tucking Viola's head up under my arm even as I grope for Kora's hand. She's there, and I grab hold, and we're running, we're finally running, leaving Michel, and Mom's body, and the monsters all behind.

18

CAR CHASE

THERE ARE NO MONSTERS BETWEEN us and the ATV, no terrible creatures made of knives, no native Zagreus wildlife. It feels like a small blessing in a day that has been noticeably devoid of blessings. There's no time to stop and dwell on it: we keep running until we reach the vehicle, and I toss Viola's head onto the seat before shoving myself behind the wheel.

"Hey, ow," she protests. "Just because I don't have a body, that doesn't make me a basketball."

"Sorry," I say, and hammer on the engine. This time, I engage the fuel line. Battery power alone isn't going to get us out of here as quickly as I need it to. "Kora?"

"Here." She drops into the passenger seat, fastening her belt before she picks up Viola's head and tucks it securely against her hip. "*Drive.*"

She doesn't mention Michel, and I'm sadly, secretly glad, because there's no way we're going back in there to get him, not after the injuries on Mom's lips and the things Viola wasn't willing to say. Whatever horrible thing is about to happen in that cave, we won't be there.

I jerk back on the controls. The ATV roars and lurches, and then we're racing away from the hole in the earth, the hole filled with murder and monsters and impossible decisions. Kora whoops, making no effort to conceal her relief. The guilt will come later, I'm sure. Michel was alive, and we left him there, and while she may not remember him right now, she will. She's known him for too long, and is too good of a person, to just let it go. Right now, though, right now we're heading for the colony, and we're going to get away. We'll get on my family's transport, and we'll take off, and Zagreus can solve its own problems. The Shipp sisters are—

The ground in front of us bursts upward as a juvenile lion-worm—this one easily five feet long, almost as long as I am tall—erupts from the crust, jaws open in a shrill, keening shriek. It slams to earth a few feet from the ATV's grill. I haul hard on the controls, barely evading a collision.

"*Look!*" shrieks Kora. Her voice is high and shrill and terrified.

I look.

Crawling out of the tunnel formed by the lion-worm's body is another of the creatures. This one is smaller than the one from the cave, which explains why it was out hunting, and not patrolling the cocoons. Its head turns toward us, its jaws gaping in a hiss I can't hear above the engine. Then it leaps, abandoning its injured prey in favor of following us.

What makes us more appealing than something as large and presumably nourishing as the lion-worm? I don't know, and while my biologist's heart yearns for information, the rest of me is way more interested in staying alive. I punch the controls harder, teasing a little more speed out of the engine. I don't look at the readings on my dash. If we're running short on fuel, I have no interest in knowing about it. All I can do right now is drive.

The thing in the cave clearly knew we were there, despite the pollen. Even if the pollen *had* been enough to shield us, it wouldn't stop the creature from following the ATV's engine, and we know they can track by sound. Fine: I need to find another way to get it off our tail.

"Hold on," I say, raising my voice to be heard above the engine's roar, and haul hard on the controls, sending us into a half-spin before we race off in the direction of the wetlands. Something that worked once may well work a second time. Even if it doesn't . . .

The goal here is not to win. The goal here is not to be the better predator. The goal is to get away. That's the one advantage we have over the creatures from the shuttle, the knives that hunt. We understand that sometimes, success isn't in the kill. It's in the escape. So we race across the taiga, and when Kora screams beside me, high and shrill and painful, I don't even need to look behind us.

"How many?" I demand.

"One," gasps Kora. She sounds utterly terrified. That's probably smart, and the reason I can't look back. I can't afford to be frightened right now. I need to keep my eyes on the horizon, and keep us moving toward something that might save us.

"One? Okay." One, I can handle. One won't have pack dynamics I don't understand, and we've already proven that they can be distracted by presenting them with a greater threat or an easier target—or both at the same time. "Hold on."

The ATV wasn't designed for this kind of speed over long distances. I still bear down harder, coaching a little more out of the straining engine. We roar toward that horizon, and behind us the creature roars in answer, the sound nowhere near as distant as I want it to be. I can't tell if it's gaining or if it's just pissed off. Either way, subprime.

"Kora, try to make it back off," I say.

"*What?!*"

"You have a gun! Use it!"

There's a long pause before Viola's head lands in my lap, faceup and blinking at me. I glance down long enough to meet her eyes. She blinks at me. This is the weirdest day I have ever had.

"I think I like your girlfriend," she says. "She's fun. And she bathes! Having someone stick you under their arm is a great way to measure their personal hygiene."

"Vi!"

"What?" She rolls her eyes. "I'd shrug, but you sort of need shoulders for that."

Beside me, Kora is unbuckling her belt and climbing onto her knees on the seat, taking aim at the closing danger behind us. I swerve to avoid a rock in our path. Jostling her out of the vehicle wouldn't exactly be a good thing right now. We can't afford to stop or go back. There's no way I could leave her behind.

"Cover your ears!" she shouts, and the volt gun goes off, loud as a lightning strike and twice as close. My hair stands on end, and the recoil from the shot washes over my skin in a static wave.

Viola makes a small, pained sound. I glance down at her. She manages to force a pained smile.

"The power cells in my head aren't as well-shielded as the

ones in my body; no room," she says. "It's fine. I'll be fine. Let her keep shooting."

"Kora?" I ask, question rising toward a shout.

"It didn't like that!" she replies jubilantly. For the first time since this all started, she sounds like she thinks we might be able to win. "Hold on!"

She fires again. This time, the creature roars in anger and pain, confirming that the bolt struck home. It sounds closer than it was. I can't tell how true that is, and so I keep driving, trying to get as much speed as I can out of the struggling engine.

We're almost finished, I think, as if the machine could hear me. *Soon as we make it back to the colony, you get to rest, and no one's ever going to ask you to do anything like this again.* I've always treated our machines—the ATV, the transport, even the servos that assemble each new air-dropped residence—with respect, like they were pets, not just tools. My parents have never discouraged it.

I wonder if that's because they always knew one day I'd find out about Viola. Not that my sister is an assembly servo or anything stupid like that. Just that . . . maybe they were encouraging empathy because they didn't know if I'd have enough otherwise.

Kora fires again, then smacks the barrel of the gun against the back of the seat, swearing under her breath. "I'm out of charges."

"It'll refuel if you give it a few seconds." The forest is looming up ahead, more welcoming than ever. The creatures are new to the planet. They don't know it as well as I do. Sure, they're knives in more ways than one, capable of cutting through virtually anything that gets in their way, but that doesn't mean they won't be impacted by any obstacles I can throw into their way.

"We don't have a few seconds!"

That's when the creature leaps onto the back of the ATV, rocking it. Kora screams. I scream. Even Viola screams, which is impressive, since she has no lungs.

"*Hold on*," I shriek, and turn us hard to the left, heading straight for the trees.

Kora, who has seen Earth cartoons before, understands what I'm about to do, and ducks down. The creature doesn't have her cultural advantage. It reaches for us, and is in mid-reach when the branch catches it across the middle of its chest, knocking it back, off the ATV, leaving us to go roaring on without its additional weight.

This isn't a solution. On the one hand, I don't think the creature has enough higher thought to actually be angry with us. On the other hand, now it's in the trees. Not exactly what I'd call a net gain on our part. I haul on the controls again, settling us on the path my family has cut through the trees, and race on toward the wetlands.

Terrain varies. That's one of the great things about terrain, from a biological standpoint, and one of the terrible things about terrain, from a tactical standpoint. The caves are located on the edge of the taiga, which gives way in turn to forests of both trees and towering mycotic blooms. The forests verge on more taiga, on deeper, more impenetrable forest, and on the wetlands.

The wetlands, where the Zagreus hippos live.

"We're gonna get wet," I say, raising my voice enough to be heard above the rumble of the engine. I can hear the creature crashing through the trees behind us. I'm doing my best not to focus on that, because if I lose focus, we're all going to be dead. Except for Viola. She'll be in the same situation she was in when we found her in the cave, only worse, because now she's just a head. She'll have to watch us get ripped apart—please let us get ripped apart, and not dragged back to the cave—and then she'll lie, forgotten, wherever she fell, until her batteries run down and she's finally allowed to slip away.

We have to beat this thing. We have to win. So I gun the engine and coax a little more speed out of the straining power connectors, sending us flying over a rise in the ground, into the marshy edge of the wetlands.

This is where things get tricky. If I'm not careful, I'll swamp the axles, getting them so stuffed with waterweeds that we can't move anymore. We'll be easy prey for the creature if that happens. I ease off on the power, just a little, and take one hand off the controls, digging into my pocket. My backpack is also digging into me, pressing into my back until every jolt knocks the breath halfway out of my body. It seems impossible that I didn't notice it before, although to be fair, I've been distracted.

The creature shrieks behind us. The ground sags beneath us. The ATV shakes around us, fighting to make its way through the growing marsh. It's a loyal little machine. It's always done exactly what we ask it to do, even when that meant damage to its systems.

Just one more great escape, I think, and gun the engine. We break free of the marshy patch, rolling onto solid ground as I pull the second vial of lion-worm pheromones out of my pocket and pop the lid off before flinging it into the waterweeds looming on our left.

This is the risky part. If any of the stuff gets on us, we'll be contending with ongoing attacks from amorous lion-worms for the rest of the day, all of them convinced that we've somehow hidden the most attractive female of their species in our pockets. But.

Lion-worms don't hunt in the wetlands, because the Zagreus hippo is one of the few creatures native to the region that possesses the size, strength, and natural defenses to make the lion-worm reconsider its choices. Hippos *hate* lion-worms, an accidental re-creation of an old Earth relationship between two animals that bear no actual resemblance to Earth lions or Earth hippos. Their usual reaction when a lion-worm—generally a juvenile, too young to know better or to have an established hunting ground of its own—wanders into the wetlands is fast, bloody, and violent.

A juvenile lion-worm that survives one encounter with a Zagreus hippo will do almost anything to avoid having a second one.

We race on, and the creature chases behind us, unable to be silent on the uneven terrain, with the waterweeds lashing at its chitinous form. It hasn't learned the territory yet. It's still the universe's perfect predator, still the knife that hunts, it's just having a little difficulty figuring out how to wield itself. Give it time, give it time.

Time's what I'm not going to give. I punch the engine one more time, and we roar forward as it reaches the patch of waterweeds I've saturated with lion-worm pheromones. It recognizes the scent and roars in anger at the presence of another predator—a roar that proves remarkably prescient as the hippo charges out of the weeds and slams its bony head into the creature's midsection.

My parents would be so proud of the way I've been using the wildlife of Zagreus to do my dirty work.

Solid ground begins just a few meters away, marked by a

small, blooming fungus that only grows where it can be sure of staying dry. It makes a grubby red line all along the edges of the wetland, fragile and easily overlooked. Mom missed it the first time, and fell into the water up to her neck.

It's a funny memory now, while I'm still in semi-shocked denial about what happened back in that cave. Maybe someday it'll be a funny memory again. I pull onto solid ground and stop the engine.

"What are you doing?" demands Kora.

"Buying us some time," I say, and draw Mom's gun from its place at my hip.

In the cave, I'd been afraid to fire, afraid to bring more monsters down on our heads. Here, I have no such fears. Here, I need to stop this thing from following us. It killed the lion-worm back in the cave. I absolutely believe it can kill a single Zagreus hippo. Maybe if a whole pod came out to finish the kill, the odds would be different, but we can't count on that, and we can't count on the creature deciding that it would rather hunt here in the wetlands than follow us back to the colony. For whatever reason, these things like human prey.

The creature and the hippo are a roiling ball of limbs and terrible natural weaponry. One of the hippo's horns has broken off near the base; it's bleeding, which only enrages it more. Adult hippos aren't used to getting hurt. They aren't used to thinking that they *can* be hurt. It slams its head into the creature again and again, ripping and tearing with its terrible bony maw.

As for the creature, it slashes with all four limbs and with its terrible tail, clearly angling for a clean shot at the hippo's throat. The purpose of the second mouth is suddenly horrifically clear. If the creature can bite down just *once*, it won't need any leverage to rip the hippo's throat out: all it will need to do is let its second mouth snap forward and bite down. It can sever arteries without ever relaxing its grasp on the main bulk of the hippo.

It's efficient and elegant and I hate it. Breathing out, I line up the barrel of my mother's gun with the two roiling forms, trying to relax into my stance.

Shooting is one of those things that works better when you're not stressed or tense. Naturally, most of the time, if you need to shoot something, you're probably going to be at least a little bit uneasy. I can't quite forget that a miss will mean the creature shifts its attention away from the hippo and maybe comes after us again. But it's going to win. The hippo is the nastiest creature on Zagreus, and the creature is going to defeat it, rip it to shreds and leave it for the scavengers, and I can't let that happen. Not out of any desire to conserve the hippo—although they may be endangered someday, the Zagreus hippo has a perfectly stable population right now—but because I want this to be over. I want to get back to the colony and know that we're finally safe, that this is finally finished.

So I line up my shot, and I breathe out, and when the rolling of the two terrible beasts brings them into the right alignment, I pull the trigger.

The recoil is immense, slamming me against the seat and nearly ripping the gun out of my hand. It doesn't dislocate my shoulder—quite—but it feels as though it might as well have done so. The impact vibrates all the way down to my bones. I don't want to do that again.

I won't have to. The entire front of the creature's long, curving skull has been blown away, sending chunks of chitin and sprays of terrible fluids in all directions. The hippo bellows—but not in triumph, as I would have expected. It's bellowing in pain.

"Hold me up," commands Viola.

I lift her with my good hand—my right arm is so much dead-weight, and probably will be for the next several seconds—and turn her so she can see the creature topple gently onto its side. The hippo is shuddering, shaking its head like it thinks it can shake the pain away, and . . . smoking? I'm too far away to say for sure, but from here, it looks like the flesh on its skull is melting away, blistering and bubbling and coming off in chunks.

"Acid," says Viola firmly. "I suspected as much. We should get out of here. The rest of the hive will come looking for the one you just killed."

"Scent tracking?" I ask.

"I think so," she says. "Nothing else makes their movements make sense."

"What are you talking about?" demands Kora. "You—you killed it. That means we *won*. That means we can go home, and everything is going to be all right. Doesn't it?"

I don't like the rising edge of hysteria in her tone. It's jus-tified, absolutely so: I'd be hysterical too, if I thought I could afford to be. But something being justified doesn't mean that it's convenient.

"It would, if there were only one of the things," I say. Perfect ambush predators, adapted for virtually any biome, with knives for hands, secondary jaws tailored specifically for ripping out throats, and acid for blood? If there had only been one of them, I would have been planning the parade.

But there's never only one. Not when you're looking at this

sort of natural disaster. They had come to Zagreus through chance, with the resources they needed to start establishing their hive, and now that they were here, it was going to take a lot more than one girl with a gun to stop them.

"We have to go back to the cave."

Kora's voice is barely louder than a whisper. I tense my shoulders, not looking at her.

"We have to go *back*," she repeats. "Michel—"

"Saved our lives by being alive enough for his heartbeat to cover for ours, but that's it," I say. "He's past saving."

She looks at me, eyes wide and wounded. "You don't know that. We went back for your sister. Why can't we go back for my friend?"

"Because . . ." I take a deep breath. We shouldn't be doing this here, in sight of the collapsing horror that was pursuing us only minutes ago. We don't have *time*. We don't know where the others are, and we don't know how much of the creature's scent is on the ATV, and we don't know whether we're all about to die.

But my arm aches from the recoil of Mom's gun, and the ATV's engine needs to cool a little if I don't want it to overload and die, and I need to catch my breath. Please, just let me catch my breath.

"Do you know what an ovipositor is?" I ask.

Kora shakes her head, expression tight.

"It's . . . it's a thing some insects have. I mean, and some mammals, too, but only the ones in really *weird* biomes, we don't see many of them, they're pretty scary, and—"

"Olive, you're babbling," says Viola gently. "Take a breath."

I do. The air burns my throat. I didn't realize how much I've been screaming. "They're used by animals that don't gestate their young inside their own bodies. Animals that use the bodies of other creatures as sort of . . . giant living wombs."

Kora pales. "What are you saying?"

"Those splits on Michel's lips weren't from impact with the ground. They were from something forcing his mouth open long enough to put an egg inside of him. He's already dead. He was dead before we got there. His body just doesn't know it yet." I look at her sympathetically. "I'm sorry."

"But your mother . . ."

"I saw them," says Viola. We both look at her. It should be comic, talking to her severed head, with its ragged-edged stump and trailing wires. It's not. It's horrific. Everything about this is horrific. The world is never going to be normal again.

She can't turn her head, but she can move her eyes. She focuses on Kora, expression grave. "I saw what they did to our mother, and if Olivia says your friend Michel had the same splits in his lips, I know what they did to him. I'm sorry. He wasn't my friend. He tried to lock me out because of what I am, even though it wasn't something I had any control over, and he nearly got my sister killed, but that doesn't mean he deserves what happened to him. No one deserves that."

"*What* happened?" Kora lunges, snatches my sister's head out of my hands before I realize what's happening. She grasps Viola by the temples, fingers tangled in my sister's hair, and raises her to eye level, glaring. "You're a machine. I'm a human. You have to tell me what I want to know."

"Okay, well, that isn't how this works, and even if it *were* how this works normally, my parents were smart people and knew that if they had one daughter who did everything the usual way and one daughter who did whatever she was told, people would notice," says Viola. "I'm not going to tell you something I don't want to tell you just because you tell me to."

Kora blinks, looking like she didn't quite follow that sentence. I know I didn't. Then she takes one hand away from Viola's head and raises her other hand, like she's about to throw my sister into the weeds.

I grab her wrist. I don't hesitate. Kora turns to look at me, confused.

"What?" she asks.

"Give her back." My voice is low and dangerous. "Right now. Or you're walking to the colony."

Offense blossoms in her face like a terrible flower. "Are you serious?"

"Give me back my sister."

Kora hands Viola's head back to me and leans back in her seat, folding her arms sullenly across her chest. I tuck Viola securely between my knees, facing to the side, so she can see as I drive, and restart the ATV.

Kora doesn't say anything. It doesn't feel like there's anything to say.

19

BROKEN WALLS

WE'RE ALMOST ACROSS THE TAIGA,
almost back to the colony, when Kora says softly, "I'm sorry."

I glance at her, but I don't say anything. This apology is hers to give, not mine. I'm not going to interfere with it.

Oh, but she's beautiful. Even now, even with everything that's happened, I can't look at her and not see how beautiful she is. The pollen is still gilding her hair, snarled so deep in the curls and twists of it that it dusts her with golden light. It's all wiped off of her skin, leaving smooth brown exposed to the world. A few motes cling to her eyelashes. I want to kiss them away. I want to stop the ATV and put my arms around her and tell her that everything's fine, everything's going to be all right, forever, because we're here, all three of us; because we're going to get away.

"I don't . . ." She pauses, seems to assess her own words, starts again. "I don't understand biology the way you do. The way you both do. If you were willing to leave your own *mother* behind, there's no chance she was going to survive. There's no chance Michel was going to survive. You weren't being cruel. You were being . . . realistic."

She says the word like it's bitter, like it burns her mouth. I want to argue with her. I can't.

"They were already dead," I say. "They didn't know it yet, but they were, I promise you." As long as they don't wake up before their terrible cargo starts hatching, they won't suffer more than they already have. It's a small, cold comfort. It's the only comfort I've got. I only wish I felt like it would be a comfort to Kora.

"I shouldn't have . . . Viola, I'm sorry. I don't get to treat you like you're not a person. You're a person. I *know* you're a person. I was just angry, and lashing out, and it wasn't okay, and I promise I won't do it again."

"It's not your fault," says Viola. "Stress generates hormones that make humans weird." A note of wry, bitter amusement enters her voice. "I guess that's one area where I'm lucky. I don't have any hormones to mess with my thinking."

"You're a talking head," I say. "You're already weird."

Kora offers me a wavering smile. "Are we okay?" she asks.

I want to say no. She threatened to throw my sister—my *sister*—away. Viola's the only family I have left, and Kora was ready to dispose of her like so much trash. But Kora was also scared, and out of her depth, and lashing out. We're all out of our depth. If I refuse to forgive Kora for being frightened, I'll be the one lashing out. That's not fair. I don't want to do that. So I nod, and return her smile, as warmly as I can.

"We're okay," I say. "I mean, we still need to get to the transport, and get off this—"

The wall finally comes into view up ahead, and the rest of

the sentence dies in my mouth, turning to ashes that blow away with the wind. I stop the ATV. I have to. I'm not safe to continue driving.

There's a hole in the dome.

The gate we came through is still closed, but it doesn't matter, because there's a *hole* in the *dome*. Eight feet across, with irregular, melted edges, like something has burned through the supposedly unbreachable plastic.

Something with acid for blood, maybe. Something that already knew there was life beyond that barrier, life and hosts for its gestating young. Something fast, and hungry, and smart enough, in its own alien way, to figure out that all it had to do to get inside was create a weak spot where none had previously existed.

Kora clasps her hands over her mouth, making a thin whimpering sound. I wish I felt like I could do the same.

"We have to go in," I say.

She shakes her head, quick and violent.

"Kora. The creature I killed, it wasn't the only one out here. We're not safe out here." We won't be safe in there either, not with the hole in the dome making it absolutely clear that the colony has been violated, but that doesn't matter. Out here, we have an ATV with a limited amount of remaining fuel, our dwindling supply of ammunition, and my family's residence, which has already been attacked once. In there, we have the entire population of Zagreus.

These things are fast, efficient hunters, but there are guards in the colony. There are people with weapons. There are doors that lock and shutters made from the hulls of salvaged spacecraft. There's no way the creatures have been able to kill everyone in the colony. There's just no way.

And most importantly of all, in there, we have a way off this stinking planet. If we can reach our transport, we can *go*, we can take off and *go*, off to someplace where people will listen to our story, off to someplace where knives don't hunt under their own power.

We can leave this floating graveyard behind, and never look back. Not even for a second.

"This looks bad, but I'm sure the guards reacted fast enough." I'm lying. "I'm sure they were able to chase the creatures away with minimal loss of life." Lying, lying, lying. "There's no way those things could have overrun the colony that quickly."

But they overran the seastead, didn't they? And the caves, when we'd been there, had been so *empty*, like most of the creatures were somewhere else, doing something else—something important enough that they'd been willing to leave their gestating young virtually undefended. The hive is always more important than the individual with eusocial creatures like these. What would have been big enough, valuable enough, to lure them away from their burgeoning hive?

What, if not the resources they needed to expand at an exponential rate? I had a sudden, terrible feeling that I knew why the caves had been so empty—why getting into and out of them had been so easy, compared to what it could have been. Yes, we'd been forced to face two monsters, and kill one of them, but there was no way we could have escaped the notice of an entire hive. Not unless something had the rest of them distracted.

We're so close to the entrance that driving doesn't make much sense, and could put us in more danger than we're already in, if the creatures hear our engine approaching. If they're still here . . .

If they're still here, the only way we get away is by somehow sneaking past them. That means being as quiet as we possibly can. I disengage the last of the controls, and the ATV slips into silence, waiting for a command that's—hopefully—never going to come. It can rust here. It can rest here.

"Vi, I'm going to put you in my backpack," I say, moving her onto the seat beside me so that I can unhook it from my shoulders. "I need my hands free."

"I understand," she says, then grimaces. "I just tried to nod. I miss having shoulders, Olive. I miss having *hands*."

"Mom made sure I had the specs for your next body," I say. "You'll have hands again just as soon as we can get someplace that builds androids. The best hands money can buy."

"Well. Maybe not the *best* hands," says Viola. "I sort of like the ones I had." Then she sobers. "I can't help you anymore. I can't hold a gun or close a door. Please be careful. You're the only family I have left. I can't lose you, too."

"I'll be careful," I say, and pick her up.

She closes her eyes as I press a kiss to her forehead. It feels the way it's always felt. It feels warm, and real, and alive. If I pretend I'm just holding her cheeks, and that there's still a body below her neck, I can pretend the last day didn't happen.

Pretending never changes the world. It just leaves you helpless when the monsters come.

Viola keeps her eyes closed as I tuck her into my backpack and fasten the compartment, sliding it over my shoulders. I look to Kora. She offers me a small, wan smile.

"What," she says, "no kiss for me?"

So I lean over, and I kiss her.

Maybe it's a waste of time. Maybe we should be smarter than this, stronger than this; maybe we should be battle-hardened and ready to do whatever's necessary to survive. But I'm seventeen. Kora's seventeen. I'm scared, and from the way she's been looking at me, she's scared, too. This isn't the world we know. There are still supposed to be adults ready to protect us, people who can say "everything's going to be okay" in a voice that makes us believe, really believe that they can keep their promises.

We've lost that. We've lost *all* that, and it happened so fast that there wasn't even time to understand that it was happening until it was already too late. So I wrap my arms around her waist and I kiss her. I kiss the pollen off of her lips until they stop tasting like nothing, until they start tasting like salt and engine oil again. I kiss her until she presses herself against me and wraps her fingers through my hair, and if the world could stop right here, right now, that would be fine. We would be safe, imprisoned in a single crystal moment of absolute contentment.

But the world can't stop. The world never stops. Before I'm ready to let the moment go, it passes. Kora steps back, taking her hands off my shoulders and her mouth away from mine. The air between us feels suddenly, brutally cold.

"Are you ready?" she asks.

I'm not. I'll never be. "Yeah," I say, and nod. "Totally prime. You?"

"If we make it off this planet, I want to stay with you and Viola," she says. "Maybe forever. I want to be your girlfriend, and hold your hand, and sleep knowing you'll watch over me. Can we do that?"

This time, I nod in silence. I want what she's describing so much that it feels too big for my body to hold, like a secret that should never be spoken in the outside air.

She smiles, teeth white as stars in the gathering gloom. It'll be dark soon. We can't be here when it's dark. "Then yeah," she says. "I'm ready."

She draws the volt gun. I draw the gun I took from Mom, the one that might break my wrists if I fire it more than once in quick succession. It makes me feel small. It makes me feel safe. I don't understand how both those things can be true at the same time, but they are. They are.

Side by side, with Viola in the bag on my back, we walk toward the closed colony gate. The hole in the dome is a silent accusation above us. We didn't try hard enough to sound the alarm. We didn't make enough of a fuss.

But what were we supposed to do, really? Everyone who'd been at the residence when Paul and my mother were taken had seen as much of the creatures as Kora and me—they knew as much as we did when we reached the colony gates. They'd learned even more in the seconds that followed, when Michel and Viola were taken. Why was it my responsibility to tell people what was happening? Why was it Kora's?

And if it was somehow Kora's, why wasn't it enough that she'd gone to her mother, and told *her* what was happening? Kora's mother was the planetary governor. It was her responsibility to take care of these people. Did she?

The answer is on the other side of the door. When we reach it, Kora produces her mother's access card and steps anxiously forward. I swing my gun into position, ready to blow the head off of anything that comes looming out of the shadows to attack her. She glances at me. I nod.

She swipes the card, and the door opens on a slaughterhouse.

For a terribly long moment we both stand frozen, trying to process what our eyes are telling us—trying to *understand*. We can't understand. This is too much for understanding. Kora gets paler and paler, until it seems like there's no blood left in her body, until her normally warm brown cheeks are the color of dust gathering in the corners of an unswept room. I feel faint. The sound of my heart is like a drumbeat pounding in my ears, and it's so *loud* that I'm sure the creatures that did this must be able to hear it, must be able to follow it back to me.

Kora takes a step back. I take a step forward to meet her. There's no other way left for me to go.

There's blood everywhere. On the walls, on the ground, painting everything in the same unrelenting shade of dull rusty matte. The people of Zagreus have always seemed to hold this ideal of sameness, and now they finally have it, because once something is covered in blood, it looks like everything else that's been covered in blood. They have finally found homogeny.

I guess I should be proud of them. All I can really feel is sick to my stomach, and relieved that Viola doesn't have to see this. She saw what happened in the cave. We didn't. I can spare her from this, if she can spare me from that. We're sisters. We protect each other.

I take another step toward the open door. Kora doesn't move. I look back at her and she shakes her head, silent, shivering. She looks like she's on the verge of passing out.

I want to grab her, to yell, to tell her that we don't have time to waste. I don't do any of those things. I move back a step, until we're close together once again, and say softly, "You can't stay here, Kora. You have to come with me."

"No." She shakes her head again, harder this time, so that her hair slaps against my cheek. "I can't. Do you see . . . I can't. We can't go in there. It's death in there."

"It's death out here." If we're outside when the suns finish going down, we might as well give up. "They weren't in the cave because they were at the colony. So they're probably not at the colony anymore, right? They're probably on their way back to the cave. This is the closest it's going to come to being safe here. We have to get to the transport. We have to get off this planet."

"My mother." She gasps as she looks at me, sudden comprehension in her eyes. "Our residence has the best locks in the whole colony. My mother—she's probably there, she probably let refugees in. Please, we have to go and get her. Your ship can take one more, right?"

I don't want to point out that if her mother has allowed refugees into their residence, she probably won't be willing—or able—to leave them behind. My family's transport can handle six passengers if we're willing to be cramped. That's a hard stop, although I guess Viola technically doesn't count right now, since she doesn't weigh as much as she usually does. So fine: maybe we could take Kora's mother *and* three of the colonists . . . but that's it. That's where the space runs out.

And what's going to stop Kora's mom from deciding that an off-world teenager whose parents failed to prevent a biological disaster doesn't need a functional transport as much as she does? She could leave me and Viola behind to face the creatures, all alone, last denizens of an involuntary graveyard.

It's a chilling, if improbable, thought, and I know I'm dwelling on it because it covers up the much greater possibility that she'll grab hold of Kora and say that no, her daughter can't leave with us; her daughter belongs with her, in a Zagreus-owned transport, surrounded by good colonists who would never dream of running if it weren't the only way. I don't want to lose Kora after everything we've been through. I'm pretty sure surviving a dark cave filled with unknown, unknowable monsters is even better than agreeing to go steady.

I take a breath.

I force a smile.

"Let's go get your mom," I say, and this time when I move toward the opening in the wall, she moves with me, toward that terrible bloody landscape, until we can smell it, the bittersweet reek of blood left to dry in the fading sunlight, and something more, something sharper and crueler and less familiar.

Acid. Not just the kind that eats through walls: the kind ants, Earth ants, use to keep track of the rest of the colony. When Viola and I were little kids, our dad set up an ant farm for us, as part of his ongoing campaign to get us interested in the natural world—Earth first, since that's where humans come from, and then the rest of the universe, in all its strange and complicated and weirdly predictable diversity.

Life seeks out forms that work. That's why we find beetles, crabs, skeletons, skins, everywhere we go. There are exceptions—even back on Earth, there are almost no absolute rules that can be applied to every single living thing—but once evolution finds something functional and easily replicated, it replicates it over and over again, from one side of the universe to the other.

Eusocial insects frequently organize the colony by laying down scent trails. They use special acids and pheromones, things the rest of the colony will be able to pick up on and understand. The smell in the air isn't *exactly* like the smell we used to pick up from our ant farm, but it's close enough to be another piece of convergent evolution, another piece of the puzzle snapping into place.

The creature that followed the ATV here in the first place left a scent trail to mark where it was going, and then it came back to the hive with proof that there was food to be found in the colony, good food, food suitable for the incubation of its young. We had drawn a straight line from the residence to the colony, a line that might as well have been a flashing sign reading "come and get it, the buffet is open."

I can't be sorry about that. I was trying to save us. I did the best I could with what I had. But I look at the blank, stricken expression on Kora's face, and I hope that she never figures out what I just figured out. I hope she never blames herself.

The streets are bathed in blood, and the walls are red and sticky, but there are surprisingly few bodies, at least out in the open. The creatures must have carried them away. I wonder how many they were able to take alive. How many of the colonists are in the caves where my mother died, stuck to the walls and waiting for their own lives to come to a horrifying, unheralded end?

The ground feels soft and spongy under my feet. I don't look down. I *won't* look down. If I don't acknowledge what I'm stepping in, it won't count, and I won't have to think about it.

Kora shakes as we walk, a fine, unceasing tremor that seems to start at the center of her belly and radiate out from there, pulling her entire body into the motion.

Then we come around a corner, and Alisa is there, gore matting her hair down to her scalp, tracing the planes of her cheeks. Her eyes are so wide that I can see the white all the way around her irises, making her seem like something out of a children's horror show, some terrible monster from the depths of a haunted space station or a forgotten colony. But she's not a monster. She's a girl, she's only a girl, and the monsters aren't part of any story. The monsters are real.

There's a gun in her hands. I recognize it as Rockwell's side-arm. Every other time I've seen it, it's been strapped securely to the guard's hip, more for show than anything else. It's not for show now. Alisa has her fingers wrapped securely around the grip, one hooked into the trigger, and it's all I can do not to step back immediately.

"Alisa!" Kora sounds overjoyed. That's good. Kora also sounds very loud. That's bad. Her voice bounces off the walls, a beacon telling anything left in the colony where we are and that we're ready to be taken. "You're okay!"

Alisa's eyes don't quite focus as she turns her face toward Kora. The urge to run is even stronger now.

"Okay?" she says, voice oddly disconnected, like she's speaking from a very long way away. "I'm okay? They took my fathers. Both of them. We were in the front room, we were getting ready to run for the transports, and then the wall wasn't there anymore, and there were two of those . . . those *things*, and then the things were gone, and my fathers were gone, and I was alone, and I'm okay? Because none of this blood is mine, I'm okay?"

"Alisa . . ." Kora sounds horrified. It's the only reasonable response. "I'm so sorry. I'm so—that should never have happened to you. We're on our way to get my mother, and then we're leaving. We're leaving the planet. You can come with us."

I think I manage not to react to Kora offering Alisa space in my family's transport like it's nothing. Maybe it's a good thing. If there are three of us, plus Viola, and we tell Kora's mother that the transport can only hold six, maybe she'll be able to leave the refugees behind. Or maybe they have their own transports. Most of the colonists have given their private vessels to the colony for disassembly and reuse, but they had the shuttles they sent up to the survey ship, they have the transports they use to reach nearby ships for trading and medical supplies. There must be more private transports on this planet than just ours. There have to be.

Maybe we can all get away from here safely, and never need to look back at what this world has become.

"Come with you?" Alisa blinks, looking briefly, heartbreakingly confused. "Why would I want to come with you? This is my *home*. I was born here. I was the third baby born in this colony. My dads have the certificate from the governor framed and on our kitchen wall. It proves this is my homeworld, not anyplace else in the whole universe. Zagreus is in my blood. I'm not going to go anywhere."

"Alisa . . ." Kora takes a step forward, one hand outstretched in a beckoning gesture. It would be sweet, if not for the fact that everything around us is covered in blood, the fact that *Alisa* is covered in blood. "You know you can't stay here. It isn't safe anymore."

"Whose fault is that?" Alisa moves surprisingly quickly, and suddenly the gun in her hands is aimed directly at me. Her hands are shaking, but it doesn't matter: at this range, she only has to pull the trigger. A shot to the gut will be just as deadly as one to the forehead. "Your parents were supposed to make sure nothing like this happened here. We paid them good money to make sure nothing like this happened here. You were supposed to *protect us*."

She snarls her final words like an accusation, like a condemnation, and I realize two things at the same time. First, that seeing her parents taken by the creatures has broken her in a way that I can almost understand, having seen my own parents die. She's lost and she's scared and she's lashing out, and it's my bad luck that she managed to get her hands on a gun before we ran into her.

Second, that there's no way we can take her with us. Even assuming she *can* be talked down from her current state of shock and rage and disassociated horror, which I doubt, she's looking at me like I'm the monster here, like I am singularly and solely responsible for everything that's happened.

"My parents didn't have anything to do with purchasing the survey ship where the creatures were supposed to have been contained for research purposes," I say. "That decision was made by the colonial government. I promise, if they had been consulted, my parents would have recommended against it." Biosecurity is not a toy.

"Really? Or did they set this whole thing up?" Her voice is getting steadily louder, peaking every few words, until I flinch and glance at the shadows around us, looking for signs that something is lurking there, dark and terrible and preparing to attack. "Who *really* paid you to come here? Who *really* thought they could get away with planting a pair of android spies in our colony?"

"A pair of—what?"

Kora's eyes widen. I see her realize what's about to happen a bare instant before I do, and then she's rushing at Alisa, grabbing the other girl by the wrists and yanking her arms up, a bare second before the gun goes off. The bullet ricochets off the remaining dome, and I can't decide whether it's stupid that the guards carry actual projectile weapons or very, very smart, since energy weapons could have been even more dangerous in this enclosed space.

Reality crashes over me like a wave. Alisa tried to shoot me. Alisa tried to shoot me and, if Kora hadn't interfered, she would have succeeded. I rush forward, snatching the gun out of her suddenly limp hands before she can react.

"What are you, stupid?" I demand. "Those things are still out there!"

"The things are in here," she wails. "You're not a real person, you're a trick, you're a trap, just like your sister was a trap, you brought them and now my fathers are dead, now everyone is dead, and we're dead, too, you just can't see it yet. We're dead too."

She yanks herself free of Kora's grasp and turns, running away into the empty, bloody streets. We watch her go, and neither of us says anything. I wonder if Kora shares my guilty relief at the knowledge that when the creatures come for Alisa, she won't be anywhere near us.

I don't ask. I just shove my newly acquired weapon into my belt, and take Kora's hand, and let her lead me deeper into the colony.

20

BROKEN HOMES

THE SCENE IS THE SAME EVERY-
where we turn: broken windows, broken doors, and blood, so
much blood that it seems almost ridiculous, like this is some sort
of coordinated, colony-wide prank. No bodies. No intact bodies,
anyway: there's the occasional *piece* of what used to be a person, a
hand or a foot or, in one case, an entire torso, devoid of any identi-
fying marks. Or limbs. The creatures may prefer to take their prey
intact and alive, but when they can't, they're brutally thorough.

Kora keeps hold of my hand as we walk, squeezing so hard
that I'm afraid I'll lose circulation. I should pull away. I need to
be able to protect us, and that means I need to be able to feel my
fingers. I don't do anything of the sort. Protecting her matters
just as much right now, and part of how I do that is by shielding
her from the worst of what's around us.

Viola hasn't said a word since I shoved her into my backpack.
I don't know whether that's a good thing or not. I don't want to

treat her like she's less real now that I know she's not flesh and blood—but she can't do anything to help us get through this, and it's easier if I don't dwell on the fact that my sister is depending on me even more than Kora is. At least Kora can run if something happens to me. Viola is completely at my mercy.

We don't see anyone other than Alisa. Maybe she's the only survivor, or maybe she's just the only survivor so shattered by what's happened here that she can't bring herself to stay inside. It doesn't matter. She's not going to trust anyone who offers to help her, and she's not going to stay quiet, and she's going to die here, in this blood-drenched slaughtering ground that used to be her home. There's nothing we can do.

I should feel guilty about that. I don't. I'm still alive. Kora is still alive. Viola is still operational, or whatever the right word is when you're talking about an android. Everything else is secondary.

When we reach the stairs leading to the residence Kora shares with her mother, she surges forward, so eager to go home that she actually drags me for a few feet before I can dig my heels into the road and stop us. She's bigger than I am. Not hugely so, but enough that for a moment, I wonder whether I can stop her, or whether she's just going to haul me up the stairs like so much deadweight.

She does stop, though, and turns to look at me, bewildered. "We're here," she says. She still has the sense to keep her voice low. I appreciate that. The sky outside the dome is dark. The streetlights are coming on, automatically, but half of them are splattered with drying blood, and the light they cast is lurid and foul.

"I know," I say. "We need to be careful. You need to let me go first." I'm the better shot, and more importantly, I'm not going to freeze if we find her mother's body at the top of those stairs. I'll still be able to react to any other threat that might be present. Right here, right now, that feels like it matters more than anything else.

Kora looks like she's going to argue. Then she catches herself, seeing the sense of what I'm saying, and offers me a small, unhappy nod. "Hurry," she says.

So I hurry.

The stairs are splashed here and there with blood, but it's nowhere near as thick or as plentiful as it is in the streets: one person, maybe two, bled out here. That shouldn't be a good sign. Under the circumstances, it's the best we could have hoped for. Even better, if I'm reading the direction of the splatter correctly, the people were running *up* the stairs when they were attacked, fleeing from something in the streets below.

A scenario is starting to occur to me, a beautiful, simple scenario that ends with us finding Kora's mother safe and sound and tucked into some quiet corner of her residence, frightened and heartbroken over the damage to the colony she dedicated her life to, but alive. It's a child's idea of a happy ending, and I cling to it all the way to the door that should separate the public stairway from the private one.

The door is broken.

The door is *shattered*, splintered off of its hinges by some titanic force, and the pieces that remain look strangely melted, like something caustic was used to weaken them. Behind me, Kora makes a soft whimpering noise. I don't try to shush her. I'd be doing the same thing if this was the approach to my home, if we were walking toward my mother.

The second door—the door to the actual residence—is intact,

and I have a momentary flare of hope before I realize that it isn't quite closed; it's standing ajar. I take a deep breath. There's no way I can convince Kora to turn back, not when we're this close to finding out what happened. There's no way I can even ask her to. Maybe we're going to die here, but if we do, we'll die knowing we did everything we could.

I push the door open.

There's a cocoon on the wall.

It's the first one we've seen here, and for a moment, I just stare at it, unable to quite comprehend. It looks like the cocoons we saw in the caves—but why should Kora's mother be so special? Why would she be the only one they did this to?

The answer, of course, is that she isn't, and she wasn't. This is the only private home we've entered. There could be cocoons all over the colony, each with its own precious, predatory cargo, all of them just waiting to hatch.

"Mama!" Kora shoves past me, running into the residence, heading straight for the cocoon on the wall. She begins to beat her hands against the hard, resinous surface of the thing, already starting to sob.

I follow more slowly. I want to tell her to stop. I don't. I *can't*.

But the closer I get, the more I can see—like the tears in her mother's lips, and the cuts at the corners of her mouth. She's not being saved to eat later. She's being saved because something is already eating her.

"We can't stay here," I whisper.

Kora doesn't hear me. Kora doesn't *want* to hear me. She's turning away from her mother's motionless form, racing for the kitchen, where she begins yanking drawers open and dumping their contents onto the floor.

"Kora, we can't stay here," I say, louder.

The cocoons in the cave, those were the beginning. Those were hidden in a safe place, a place that could be defended and claimed, but that would never make a perfect hive. It was too low, too dark, too subject to random attacks by lion-worms and other native predators. The creatures are terrifying. They can kill anything that comes for them. But that doesn't mean they won't have the drive to defend their young, to find the best possible place to keep their offspring and their incubators safe.

The colony will make a magnificent hive.

I don't know whether these things are builders—being able to extrude a fast-hardening foam and glue your incubators to things isn't "building" so much as it's "one more horrifying piece of a horrifying reproductive strategy." If they are, the colony will give them a frame to build *on*, with its lattices of steel and hardened glass and its ready-made chambers. The presence of people must seem like a welcome gift: here's your new den, and look, we put a bassinet inside it, waiting for your use. If they're not builders, they can just use the place as it is right now. Zagreus will be home to a city of monsters, a civilization of knives, and it will never belong to humanity ever again.

Kora has what she was looking for, some kind of heated knife that vibrates in her hand. It's probably intended to cut roasts and other large family dinners, and I can't imagine it got much use with just her and her mother living here. I step back as she runs at the cocoon, and I want to interfere, and I can't. I just can't.

I should leave. I should choose myself and my sister over this girl who kisses me like it's an interrogation, whose lips always taste like engine oil, who's just as much an orphan as I am. I should head for the transport before she brings the creatures down on our heads, letting her be the distraction that gets me safely off this doomed planet. I don't move. I stand and watch as she hacks chunks of cocoon away with her stolen kitchen knife, and all I can think is that this isn't fair.

We didn't deserve this. Neither did Alisa, or Paul, or even Michel. We'll be adults soon, but we're not there yet, and we didn't have any say in the choices that brought the monsters to our doors. This is a terrible fairy tale, a story told to children to make them behave. Only fairy tales were never this bloody, and there's not going to be any happy ending, and if there's a moral, it's something horrible, like "sometimes your parents will make mistakes, and then you'll have to pay for them, in blood and bone and viscera."

The bills always come due, and there's no way to get out of making good. There's just no way.

"Olivia, help me!" Kora has managed to slice away more of the cocoon than I would have thought possible, letting it fall to the floor in cauterized chunks. Her mother is still suspended, but there's a chance we could break her free now.

"What do you want me to do?"

"Catch her." She goes back to hacking. I don't ask her for the knife. If she slips and hurts her mom, she may never forgive herself, but at least she can try. If I slip and hurt her mom, she'll never be able to look at me again.

This is all too complicated. I should have stayed home with Viola, taken my classes over the network, and never tried to put down roots. I should never have fallen for Kora, never learned how soft her hair is or how nice her skin smells. Maybe then I wouldn't be standing here, instead of running for the transport as fast as my legs can carry me.

Or maybe I'd already be dead, and Viola would be running down in that cave, sitting at my feet instead of at our mother's. You can't live in might have been, maybe, or almost. Those will eat you alive as surely as a monster out of space.

So I move where Kora wants me to move, and I put out my hands, arms spread wide, and when she slices away the last sliver of cocoon, her mother falls against me, surprisingly light and surprisingly heavy at the same time. She's completely limp, but I can feel her breathing; she's still alive.

This would be so much kinder if she weren't.

Kora drops the knife and hurries to help me lower her mother to the ground, the two of us keeping her propped into a sitting position as Kora rubs her back and whispers, over and over again, "Please, Mama, please. Please, wake up. Please, Mama, please."

It's a prayer masquerading as a plea, and it almost exactly matches the rhythm of the heartbeat I can feel pulsing in Delia Burton's throat. It's weak and too fast, but it's *there*.

Even as the thought forms, Delia gasps and opens her eyes, clutching wildly at Kora's arm as she looks around the residence, clearly terrified.

"Mama!" Kora slings both arms around her mother, holding her tight, making no effort to hide her joy. "You're all right!"

No. She's not.

As if she could read my mind, Delia makes a wordless sound of dismay and shoves Kora away, saying, in a raspy, raw-throated voice, "No. I'm not. What are you doing here? I thought you were already gone. I thought—"

She glances at me, blame and needy hope both naked in her eyes. She knows something's wrong. She may not know exactly what it is—oh, I hope she doesn't know what it is, hope she can't

258

feel herself being eaten alive from the inside—but she knows she's not right.

"I thought you and Olivia were going to get off this planet," she says. "You were supposed to be gone."

"Mama, what happened?" asks Kora. "Where is everyone?"

Delia laughs, low and bitter and broken. Then she coughs, and that's somehow worse, because when she coughs, I can hear the bubbling sound of all the things that have been ripped and ruptured in her throat. She's dead. She's dead, and she knows it, and I know it, and Kora's the only one who doesn't know, and yet somehow, I'm still a little jealous. Kora gets to see her mother one last time.

"There is no 'everyone,'" says Delia. "They're all gone. You may be the last people alive on this planet."

She doesn't include herself. She knows, she knows, and if this can get worse without something actually crashing through the window to kill us all, I don't know how.

"We have a transport," says Kora. "I mean, Olivia has a transport. I mean—we're leaving, Mama, all of us. We're all leaving. Right, Olivia?"

My mouth moves soundlessly. I can't speak. I want to tell her all the reasons this isn't going to happen, but I can't. She's holding on to her mother like a lifeline, and telling her the truth will break her heart.

Telling her a lie will kill her. I'm only seventeen. I shouldn't have to make these choices.

"I can't listen to this anymore," says Viola, voice only slightly muffled by the fabric of my bag. "Olive, I need you to take me out of here."

"What in the world . . . ?" asks Delia.

I shrug out of my backpack, open the main flap, and withdraw my sister's head. It doesn't look as strange to me as it did at first. Give me enough time and maybe it won't look strange at all, and having a sister who fits in my bag will be perfectly normal.

"Hi," says Viola.

Delia blinks, slowly. Then, with the poise that saw her become a colonial administrator, responsible for the lives of almost five thousand colonists, she says, "Hello."

"We didn't get to meet while I had a body; I'm Viola Shipp," says Viola.

"I know who you are." Delia looks tired. One hand is resting on her stomach, rubbing in small, concentric circles, like a pregnant woman trying to relieve the pressure on her bladder. I wonder if she's aware she's doing it.

Somehow, I don't think she is.

"Good. That makes this easier." Viola looks to Kora. I shift the angle of her head slightly, allowing her to fully face the other girl. Okay. That part's still sort of weird. "Kora, I'm sorry, but your mother can't come on the transport with us."

Kora's eyes widen. "You take that back. You don't get to say that. You don't get to *decide*. She's alive, and she's coming with us, and it's not up to you."

"No," I say softly. "It's up to me, and Viola's right. Your mother can't come."

I would have faced a hundred monsters—a thousand—before I voluntarily put that look on Kora's face.

"What?" She sounds utterly, profoundly betrayed. "Why would you say that?"

"Because one of those *things* is inside me," says Delia. She looks down at her hand, resting on her perfectly flat stomach, and grimaces. "It's not ready to come out yet, to hatch or be born or whatever the term is for having a creature use your body like this. I don't think it's going to be gentle when it does. It wasn't gentle going in."

"Mama," Kora whispers.

"The creatures, whatever they are, they're closer to insects than anything else," says Viola. "Insects with armor and blades for hands and acid for blood. I don't want to see the rest of what lives on the planet where they evolved. A lot of insects—especially predatory insects, whose young tend to have a high metabolic drive—will use the bodies of other things to hatch their eggs and incubate their larvae. I told you this, remember?"

Kora looks at her, blankly. Delia nods. It's a small gesture. It's impossible not to read the relief that it contains. Yes, Kora knew all this, but for Delia, this is the first time she's hearing it, and there's comfort in facts. Cold comfort, to be sure, especially in a situation like this one, where every word Viola says is essentially "you are going to die," but even cold comfort counts.

"There's one of them inside me, honey," says Delia, drawing Kora's attention back to her. "Those things came here, and they killed the people they couldn't capture, and the people they *could* capture, they . . . they stuck us to the wall and brought these terrible *things*, like flowers, like flowers made of living meat and bone, and when they blossomed . . ."

She shudders, turning her face aside, and touches her stomach again.

"I'm already dead," she says softly. "You have to go, and you have to go now. I don't want you to see the way this ends. I don't want the thing that's feeding off my body to see *you*. I'm so sorry, sweetheart, I'm so, so sorry. I was greedy and I was foolish and it's only fair that I should pay the price for that, but there's no reason for any portion of that bill to fall to you. This isn't the way things were supposed to go."

"Mama," gasps Kora, tears running down her cheeks. She grabs for Delia.

Delia pushes her away, gently but firmly. "No," she says. "*Go*. Leave me here, and let me die knowing that you got away. That's the only thing you can do for me now, and it's enough, baby, it's so much more than enough. Run. Run, and never blame yourself for what happened here. If there's anyone at fault, it's me. I love you. Run."

She sounds so much like my mother that I have to look away. Kora sobs, and I know they must be embracing, mother and daughter clinging to each other for the last time. I look down at Viola, my hands cradling her cheeks.

"I need to put you back in the bag now," I say softly.

"I know," she says, and smiles, somehow looking more untouched than should be possible, given that she doesn't have a body anymore. "We're almost out of here. It's going to be fine, you'll see. We're going to get to the ship, and we're going to be *fine*."

Tempting fate is never a good idea.

That's when the floor explodes.

21

ADAPTATION

IT'S NOT A LITERAL EXPLOSION, although it feels that way in the moment. Chunks of masonry and artificial wood fly everywhere, driven upward by the force of the impact. Kora screams, clinging to her mother as the beast breaks through the floor between us.

"Oh, *crap*," says Viola, and she speaks for everyone in this room, and I can't stop staring.

It's definitely one of the creatures that have been chasing us across Zagreus, and it isn't at the same time. It's *wrong*.

Its head is still a long curve of black chitin, featureless and awful, but its jaws aren't blunt, toothy things anymore. Instead, they push out into a beak, and when it opens its mouth and hisses, the second mouth that emerges for a moment is like a terrible serrated flower, cutting surface upon cutting surface upon cutting surface. It looks like it could gnaw through the foundations of the world.

It's larger than the others, with a thicker body, a shorter neck. Its arms are as long as the rest, with clawed hands prepared to rip and slice, but below them waves row after row of golden cilia. It looks like one of the creatures somehow successfully melded with a lion-worm.

That's impossible. Even if they were genetically compatible—which they're not; the lion-worms are virtually mammalian, and the creatures secrete an acid powerful enough to dissolve glass and steel; there's no way their biology could blend—there hasn't been *time*. There's no way they could have mated, reproduced, and raised an offspring to this size in the time they've had available to them.

But somehow, they have. The proof is in front of me, roaring its terrible roar, pulling itself up through the floor.

"*Kora!*" I scream. "Get *back!*"

Delia should be safe. She's not in her cocoon, but she's gestating one of those creatures in her abdomen. They won't attack their own young. That would be reproductively unsound.

The creature lunges toward Kora. Delia responds by shoving her daughter away from the creature's clashing jaws, grabbing a gun from the rubble of the cocoon. I realize with a pang that it's Rockwell's gun, the one I took from Alisa.

Delia lines up the gun on the creature's head, aiming for the place where the eyes *should* be, and she fires, again and again, cracking the chitin without breaking it. That, alone, is horrifying.

The creature howls in fury, the sound filled with strange, terrible harmonics that make my skin crawl until it feels like it's going to rip right off of my body. Then it lunges for Delia. Delia, who has another creature growing inside her, Delia, who is already dead. Delia, who should be safe.

It grabs her head in its jaws and her hips in its claws and it tears her in half like she's nothing, like she's a discarded flimsy bound for the recycle bin. Kora screams as her mother's blood drenches her in a wet wave. I shove Viola's head back into my bag, not bothering to zip it as I sling it over my shoulder and run across the room to grab Kora's wet, wildly waving hand.

Delia is still thrashing, and that seems to be enough to keep the creature's attention on her, at least for the moment. Something pale and broken and not yet ready to survive slides out of the hole where her midsection used to be. The creature, unheeding, steps on it, and it splatters, yellowish goo like sticky paste spraying everywhere and beginning to eat through the floor and Delia's flesh and everything as soon as it makes contact. More acid.

Kora is wailing, the sound high and shrill and unrelenting. I pull harder, until she staggers to her feet, letting me haul her toward the door.

"Mama," she gasps. "Mama."

"She's gone, she's gone, it's over," I chant, rapid-fire, and keep pulling her until she gets her feet under herself and starts moving under her own power. That's how we make it to the door, and out onto the landing, with the sound of the creature ripping her mother apart still echoing in our ears.

That *thing*, it was like a mixture of the creatures from the shuttle and the lion-worms. I think of the lion-worm we saw outside the cave, the one that looked like it had burst from the inside out. Is it possible that their eggs or embryos or whatever they are can somehow *take on* attributes from the non-creature parent? Will the ones that hatch from the colonists be smarter, or more dexterous? It's a horrifying thought. We don't need these things to *improve*.

But maybe that's why the creature we just saw was willing to kill Delia despite the fact that she was being used as an incubator. It didn't recognize the infant inside her as a member of the same species. For a moment—just a moment—I allow myself the fantasy of the creatures going to war against themselves, the two breeds plummeting toward a mutual extinction. I don't allow the image, pleasant as it is, to slow me down, because I know it's just that: a fantasy. If that thing *is* a blend of the creatures and the lion-worms, clearly something about their biology allows them to harvest DNA from other life-forms, probably in the pursuit of making themselves over into better predators, better suited for the worlds they've come to devour. There may be some initial hitches in the process, but it has to settle out eventually, or it wouldn't happen.

These things are too efficient, too good at filling their evolutionary niche, to go around holding on to an adaptation that doesn't benefit them.

We run down the stairs, and Kora weeps silently the whole way, tears running down her cheeks and snot running over her upper lip. I want to comfort her. We can't afford the time. We have to run and keep running, away from the ripping, tearing sounds still coming from her residence, which is never going to be home to her again.

We speed up once we're through the door and back outside. There's no telling how many more creatures might be here, patrolling, hunting for survivors like Alisa—although I don't think there are many, if there are *any* by this point. Alisa was an aberration, like the antelope that walks through the middle of a pride of lions without being taken down. Even prey species can get cocky when they start to think of themselves as somehow inexplicably invulnerable.

If she's not dead already, she will be soon. I haven't seen any signs of other humans. There are probably survivors, but they're probably all like Delia, silently affixed to the walls, waiting to die. This is a killing field now. The best thing we can do is get away.

We run until we reach the bottom of the stairs, and then we run across the street, past the first three turnoffs, to a small, artificially forested cul-de-sac ringed in old Earth trees. There isn't much blood here, maybe because most people don't like to come here. The Earth natives find it too much of a reminder of everything they've lost, while the Zagreus-born generation can't understand why their parents bothered to bring such funny-looking plants across the great vastness of space. We always forget where we came from, if given enough time. That's part of how we adapt. It's part of how we *survive*.

We stop in the shadow of the trees, both panting, and I put my hand on the grip of Mom's gun as Kora sinks slowly to her knees, covering her face with her hands. We can't stay here. This isn't any safer than anyplace else in the colony. If I don't give her a moment to grieve, she's going to start screaming, and then we'll both die. This is practicality in mercy's clothes, and it's the only thing I have to offer her. At least for right now, there's nothing else that I can do.

"Olive." Viola's voice is low, flat, and pitched barely loud enough for me to hear it. "I need to talk to you."

My backpack is only slung over one shoulder; I'm lucky I didn't lose her during our flight. The thought turns my stomach as I shrug out of the bag and swing it around in front of me.

My sister looks up at me from the nest of supplies, blue eyes wide and somewhat pained. The reason becomes apparent when she speaks.

"You have to leave me here," she says.

"What?" My voice comes out louder than I intended. I swallow, hard, and follow it up with a whispered, "What? You're not—I'm not going to leave you behind, Vi. We're almost in the clear. All we have to do is get to the ship and we're free. We can leave. You and me. Shipp sisters forever."

And Kora, who is still crying, hands still covering her face, shoulders shaking like the world is crumbling around her, which it is, in a very real way. She watched her mother die. That breaks something that never heals.

I should know.

"Back in the cave, when you called the lion-worm to fight the creature," says Viola. "Some of the pheromones got on my skin, in my circuitry. Olive, I think that creature just now came because it has enough lion-worm in it to follow the scent. It thought it was chasing prey. It *was* chasing prey, because you, and Kora—don't you see? This is where you leave me behind to save yourself. I'll attract the thing to me, and you'll have more time to get away. This is how I save you." She smiles, thin and pained and terrified. She's a head without a body, she's an orphan as much as I am, and she's still worried about saving me.

I have the best sister in the universe.

"No," I say. "We save each other, remember? That's how this is supposed to work, now and forever and always. I'm not leaving you."

"You *have* to." Viola looks at me gravely, smile fading. "If you don't leave me, that thing, and any others like it, will keep following the scent. You shouldn't even be standing here. You should already be running. I'm not worth it."

"Not worth—you're my *sister*."

"I'm your sister, and there's a backup of my program on the

transport." She grimaces. "I'll lose everything that happened here on Zagreus, but you'll be able to bring me back, if you want to."

Mom and Dad don't have that option. They're gone, forever. I stare at Viola, trying to find the words to tell her how offensive this idea is, and how unfair. I'm not going to save myself at her expense.

Kora rises, cheeks still wet with tears, and moves to stand next to me, so she can look down into the open bag. Viola's eyes dart to her, studying the puffy, tear-streaked lines of her face. Then she relaxes, and actually offers Kora a smile.

I know that smile. It's her "I'm going to get away with something" smile, the one she uses when she wants our parents to let us stay up late, or let her order some technically restricted piece of media or information file. I've been protecting myself against the consequences of that smile for my entire life.

"You understand why it's essential to leave me here, don't you?" she asks. "I'm a liability. I can't fight. I can't help you escape. I'm deadweight—and worse, I'm deadweight that's going to attract monsters to your location. Tell Olivia to leave me. She'll listen to you."

I don't have time to get mad at my sister for thinking I'll prioritize my girlfriend over her, because Kora is already shaking her head, a firm negative that only gets firmer when she opens her mouth.

"We're not leaving you," she says. "There is *no way* we're leaving you. Olivia, do you have any more of that pollen?"

I blink at her. "What?"

"If the thing is tracking Viola by scent, we cover her in the pollen that makes it impossible to smell us. Easy. Right?"

"Maybe," I say carefully. "I mean, it might work. I don't know whether it does, and it doesn't matter, because I don't have any more. We used it all."

"Oh." Kora's face falls. Then she shrugs. "Doesn't matter. We're all orphans now, Viola, and we went too far to get you back. I'm not leaving you. I'm not telling Olivia to leave you. We get away together, or we don't get away."

I want to put my arms around her, to hold her until it feels like there's nothing left between us. I want to kiss her until I find that engine oil taste under the sweat and the fear and the blood, and then I want to keep kissing her, maybe forever. I haven't decided yet. But there isn't time, there isn't time for any of that, so I just offer her a thankful smile before turning my attention back to Viola.

"We head for the launch, and we get in our transport, and we go," I say. "The three of us. We're all that's left of Zagreus, and we're going to make sure people know what happened here. People *have* to know."

This isn't just a matter of biosecurity. This is a matter of survival, maybe for the entire human race. That feels like a big way of putting it, but . . .

These things can survive in conditions that would kill almost anything, can survive *reentry* without it noticeably slowing them down. They're fast and they're hungry and without an accurate count of how many were on that first shuttle, I can't even begin to guess at their reproductive rate, but it's more than high enough to constitute a threat to even the most advanced colonies. This isn't the sort of thing we can afford to let be buried. This has to get out. Otherwise . . .

Otherwise, this is only the beginning. Colonies like Zagreus, they're not prepared to defend themselves against things like this.

I don't think *anyone* is prepared to defend themselves against things like this.

We have to live, or a whole lot more people are going to die.

"Don't you ever ask me to leave you behind again," I say to Viola. "We need to move. Did you want to say anything else before I put you back in the bag?"

She smiles lopsidedly. "Only that I'm glad you're my sister. I don't think I could ever have found myself a better one."

"Me either," I say, and press a kiss against her forehead before I tuck her back into the bag. She closes her eyes, and somehow that makes it easier to fasten the flap, shutting her away from the world. She can rest while we run. That's fine. We're going to need her soon enough.

I adjust the backpack until it's good and secure on my shoulders, trying to take as little time as possible, then turn to Kora.

"Are you ready?" I ask.

She nods, although her expression is unsure. "I don't think I have a choice, do you?" she asks, and there has never been anything truer on this distant, backwater world, under that ashen orange sky.

I take her hand. She steps closer.

Together, we walk away from our momentary peace, and into whatever hell Zagreus has left to offer us.

22

FLY AWAY HOME

WE'VE ONLY BEEN WALKING FOR A few minutes when we find Alisa. She's sprawled in the middle of the blood-soaked street, and there's a hole where her throat used to be, red and raw and gaping. She has a surprised look on her face, like she can't believe this is how her story ends; like she thought she was somehow going to be the one who made it out, the one who got away.

I guess everyone feels like that. I guess everyone *needs* to feel like that, because the second you stop believing that you can somehow be the one to bend probability and get away, that's when you die.

Kora pauses when she sees Alisa, putting her hand briefly over her mouth, but she doesn't stop walking, and neither do I. We haven't lost faith in the idea that we're going to survive yet, and stopping . . . stopping would chip away at that faith. At least Alisa isn't glued to a wall somewhere, waiting for the moment when her deadly cargo decides it's time to emerge.

I can't stop thinking about the thing I saw slide out of Kora's mother when the creature ripped her open. It had been small, and pale, and not ready to survive in the world yet, but it had been close to being ready—I'd seen that closeness in the angle of its long limbs and the slope of its eyeless head, in the way it had twitched and thrashed before going finally, lifelessly still. It was *so close* to being ready, but there was no way it had been inside her for more than a few hours. These things don't just reproduce fast, they mature fast, and that means we're not running out of time: we *are* out of time.

I don't say any of this. Kora knows how high the stakes are, and all I can do now is frighten her. Scared people don't move faster or more efficiently. Scared people fall apart. We're plenty scared enough already.

The colony lights click on as the last of the sunlight slips out of the sky, and everything is bathed in the cool electric glow of the power grid. It's a sterile light, with none of the color of the Zagreus sunlight, and that somehow manages to make things even worse. This light is unforgiving. This light calls out the blood on the ground, on the walls, on the windows. There's a perfect human handprint on a partially open door, and I know that if I stopped long enough to look inside, I'd find a cocoon at best and a creature at worst, and either way, it wouldn't make this any easier.

Viola's weight is nothing compared to the rest of what's in my bag, but it's still welcome, a reminder that I may be the last Shipp living, but I'm not the last Shipp on the planet. She's coming with me. The person I love best and the person I want to love me are both coming with me. We're almost there. We're almost in the clear.

Then we come around a corner and the launch port is in front of us, a shallow bowl with high metal walls, perfectly centered under the opening at the top of the dome. If the automated guidance systems are still online, activating the transport will lift us straight toward that hole, and we'll be able to shoot out of the colony and into low orbit before engaging our primary launch systems.

I've known how to operate the transport under emergency circumstances since I was twelve. This is still enough to make my stomach flip idly over. I won't have room for errors. I won't have anyone else to back me up. I can show Kora how to operate the controls once we're free of Zagreus's gravity, but until then, this is entirely on me.

No pressure.

Kora squeezes my hand. I glance at her, and her face is lit up, bright with the anticipation of escape.

"Come on," I say. Maybe I can't be strong for myself any longer, but I can be strong for Viola, and I can be strong for her. Maybe that will be enough.

We approach the launch port as quickly as we dare, all too aware that every step could be the one that pulls the creatures down on our heads. In the end, nothing comes to attack us, and we reach the end of the colony streets, facing the long stretch of open space between us and the port wall.

Mom always says that it's a sign of a frightened colony, when they build their city up around their launch port. There are too many things that can go wrong during takeoff and landing. If you really care about having a stable, self-sufficient colony, you put your launch outside the main city, where a crash or a fuel line explosion won't kill people. But if you do that, sometimes you'll have to acknowledge that the planet around you is the planet you have to live with. Sometimes you'll have to go out into the open, and face the dangers waiting there.

"People who build like they built here are scared," she'd said, the night after we moved from our temporary quarters inside the colony to our private residence outside it. "They don't care about doing things right or doing things better; they care about doing things as safely as they can. It's all right to feel sorry for them. Just don't let them convince you that they're in the right."

They haven't convinced me. Their idea of safety was what let the creatures tear through them so quickly, and with so little chance for anyone to get away. That same idea of safety is why I'm hesitating now. Twenty yards is a lot of open ground, and these creatures can *move*. If one of them comes after us while we're out in the open, there's going to be nothing we can do to save ourselves.

If we stand here, there's going to be nothing we can do. "Subprime either way," I mutter, and squeeze Kora's hand before letting go and bolting for the nearest door.

The world narrows itself to nothing but running, the feeling of my heart pounding in my chest and the sound of Kora's feet striking the ground behind me as she hurries to keep up. She doesn't shout for me to slow down or stop. I don't allow myself to look back. If there's something chasing us, I don't want to know. We're committed to the run now.

The door to the port is closed. I don't know whether that's good—maybe the creatures never got inside—or bad. I skid to a stop, looking toward Kora.

She answers my glance with a nod, pulling out her mother's access card and swiping it across the scanner, which beeps but doesn't disengage. Kora frowns and swipes it again. The beeping is obscenely loud in the quiet colony. This would be a stupid way to die.

"Hang on," I say, sotto voce, and grab the door handle. "Try now."

She swipes the card a third time as I pull. The panel beeps, and then the door clicks and swings open in my hands. Kora sags with relief even as she tucks the card back into her pocket. It's useless now. It has no more doors to open, no more access to grant. But it belonged to her mother, and she didn't have time to raid their residence for remembrances. That card may be the only thing she has of Delia's. I can't blame her for being careful with it.

The narrow stretch of hall on the other side of the door is mercifully pristine. There's no blood on the walls or floor; the overhead lights are glowing steadily, with no sign that they've been broken or compromised in any way. I don't want to be hopeful, but I am. If the creatures haven't violated the launch port, we can get to the transport and be off this planet before they realize that we're getting away.

This could be almost over.

I step into the hall, breathing in the cool, sweet air. It leaves a faint metallic taste at the back of my throat, the taste of sterile facilities and industrial cleaners and engine oil. Wait. I shoot a startled glance at Kora as she follows me inside, pulling the door closed on her way in. It seals with a clang and a hiss.

"How much time do you spend in here?" I ask.

She blinks, looking surprised. "How did you . . . ?"

"Every time I kiss you, your lips taste like engine oil."

She reaches up to touch her lower lip with the fingers of one hand, and for a moment it looks like she's going to smile, despite everything we've been through today. The thought is encouraging. If she can still smile, things might be okay. We might both be able to recover from everything we've seen, and survive.

"I never thought that was what would give me away," she says. "My father is—was—an engineer. He built colony habitats. He taught me a lot before he and Mama split up, and I liked it. I like working with my hands. So I come down here when I don't have school or chores, and I let the launch technicians teach me whatever they're willing to share." Her face falls, all hint of a potential smile fading away. Subprime.

"I guess that's good, since it means I can probably fix your transport if anything goes wrong once we get off-world," she says. "But I guess they're not going to be teaching me anything else, huh?"

"I guess not." Dying isn't only physical. It's cultural, and social, and Kora is attending a dozen funerals inside her heart right now, and I'm sorry, I'm truly sorry, but there isn't time to let her grieve. "Do you know the way?"

"To your transport?"

When I nod, so does she.

"I sure do. It isn't on the docket for repairs, and that means it's in the pre-launch ring, in case it's needed. Come on." She beckons for me to follow her as she turns and starts down a narrow hallway off to our right.

We're halfway to the next door when the smell of blood

overwhelms the more ordinary scents of the launch port. I stop dead, looking frantically around. Kora makes it another five or so steps before she realizes I'm not with her and turns around.

"Olivia?" she asks, uncertainly.

A drop of red falls from the ceiling and lands with a small splashing sound on the metal floor between us.

Unwillingly, I look up, tracking the path of the drop's descent, until I find myself looking into the dead, staring eyes of the man stuffed into the open lattice of the ceiling. It's a narrow space. I wouldn't have thought a human body could fit there, and maybe a complete body couldn't: only half of this man is present. Everything below the waist, and one of his arms, is missing, leaving only a shattered streak of meat in a vaguely human form behind.

I take a deep breath, trying to shove back the scream that threatens to burst out of me. In a space this enclosed, it will echo. If it echoes, it will draw the creatures to us, and we'll die, all because I couldn't be strong enough, couldn't be brave enough, couldn't be fast enough to save us, to save Viola, to save—

Kora screams, drawing my mother's volt gun. The sound hasn't even had a chance to fade before she shouts, "*Move!*"

I don't look behind me. I don't argue with her.

I move.

The hall is narrow, but there's room for me to lunge toward the wall and forward at the same time, so that my first frantic motion turns into racing toward her as she takes aim and fires at something behind me. I'm not quite in her line of fire, but I'm close enough that I feel the lightning brush by me, standing every hair on end and making my skin tight and hot and tingling.

Something snarls, and I know what she's shooting at, even as I'm unholstering my own gun and drawing up level with her. I whip around, barely taking the time to aim. The recoil from the shot travels all the way up my arm, knocking me back against the wall even as the bullet strikes the creature squarely in the middle of its armored, chitinous chest. It's paler than the others, pigmentation stolen from the lion-worm whose corpse gestated and fed it. It bellows at the impact, the sound a mixture of creature and lion-worm, and the cilia along its side waves wildly.

This is my parents' life work. This is Zagreus. This is the hubris of man. It's all those things in the same breath, and it's here for me, it's here to carry me away, forever.

"Run!" shouts Kora. "I'll be right behind you!"

I don't run. Instead, I take more time to aim, trying to get a clear shot at that head, that gnashing, furious mouth. Nothing's so tough that a bullet in the throat won't kill it. Nothing.

Kora shoots again, and maybe that's the last straw. The electricity doesn't seem to do the creatures any permanent damage, but it hurts and disconcerts them, and that's enough. The thing moves, so fast my eyes can barely follow, and backhands her against the nearest wall with one curved, claw-like hand. She screams before her back hits the metal strut, hard enough to dent it, and then she falls, motionless, to the floor.

The creature bellows again, triumph and hurt and anger, and starts to move toward her, slower now, cilia waving in that familiar lion-worm way, tracking the movement in the air. It will know the instant I move, and that's fine, because for an instant, I *can't* move. For an instant, I'm frozen in a horrible mixture of loss and fear and rage, and I want to bellow with the creature, want to let it all out in a primal wail that shakes the walls. I can't. I can't make a sound.

Kora's hand twitches.

It's a small motion, barely noticeable, and for a second, I think I imagined it. Then it happens again, and I know—I *know*—that she's still alive, she's *still alive*. I can fix this, if I move quickly. If I'm willing to take the risk.

"Vi, I'm sorry," I breathe, voice barely even loud enough to qualify as a whisper, and fire again.

This time, the recoil slams me against the wall so hard that I worry, briefly, that I've broken a rib: the pain is immediate and immense, filling my entire body. The bullet strikes the creature in its right shoulder, sending a spray of blood onto the wall, where it begins to eat its way through the metal. I don't see whether any of it lands on Kora. Oh, I hope it didn't. If I've killed her . . .

The creature bellows, and the sound is nothing but pain and fury. It doesn't care about territory anymore, or about whatever confusing signals the lion-worm pheromones may be feeding to its hybrid brain. It only cares about getting vengeance against the thing that's dared to hurt it. I can't worry about Kora anymore. I have to worry about myself.

Spinning on my heel, I break into a run and race back the way we came, back to the main hall. It may not be the most efficient way to reach our transport, but I'm not aiming for the transport anymore.

I'm aiming for the catwalks.

The creature has attributes from both of its "parents." I don't know whether that's the correct term, biologically speaking, but I don't have time to stand around and debate taxonomy right now. It looks mostly like the things from the shuttle, and it can burrow through the ground like a lion-worm, it can bite through metal like a lion-worm, and worst of all, it can follow the pheromones that spilled in Viola's hair back in the cave.

Although right now, that's what I'm counting on. If it follows the scent—if that's enough to make the part of it that's almost native to Zagreus *even angrier*—that means it's going to forget about Kora. She's not a threat anymore. She's downed prey, she's defeated, and it can come back to her later. It can kill her later. Right now, it needs to be killing me.

It has thicker arms than the original creatures, a thicker torso, a shorter tail. I'm hoping that means the adaptations that make it suited to life here on Zagreus will make it *less* suited to the environment the creatures originally came from—the narrow spaces and high lattices of a survey ship, where space is always at a premium, where nothing is allowed to go unused.

I'm gambling my life on everything I've gleaned about these creatures through observation, and since most of that observation has been done in a state of mind-numbing terror, this is probably a bad idea. It's the only idea I have. So I run, and the creature pursues, and all I can think, over and over again, is *Kora, wake up. Kora, run. Kora, wake up.*

Kora, run.

Run.

Run.

23

RUN

I CAN HEAR THE CREATURE THUN-
dering behind me as I race toward the hallway. There's a small
amount of comfort in the fact that it's staying on the ground, its
claws scraping the metal floor, its tail occasionally striking one
of the walls with a louder metallic clang. If it had been one of
the original creatures, it would already be using the ceiling to get
the tactical advantage. These "Zagreus local" versions aren't as
suited to an arboreal existence.

Of course, this one is also larger than any others I've seen,
which isn't an *improvement* by any reasonable measurement. I
have to stay farther ahead to keep from getting grabbed, and the
cilia on its sides seem to be keeping it fully aware of how much
space it has to maneuver. This is a nightmare.

The thought is almost freeing. Yes, I know this is really
happening, I know I'm not going to wake up and find myself
suddenly back in a world that makes sense, but what if I pretend?

What if I let myself act like this is all a dream? Can I be braver, if it's not real?

Yes. For Kora, for the chance to get Viola away from here, I can.

I keep running, digging down deep until I find another sliver of speed, another scrap of endurance. The hallway ends, opening up on the wider hall that serves as an artery for the launch port as a whole, and there it is, my last chance, my salvation: a ladder leading up to the network of catwalks that crisscrosses the entire structure. Engineers use them to get between transports without needing to descend and repack all their tools. Fuel lines are affixed to their sides, ready to be attached to a transport preparing for launch. It's a sterile, efficient environment. I have no place going anywhere near it, much less leading a monster into its midst.

I grab hold of the nearest ladder and begin climbing, ascending as quickly as I can into the vaulted dome above me.

There's a hissing snarl of outrage, and the ladder shakes, nearly jerked out of my hands. A fall now wouldn't be fatal, but a fall with that *thing* on my heels doesn't need to be fatal: it just needs to slow me down for a few seconds. Maybe not even that long, depending on how close it is now. I don't look back. I don't want to see where it is, because knowledge is only going to hurt me right now. Either it will make me complacent and potentially slow me down or it will tell me this is hopeless.

I keep climbing, and the ladder keeps shaking, the creature pulling its considerable bulk along behind me, making the whole world feel like it might fall apart at any moment. Then I'm at the top of the ladder—prime, prime, *prime*—and I'm running, racing along the catwalk, trying to scrape every possible scrap of lead out of the situation that I can.

The creature is faster than I am over straight, smooth ground. I know that from the way it attacked Kora, the way it attacked Delia. I can't beat it in a fair race, and there's never going to be anything fair about a conflict between one human girl and a monster from the stars. I have to cheat. I have to move, and I have to make sure the environment works for me, not for it.

The catwalk shakes as the creature makes the transition from ladder to flat. I put on what little speed I have left in me, fully, horribly aware that the creature is almost certainly gaining. I got away before because it was distracted, trying to deal with the pain in its shoulder and to overcome its own instinctive desire to stay with the prey that had already been wounded and would present no further challenge.

From up here, I can see the blood on the ground, the bodies of the workers who'd been caught inside the launch port when everything went wrong. There aren't many of them, and I don't see any cocoons. They had too many weapons. Unlike the rest of the colonists, they'd been in a position to fight back, and the creatures had been forced to kill them rather than taking them alive. I'm proud of them for standing their ground, and more, I'm relieved, because no cocoons means no rapidly gestating embryos. There's no guarantee that another creature won't find its way in here, but . . .

But I don't think so. This one followed us because of the pheromones. I haven't seen any other hybrids like it, and if there were more than one, I'm sure they would be here now, making a terrible situation even worse, making things completely hopeless. It's one-on-one here at the end of the line, and if I can just stay alive for a few more minutes, maybe I can figure out a way to win.

My lungs burn and my knees ache. Everything about me

hurts, and the weight of my backpack is almost unbearable. If it weren't for Viola, I would throw it away, hoping that the motion would be enough to distract the creature. I can't do that. I have to protect her. I have to keep my sister—

As if the thought were enough to make the universe get in one more blow, something snags the pack, jerking me to an abrupt, bone-rattling halt. I scream, unable to stop myself, and try to start moving again even as the creature rips the pack away from my shoulders. The fabric digs into me before it lets go, that solid construction suddenly turned into a potentially fatal flaw.

Then, from inside the bag, I hear my sister's voice, loud and hectoring.

"Look at you, you useless lump! Do you even know what you are? Do you have any idea? You're ugly even for a lion-worm. Evolution really messed up with you, huh? You should've stayed in orbit, at least there nothing would have to see you. I bet your own mama tried to squash you once she realized what she'd done—"

I should feel grateful. I know what she's doing. All I feel is numb.

The backpack is gone, ripped away by the monster that now has what remains of my sister. To save her, to save Kora, to save myself, I can't turn back now. My only hope—*our* only hope—is somewhere up ahead, half-formed and still potentially disastrous. But it's hope, and so I run, until my sister's litany of abuse ends in a short-lived scream.

I don't know whether the creature has crushed her, whether anything remains to repair, whether this is the end. But I know she bought me time, and I am running, I am running as fast as I can.

The catwalk stretches above the launches, transports rowed

and ranked and ready for departures that will never come. There aren't as many of them as there should be for a colony this size. Too many have been dismantled, recycled, reused. I see my family's transport, sitting at the center of a cluster of docking pads that were empty when we arrived and will be empty forever now.

And I see the construction equipment.

One of the docked transports is halfway through the process of being stripped down and turned into so much scrap. In the normal course of things, it would have become another building, another bridge, another piece of the slowly expanding body of the Zagreus colony. The work has stopped. The workers are all dead.

The tools they were using are still in place. They jut into the air, carelessly thrown aside, transforming that small patch of the launch port into a forest of jutting blades, razored cutting tools, and jagged metallic edges. A catwalk runs directly above it, held in place with suspiciously narrow struts. I breathe in through my nose, out through my mouth, and run like death itself is on my heels, maybe because it is.

It is faster but I am smaller, and I am better equipped to make quick adjustments to my trajectory. When I hear the catwalk shake behind me, I know, without question, that it's preparing to jump. So I wait as long as I can, and when I hear the softest clatter of claws against metal, I throw myself from the side of the catwalk, into the sickening void below.

There's a moment—only a moment, more than long enough—when I'm actually falling, my heart in my throat and the hot taste of fear clogging my sinuses, making it impossible to breathe. Then I grab hold of the struts beneath the catwalk, jerking my arms in their sockets, leaving me suspended in midair.

The hybrid creature strikes the catwalk where I was standing only an instant before. It snarls, rage and confusion and what feels almost like petulant disapproval, like it can't believe I would thwart it like this. I wish I knew how intelligent it was. I wish I could tell whether this was instinct or actual anger.

It doesn't matter. In the end, the only thing that matters is that one of us is going to live and one of us is going to die, and I intend to make sure I'm the one who walks away. I take one hand off the strut that holds me and draw Mom's gun, heavy and deadly and mine now, mine forever after this. I take careful aim, and I fire twice in quick succession, pulling the trigger the second time before the recoil even has the chance to travel up my arm. The pain is immense, enough that the world goes gray for a potentially fatal second.

But I hear the struts that hold the catwalk beneath the creature in place give way, their delicate connections shattered by the bullets. The entire section crumples and falls, leaving the creature with no leverage, no way to leap for safety. It falls, clawing at the air, tail lashing and cilia waving, and lands, as I had hoped, directly on the jagged piles of construction equipment.

Chitin makes fine armor, but it's not enough to protect against impalement. The creature shrieks, loud and agonized. Then it begins to thrash. The motion drives the spikes and cutting metallic edges deeper and deeper into its body. The bleeding has already started, but for once, I don't think acid is the answer; it won't be able to melt its way free. Not with those injuries.

It isn't the only one injured. My arm is still numb, and when I try to lift it, it barely responds. I let it dangle, so much deadweight, as I laboriously kick one leg up, over one of the remaining supports, and begin pulling myself to safety.

It's hard; almost impossible at times. I don't have the upper body strength for this. I've never needed it before. I nearly fall several times. I nearly join the creature in its agonized thrashing. But I don't. I know that if I fall, no one will ever come to save my sister. I know that if I fall, Kora dies here, as soon as the next creature shows up looking for easy prey.

I don't rush, either. I try to think about Viola, about giving her a new body and a new chance on Earth, or somewhere else even, somewhere far away from anyone who's ever heard of Zagreus. I go as slowly as I dare, and I still feel like it's not going to be enough, not until the moment when I land facedown on the catwalk, safe. No longer a plaything for gravity.

I take a few seconds to let myself cry for everything we've lost, everything *I've* lost.

Then I stand. There's still work to be done.

My backpack is about ten yards back, caught against the rail. I pick it up with my good hand, unable to work the zipper. "Viola?" I ask.

"Here," she says, voice soft, subdued. She sounds hurt. Can androids be injured? Losing her body didn't seem to slow her down, but this is one more thing to worry about in a day already full of them.

"We're almost clear," I say, and sling the bag over my shoulder, and walk on.

Descending the ladder is almost impossible. Feeling starts to come back into my arm when I'm about halfway down, which helps a little, but not as much as I would have liked. Still, I make it. Shipps always make it.

"Shipp sisters forever," I whisper, and step back onto solid ground. I start walking, not toward the hallway where Kora may or may not be waiting, but toward the construction site.

The creature is thrashing when I get there, the tools that pierce its armored skin more than halfway melted. It senses my approach and turns its head toward me, hissing. No pleas for mercy here, no tricks; it still wants me dead.

The feeling is mutual.

"Fuck you," I say, and switch the gun to my good arm, using my weak one to brace myself as I fire the rest of the clip into the creature's skull, shattering it.

By the time I lose feeling in my arm, the creature isn't moving anymore. It looks smaller now that it's been broken. It looks no less horrific, no less alien. It and I were never meant to share a world.

So let it have this one. Zagreus is a graveyard. Let these things be its ghosts.

I'm leaving.

I turn away, shoulders slumped, and walk off to find out whether Kora is still alive.

24

THE LONG WAY TO THE STARS

KORA HASN'T MOVED. I ROLL HER onto her side, away from the acid that has eaten a hole in the wall, and grimace at the acid burn on her shoulder, at the slack set of her jaw. But she's breathing, and there are no splits around her lips. She hasn't been impregnated with one of those horrible *things*.

She could still be okay.

My right arm is almost back to normal, although my shoulder aches like it never has before, and my left arm is mostly useless. Still, I'm able to rock her to her feet, slinging her arm over my shoulders, and start walking toward the berth where my family's transport is waiting, her feet dragging on the ground.

"I don't feel good," whispers Viola.

"I'll check your schematics as soon as we're on the transport," I say. Maybe she needs power. The machines that were supposed to monitor her health back when I thought she was alive, they were probably keeping her batteries charged. With most of her body missing, I don't know how much battery her head has.

"Thank you," she says, and doesn't say anything else.

I keep walking, and when Kora starts picking up her feet and putting them ploddingly down, I almost topple over.

"Kora?" I ask.

"Hurts," she says.

"I know." I do know. My arms ache, and I think I may have fractured my collarbone, and all I want to do is leave. This world, this launch port, this colony, let it all fade behind us. Let it be forgotten.

It's just another graveyard, after all.

"Can you walk on your own?" I ask. I hate to make her do it, I don't want to let her go, but my arms ache, and I hate the idea of dropping her even more.

We keep walking, another step, and then another, and finally Kora says, "I can try," and pulls away from me, taking her first wobbly, independent step.

We're going to get away.

It becomes a chant in the back of my mind, motivating me forward, keeping me moving, until we turn a corner and there's my family shuttle, dull and old and serviceable and waiting for us. Ready for us.

I have more strength than I thought I did.

I have enough strength to run.

I reach the door and punch in the code, and the door opens and the air that flows out is cool and sterile and doesn't smell like acid or blood or anything other than freedom, freedom, freedom.

I turn, my sister's head safely bundled on my back, and I wait for Kora to reach us, and then I close the door. I close the door on Zagreus. I close the door on everything that happened.

I can't forget everything I saw. I can leave it behind me.

Kora settles in the co-pilot's seat. I pull Viola's head out of the backpack before sitting down behind the controls. I place her in my lap, eyes turned toward the screen. Then I punch in the code to let us leave this place, this haunted, haunting place.

For once, nothing goes wrong. The engines engage; the magnetic launch pads let us go; we lift off, and then we're gone, racing through acceleration and out into that orange sky. For a moment, I can see the curve of the horizon, and I wonder how long it will take for the creatures to conquer Zagreus, to make it a hell in more than just name.

Kora moans softly. When I glance at her again, her eyes are closed. She's hurt. I knew that when I saw her on the floor. But she made it to the ship, and she's with the Shipps, and we're going to be okay. All three of us are going to be okay.

We have to be.

Our shuttle isn't designed for interplanetary travel. It's meant to go from big passenger or survey ship to the surface and back again. We're never going to make it to an inhabited world, not on our own. Maybe we could find a moon with an atmosphere, maybe, but it won't heal Kora's injuries, and it won't build Viola a new body. So as soon as we're completely free of Zagreus's gravity well, I flick on the emergency beacon and reach for the comms.

What I say now has to be precise. It has to make it clear that we need help, and that we were attacked, not infected: there is no disease on Zagreus, not in the traditional sense. If we get dropped into quarantine . . . that would be bad. That would be very, very bad. We need a rescue, not a mercy killing.

I take a deep breath, and I begin.

"This is the privately held vessel *While There's Hope*, requesting immediate medical assistance. My name is Olivia Shipp. I have one badly injured passenger. Do not make landing on Zagreus, repeat, do not make or attempt landing on Zagreus. The planet has been compromised by . . . things . . . they've killed everyone. They've killed . . . everyone. This is the privately held vessel *While There's Hope*, requesting immediate medical assistance—"

I reach over and take Kora's hand, cradling Viola's head against my chest. Neither of them responds as I speak into the void, over and over again, pleading for help. Space is vast. We're so small.

Someone will find us.

Someone has to.

We got away. Doesn't that mean we deserve a happy ending?

I close my eyes and keep calling, and I wait for someone to answer.

ACKNOWLEDGMENTS

This was so. Much. Fun.

I don't have a lot to say here, but what I do have matters, so:

Thanks to my mother, who let me wrap myself in my sleeping bag and spend every Saturday night of my childhood watching horror movies in our living room. She raised me with a heart full of monsters and a keen awareness that inside everyone is a skeleton just waiting to break free.

Thanks to my agent, Diana Fox, who knew as soon as she heard about this book that I wanted to be the one to write it, and to my editor, John Morgan, who was a genuine delight to work with.

Thanks to Ripley and Newt, and to every Final Girl who ever hacked, slashed, and screamed her way to the finish line. In a very real way, this book is for them. They were my heroes and my idols as a child, and I am so proud and so honored to add Olivia Shipp to their number.

Thanks to all my horror movie buddies, past and present, but especially to Michael, Chris, and Brooke, who have watched more people melt than is strictly kind. You are all very good sports, and I adore you.

They say that in space, no one can hear you scream. In my living room, on a Saturday night, they definitely can.